Riders Down

Books by John McEvoy

Blind Switch
Riders Down
Close Call

Great Horse Racing Mysteries: True Tales from the Track

With Julia McEvoy
Women in Racing: In Their Own Words

Riders Down

John McEvoy

Poisoned Pen Press

Poisoned
Pen
Press

Copyright © 2006 by John McEvoy

First Trade Paperback Edition 2008

10 9 8 7 6 5 4 3 2 1

Library of Congress Catalog Card Number: 2005934986

ISBN: 978-1-59058-497-2 Trade Paperback

Poisoned Pen Press
6962 E. First Ave., Ste. 103
Scottsdale, AZ 85251
www.poisonedpenpress.com
info@poisonedpenpress.com

*Again, to my wife Judy
and our family, which
now also includes
Taskin, Teoman, and Sinan.*

Acknowledgments

For their aid and encouragement, my thanks go to Lucy and Kirk Borland, Dee Hannan, Elsie and John Hoban, Dana Lubotsky, Rose Nigro, Carolynn and Bill Sheridan, Gayla and Chuck Tilton, and Barbara Peters and Robert Rosenwald.

"I was nuts about horses... There's something about it, when they come out and go up the track to the post. Sort of dancy and tight looking with the jock keeping a tight hold on them and maybe easing off a little and letting them run a little going up."
—Ernest Hemingway
("My Old Man")

"Once the horse moved man's physical body and his household goods and his articles of commerce from one place to another. Nowadays all it moves is a part or a whole of his bank account, either through betting on it or trying to keep owning and feeding it."
—William Faulkner
("Sports Illustrated")

Chapter One

Bernard ("You may call me Bernie") Glockner, at age ninety-eight Chicago's oldest active bookmaker, reached forward and again cautiously parted the curtains covering the east window of his living room on the condominium building's ninth floor. He peered down. The street below, lined with dirt-coated snow mounds, was virtually traffic-free, only an occasional taxi trolling the salted asphalt in search of customers. At 11:48 on this bone-chilling night, the scene below was nearly as quiet as its aged watcher.

A widower, Glockner had lived alone for some thirty years in the same condo unit, self-sufficient, comfortable, feeling safe. Until now. In the silence of this familiar home on the city's near north side, Glockner pulled back from the window. As removed as he was from the frigid night air, and wearing a warm robe that swaddled his diminutive frame, Glockner nevertheless shivered. He had made his living making odds. Tonight, he figured the price on his waking to another dawn was one-to-five against. And it was his own fault. "Stupid. I was so stupid," he said disgustedly.

Glockner reached for the phone, then replaced the receiver without dialing. "I got myself into this," he said aloud. "I'll deal with it." He chuckled mirthlessly at his bravado as he settled back into his leather armchair. He thought of his wife Betty who, like most of his original contemporaries, had pre-deceased him by decades. "She never would have let me wind up in a jackpot like this," he said of the woman who for so long had loved him and gently curbed his few dangerous enthusiasms.

Ordinarily on a night like this Glockner, a lifelong insomniac, would be listening to his favorite Chicago radio talk show, one remarkable in that usually raucous field because it elicited opinions from many citizens who apparently had benefited from a decent education. Several of the callers each night actually knew what they were talking about. Glockner himself occasionally phoned in his views on various political and ethical matters. He delivered them in his soft, assured voice, identifying himself only as "B. G. from Chicago, a practicing Democrat." Bernie's most provocative statement had come during the last year's gubernatorial election campaign when he said that "Many Democrats, unfortunately, feel somewhat guilty about their acquisition of worldly possessions, while most of the Republicans I've known are convinced they have coming to them everything they've inherited or stolen." Bernie never let on that years previously, before he went into bookmaking on a lucrative full-time basis, he had used an academic scholarship to earn a degree in philosophy from the University of Chicago. A memory of the university's broad midway in early spring, its new grass and budding trees bright in the morning air, came to Glockner as he shifted restlessly in his armchair. "Happy days," he whispered. Then the pressing concerns of the moment resumed command of his consciousness.

It had been gambling, not Schopenhauer or Nietzsche, that defined Bernie Glockner's life, beginning with his childhood on Chicago's near west side where he was widely known as "the kid who murders numbers." In his primarily Italian and Jewish neighborhood, Bernie handicapped foot races down Taylor Street ("Anthony, ya gotta give Sammy a yard and a half head start going a block.") He could still picture himself and his buddies running to Mario's Italian Ice stand at the end of a long, hot, summer afternoon.

A few of those kids he grew up with became Chicago Outfit guys. It was at their urging, and with their blessing, that Glockner, tucking his UC diploma in a drawer, began using his impressive mathematical skills to establish betting lines on sporting events. Again, with the permission of "the boys," he began booking the wagers of a small group of high rollers. His pleased associates dubbed Glockner "The Wizard of Odds." So did the authorities, who were never able to nail him in the course of his seven decades of illegal gambling activity.

Glockner rubbed together his small, brown-spotted hands. They were well cared for, as was the rest of this remarkably healthy and acute nonagenarian. Again, he shifted uneasily in his chair, as he had been doing frequently for the last three nights. The prescience that had carried him unscathed through a long career in association with some of the city's most vicious men evidenced itself in the sheen of perspiration across his forehead. After all this waiting, it was almost with relief that Bernie felt a quick rush of air on the back of his neck, heard the movement behind him as his front door was closed and locked again. He had hoped he was wrong in believing this was coming. But he wasn't wrong.

The old man tried to rise but a large hand pressed heavily down on his right shoulder. Bernie sat back resignedly. He shrugged when another large hand extracted the revolver Bernie had hidden beneath the chair's cushion. A remnant of his education flashed into his mind. Socrates, he thought it was: "When a man has reached my age he ought not to be repining at the prospect of death." Still…

The taller of the two invaders maintained his iron grip on Bernie's shoulder. Bernie could see him in the wall mirror across from where he sat. He was dressed in a brown leather car coat and jeans.

The other man—shorter, broader, powerful looking—moved around the chair to face the old man. He wore a gray tweed sport coat with leather elbow patches, a black turtleneck sweater, black slacks and well-worn New Balance cross trainer shoes. His large, shaven head was bordered by two of the smallest ears Glockner had ever seen. Smiling, the man said, "Hello, Bernie. It's truly a pleasure, and I mean it, to finally meet you." Behind steel-rimmed glasses his gray eyes were alight with amusement as he rubbed his large hands together. Bernie recognized the voice. During their first phone conversations, he had thought to himself that the man's husky tenor reminded him of a sinister-sounding Garrison Keilor. The man noticed Bernie glancing at the mirror. In a quick, fluid motion he pivoted and with a karate kick shattered the glass inside the frame.

"So, the so-called Professor," Glockner spat out. "Believe me, the pleasure is all yours."

Glockner felt a combination of fear and embarrassment as he recalled the long conversations he had had with the menacing figure that now stood before him. Some six weeks earlier, the man had first identified himself in a letter as Professor Harlan Kornkven of the University of Wisconsin economics department. The envelope containing the letter carried a post office box as a return address. The Professor had written that a certain mutual acquaintance of theirs had identified Glockner as one of the country's "greatest experts on gambling." The Professor said he was engaged in a study of pari-mutuel horse racing to be included in a book he was writing on "gaming in contemporary America." It was for him, he wrote, a brand-new field of study. Could he submit some questions for Mr. Glockner to answer in writing?

No, Bernie had replied in a short, formal note, he would prefer to provide any information via phone calls. The Professor called Bernie two days later. He asked permission to tape their conversations. Certainly, Bernie had replied—this, after a career of assiduously avoiding *any* sort of recording device. But that, Bernie would come to realize, was what vanity and boredom could do to a man on the far side of his better days.

Glockner and the Professor set up a schedule of thrice-weekly calls, usually in early evening. The Professor said he would describe Glockner in his book as a "rare research source," but would not identify him by name. That was fine with Bernie. In the course of the fourth week, the Professor confessed that he had become "intrigued by the race-fixing aspect of the sport. How common are fixed races?" he asked. "What methods are most effective?"

Bernie had responded readily, an old man's pride in his knowledge serving to stoke his volubility. He gave his questioner an extensive overview of how the outcome of horse races might be manipulated, then went on to provide details of past betting coups, plus a description of the few potentially successful avenues still open in this sport that was so stringently regulated and overseen by state authorities. Tonight, remembering how he had prattled on, Bernie blushed. "Forget about doping horses," he had said, "the laboratory tests are too good now. Somebody doing that would eventually be caught and then banned and maybe imprisoned.

"For a brief time there was a window of opportunity involving computers. Remember the Breeders' Cup Pick Six scandal a few years ago? A kid programmer who worked in computers for the big totalizator company got into the system and changed bets after the races had been run so that he a couple of his buddies held the only winning tickets of the day. Talk about past posting! But they were caught within weeks. And racing officials soon installed new security systems to prevent that from ever happening again. So, that door to larceny is nailed closed.

"So your best bet today, as always," Bernie had continued, "are the jockeys. They have more control over the outcome of races than anyone. Al Capone, when I was new in the business, had so many jockeys in his pocket they were bumping into each other. And Capone had big pockets.

"Oh," Bernie continued wistfully, "having a jockey or two under your control, that's the best way. Nobody can lose a race better than a jockey who wants to."

The Professor had asked for elaboration and the old bookie eagerly complied. "Let's say you're betting a Pick Four. That's when you have to pick the winners of four races in a row, which is not easy to do, believe me. The horse you want to lose would be the favorite, or maybe the second favorite, in one, maybe two, of the races involved. You'd want them to lose because most of the bettors are depending on them to win. If you know that is going to lose, then you structure your bets to include all the other horses, most of them at good odds. You'd be assured of a profitable payoff. If you get real lucky, you'd get at least one real big long shot to win one of the races. Then you're talking very big money.

"They've got these National Pick Fours now, where you have to pick four straight winners at races at four different tracks around the country. There's usually one race in the East, a couple at Midwest tracks, the windup on the West Coast. Sometimes the order changes but whatever way they do it, these National Pick Fours attract huge amounts of money, in the millions, even though it's a hard bet to win, like hitting back-to-back daily doubles. If you had jocks holding the big favorites in a couple of those races, you'd have yourself some kind of Saturday.

"But, Professor, things have changed," Bernie went on. "Today you'd have a problem with the jockey faction. First, the vast majority of jockeys are honest. Then, the jockeys who are adept enough to convincingly pull off this stuff without getting caught are already making so much money they have no motivation to take yours. It's no good fixing races at the smaller tracks. Their betting totals aren't big enough to make it worth your while. And to fix races at the major tracks you would have to try to deal with the best jockeys. I don't believe it's possible anymore. As I said, your bribe money wouldn't be enough to attract the top riders even if you could find some crooked ones."

Bernie now recalled the Professor remarking softly, almost as if speaking to himself, "Then you'd have to find a motivation other than money, wouldn't you?" He had then quickly changed the subject.

◇◇◇

It was nearly midnight. Looking down at the little bookmaker who was regarding him with a combination of defiance and dread, the Professor said, "Aren't you going to ask how we got in here?"

"No," Glockner said. "I figure you came in through the service door in the rear of the building. You probably made a copy of the master key to the building. People don't know it, but they're easy to make, they fit doors all over the city. I've warned the building management about this for years. Nobody listened.

Once you got in you came up the back stairs, nobody to see you at this time of night, and the master key got you in here, too."

The man nodded approvingly, his eyes bright, obviously relishing the sense of power he felt. His expression as he regarded the old bookmaker bordered on the benign.

"I want to ask you something," Glockner said. "Who the hell are you? And why are you doing this? I presume you are no professor. And I think I have the right to know," he added.

The Professor nodded, looking down at Bernie with apparent fondness. "My name, Bernie," he said softly, "is Claude Bledsoe." He looked at the watch on his thick wrist. "You have about, oh, perhaps six minutes during which to remember it. Bernie," he continued, "when I picked your brain, I cashed big, as your clients would put it. Too bad for you that you were so smug, so vain, that you weren't able to see through the flood of flattery I hit you with. Had you done so, you would never have gotten yourself into this position."

"So, smugness...vanity...these are reasons for me to die?"

"No. What's going to kill you isn't what you are, but what you know. When we succeed with our first big betting coup, you'd hear of it. You'd start thinking about who had questioned you about fixing races at big tracks. You'd put two and two together. That's what you were good at, wasn't it, Bernie?"

When the Professor's phone calls had abruptly stopped coming two weeks earlier, Bernie had been at first disappointed, then puzzled. He did some research. Using his computer he examined the University of Wisconsin faculty roster. No Harlan Kornkven. A phone call to Madison confirmed that no such person had ever taught at the UW or had a local phone number. Bernie chewed on that information for a day and concluded that he had been deftly misled. It didn't take him long to figure out why, and that is when the possibility of this frightening night became alarmingly real to him.

Bernie looked on impassively as Bledsoe put on a pair of thin rubber gloves and walked over to the computer. As the screen came alive Glockner said, "Okay, so you're plotting to pull something off, using information I was fool enough to give you."

"Oh, yes," Bledsoe smiled, "that's what we are preparing to do." He began writing on the computer.

Bernie said, "Well, so be it. Do what you want. But what makes you think I'd tell anybody about you? Do you know who you're dealing with here? My connections? I've made a good, long life by keeping my mouth shut, never having contact with the cops or the feds. Why would I start now, at my age?"

Bledsoe paused in his typing. His look bore into Bernie. "You think I'd want to worry about you the rest of my life? *Not* a good idea." He resumed typing.

A minute later Bledsoe hit the print command on the computer. He waited for the single page to emerge from the printer, rapidly scanned it, then nodded, satisfied, and placed it on the small table next to Glockner's armchair.

"What's that?" Bernie said.

"It's your suicide note, Bernie. Shall I read it to you?"

Glockner's breath seemed to catch in his throat. Finally, he said, "You're a cold-hearted bastard. May you rot in hell. I'm done talking to you." He turned his head away. The second man's iron grip continued to hold the old man down.

"Bernie, Bernie," Bledsoe said, smiling again, "you're the maven with numbers, percentages. You're the fucking 'Wizard of Odds!' Tell me why I should even *consider* taking the chance that you, maybe when you finally hit your dotage, are in some Alzheimer's moment and start talking about me. Perhaps someone figures out what you're rambling about. Would that be smart business for me? *Au contraire*, Bernie," he said, mockingly drawing the syllables out. "There wouldn't be any percentage in that for me, would there?"

Bledsoe didn't expect a reply and didn't get one. He stood up from the computer table and made an over the shoulder motion with his right hand, thumb protruding. His smile seemed to widen as, for an instant, the old bookmaker struggled stubbornly, attempting to hold onto the arms of his leather chair.

But the man standing back of Glockner lifted him with ease. He was almost as solidly built as the Professor, and at least four inches taller. Placing a huge hand over Glockner's mouth, he moved swiftly to the window that the Professor had opened wide. Then he sailed little Bernie Glockner out into the frigid Chicago night.

Bledsoe turned off the lights. As the two men hurriedly moved to the door, the taller one, Jimbo Murray, said, "I give him credit. The little fucker never made a sound going down."

"I'll lay you 1-to-10 he did when he hit the pavement," Bledsoe said.

Bledsoe drove rapidly but carefully from the Ohio Street ramp onto the Kennedy Expressway heading north. He was tapping his fingers on the steering wheel as he zipped past slower vehicles. Jimbo was silent, looking out his passenger seat window at the sparse traffic. Finally, he said, "You know, Claude, you kind of took advantage of me with this deal."

Bledsoe looked at him. Sharply he said, "What's your complaint?"

"You never said anything about us tossing that old man. 'Scare him into silence,' you said." Jimbo shook his head and turned to look out the window again. "I've never killed anybody before. I never *wanted* to kill anybody. I don't know why the hell I let you lead me into this." His big jaw set, Jimbo stared straight ahead as they passed the Tuohy Avenue exit.

"Well, Jimbo old buddy," Bledsoe said angrily, "isn't that a goddam shame? I told you this was the first step in a plan to make big money for us both. You were cool with that. I didn't seduce you, you dumb son of a bitch. You wanted in, and I put you in, and now we're going to put my plan in motion."

He curved around a pair of huge, speeding trucks before adding, "What did you think, we were going to come down here and pick up some cash lying in the Chicago streets?"

Cowed by Bledsoe's angry statement, Jimbo sat quietly. "Don't fuck with Claude" was a motto he had come to live by not long after first getting to know Bledsoe.

Bledsoe broke the silence. "The thing is," he said softly, "it doesn't make any difference to me *how* you feel about it. You're in. End of story, my man."

Bledsoe reached into the rack of tapes he kept next to his seat, then popped in "Uncle Anesthesia" by his favorite grunge band, Screaming Trees. The sound was so loud Jimbo cringed. Bledsoe just snapped his fingers and bobbed his big head, grinning, as they left the Edens Expressway and continued north on the interstate.

Chapter Two

On a brisk April afternoon in Chicago, some two months after Bernie Glockner's fatal descent in the night, the field for the fourth race at Heartland Downs Racetrack curved around the final turn, heralded by cries of excitement from the few thousand bettors on hand. Matt O'Connor, two-thirds of the way through writing his daily column for *Racing Daily*, the national newspaper for which he had worked for eleven of his thirty-six years, glanced up from his computer screen and looked out the press box window at the wide strip of brown earth over which nine horses were churning. The race in progress was a low-level claiming event, newsworthy only if a horse or a jockey died during it, or a long shot winner emerged to pay more than $100. O'Connor resumed writing as the horses pounded toward the finish line, located three stories below the press box that sat atop the Heartland Downs grandstand.

"Damn!" came a shout from O'Connor's left. Then there was the sound of a pair of binoculars being thumped onto a desk top, followed by the crash of an overturned chair. Source of this activity was O'Connor's press box colleague, Rick Rothmeyer, handicapper for the *Beacon*, a Chicago daily. Rothmeyer had picked another loser and was beginning another of his blame-assigning tirades. He stalked behind the row of desks, muttering angrily. He was a large, somewhat overweight man of forty-one, and people tended to stay out of his way. Rothmeyer's big, round face reddened as he ranted.

O'Connor shook his head resignedly, rose, and stretched. A tall, sandy-haired man with the solid physique of the college third baseman he once had been, he walked over to refill his coffee cup. He was very familiar with Rothmeyer's outbursts and knew he would not be able to concentrate on finishing his column until his friend's harangue was over. The late-in-the-day press box coffee was terrible. O'Connor's nose—broken years before in a home plate collision with a catcher's shoulder—wrinkled in disgust. He dumped the coffee into the sink.

Though he had worked as a respected racing handicapper for more than fifteen years, Rothmeyer had yet to admit that his occasional "cold streaks" resulted primarily from his own misguided calculations. To his mind, the fault almost always lay with others: either trainers who had poorly prepared their horses or, far more frequently, the horses' riders—"inept pinheads," as Rothmeyer termed them.

Rothmeyer said, "That nitwit Anderson rode right up into a closing pocket, couldn't get through, finally decides to go outside, then gets beat a nose. How dumb can he get?" Arms raised imploringly he added, "How dumb can *I* be—to pick a horse he's on?"

O'Connor said, "What was the last horse you rode? A big blue and white one on a merry-go-round?" O'Connor knew that Rothmeyer not only had *never* ridden a horse but, from observing him on the rare occasions that he visited the backstretch or the paddock, suspected that his colleague was probably afraid of these powerful, often fey creatures.

◇◇◇

Sometimes, listening to one of Rothmeyer's diatribes, O'Connor questioned his own decision to enter racing journalism. Rothmeyer could have that effect on him. But these doubts about his job choice rarely lingered for long.

Prior to joining the *Racing Daily* as its Chicago columnist, O'Connor had enjoyed an upwardly mobile career at three mid-sized Midwestern daily papers following his graduation from Marquette University's journalism school. He'd worked city side at the first two. After becoming increasingly hardened while writing stories about subjects that he came to see as mundane and/or depressing, he had switched to sports at the third paper. Eighteen months of covering college and high school athletics had leached most of the vocational enthusiasm from him—he couldn't decide, following the games, if he was more bored listening to the players or to their coaches. Then O'Connor learned of the opening for a columnist on the national horse racing daily, applied, and had been hired by editor Harry Cobabe.

The racetrack proved to be a wondrously different place. Matt had suspected as much when he was a kid going to the races with his father, a tools salesman with a love for horses and a conveniently elastic work schedule. Matt came to regard the world of the racetrack as an intriguing microcosm, its citizenry running the gamut from millionaire horse owners to $300 a week stable employees, with a lively middle ground in between through which money flowed in a steady stream.

There were the horses, thousand-pound, graceful creatures that ran thirty-five miles an hour on legs that looked designed to hold up nothing heavier than coffee tables. There was the vibrant, early-morning atmosphere of the track with hundreds of these beautiful animals exercising, the sounds of their hooves and their breathing providing a percussive counterpoint to the called-out greetings their riders sent into the cool air. And there was the afternoon pleasure of being able to observe nine contests each day between equine competitors and their gifted riders—men and women who, O'Connor was convinced, were pound-for-pound the world's best athletes.

O'Connor often marveled at the camaraderie that existed in a sport/business replete with individualistic natures, one in which fierce daily competitions determined who got the money and the bragging rights, who got the goose eggs and was left with the stomach-churning nights. Racing was a world unto itself, filled with hustlers, dreamers, schemers, and hard-working citizens. As Matt once said to his father, "If a man can't find something to write about in horse racing, he's either lazy or dead."

Back at his press box desk, O'Connor said to Rothmeyer, "Watch the damned replay. Anderson was pinned down there because a hole didn't open—like he thought it would, and like it usually does. It wasn't the kid's fault. It was just the way the race played out. If the hole opens, he shoots through and looks like a genius. Even to you."

O'Connor shook his head. "No, I take that back—not to you. You're too stubborn to admit the truth. Every time one of your Best Bets loses, it's the jockey's fault. That's bogus. I'm done arguing with you, you goddam hardheaded Kraut."

Rothmeyer was replying, "And screw you, too, you dumb Mick," when the phone on O'Connor's desk rang. He picked up the receiver as Rothmeyer stomped off. "O'Connor here," he said.

"Glad to hear it," came a familiar voice. It was Moe Kellman, a wealthy Chicago businessman and horse owner with a reputation for being lengthily, discreetly connected to the Chicago Outfit.

O'Connor said, "Mosey, what's up? Did you get me those Cub tickets for next week?"

"Matt, hold on. That's not why I called. I need to talk to you about something important. Not on the phone. When can you do it?"

"Tomorrow after the races okay?"

"Good. Come to my office. And thanks," Kellman said. The line went dead.

O'Connor sat before his computer, thinking about Kellman's request. Courtesy would have compelled him to comply with it. His newsman's innate curiosity compounded his inclination to do so, for Kellman had never before sounded so serious in all the conversations they had had.

His reverie was interrupted when Melanie Dorsett, the press box aide who served as receptionist/secretary/coffee maker/publicity notes writer placed copies of the next day's racing entries onto his desk. Looking up, Matt said, "Thanks, Melanie," and watched as this very tall, young, redheaded woman approached the desk of her nemesis, Rick Rothmeyer. "You're late again, Stretch," Rothmeyer growled in greeting. Melanie gave him a scornful look. "The way you've been picking horses, you might as well use a hatpin instead of your so-called system," she said. She turned her back and walked away, continuing to distribute the sheets on other press box desks.

Melanie, a Northwestern University junior on a basketball scholarship, was spending the spring and summer as a Heartland Downs press box employee. Her father, Stan Dorsett, was a professional clocker who worked at the track timing the races and whose influence had helped get her the job. Those bloodlines were enough to raise Rothmeyer's hackles, for he held most clockers in low esteem. "Some of them couldn't accurately time a hippo waddling twenty yards," he often said, "and the ones that can clock accurately don't always report the best workouts. They'd rather keep that information for themselves. I remember reading that during World War II the Defense Department was planning to hire some New York clockers to hand-time artillery shells on a test range in New Jersey. The plan never got off the ground. But it was just as well, somebody said, because those clockers would probably just hold out the fastest ones anyway."

"Why do you give Melanie so much grief?" Matt had once asked.

Rick said, "She's interning here, right? Well, I'm helping prepare her for real life."

Matt was still thinking about Moe's call when Rick said, "C'mon, lighten up, Matt. I'll buy you an adult beverage. And I won't say another word about the mental and physical midgets they put up on these horses. Swear to God."

The two men packed up their laptops, briefcases, put on their sport jackets and walked to the press box elevator. Its uniformed operator, a portly senior citizen, put down his track program and waved them in. "Tapped out yet, Leon?" asked Rothmeyer.

"I'm alive in the late double," Leon confided as he closed the elevator door.

As they rode down, Leon complained about the "tough beat" he had suffered in the feature race. Matt and Rick smiled at each other behind his back. Leon's litany of lousy luck was legendary. Yet they—and Leon, too—knew that he would be back at the pari-mutuel barricades the next day, optimistic and confident as ever.

Leon the Operator had entered local racing lore several summers before. On a blazingly hot August afternoon, Leon's elevator broke down between floors. It remained stuck for nearly ninety-five minutes. Trapped in the sweltering confines of the car, Leon removed his uniform as he anxiously awaited rescue. When the repair work was finally finished, one of the electricians drove the elevator to ground level. It arrived there with Leon lying on its floor, flushed, sweating, dehydrated and wearing only his underwear. As paramedics prepared to place Leon on a stretcher, Leon's worried supervisor asked if there was anything he could do. "Yeah," Leon gasped after ripping off the oxygen mask, "get me a dollar trifecta box in the eighth race on the three-four-nine. And hurry! It's got to be almost post-time!"

The doors opened and Leon said good night to his two passengers, who exited the clubhouse and began walking past the paddock toward the track's media parking lot.

"I've got time for a quick two," O'Connor said. "Where?"

"My new favorite watering hole," Rothmeyer said. "Five blocks down on Wilke. It only opened a couple of weeks ago. Place called Jeers. Where nobody gives a shit about your name but everybody knows your business."

Matt turned to his friend. "You haven't pulled your 'happy birthday' hustle in there, have you?" He was referring to a practice that Rick had used for years when patronizing what was to him a new bar. Rick would enter, order a drink, get change for the juke box, and play three selections. The last one always would be the last song on every juke box list, "Happy Birthday." When the song played, other patrons would look around, wondering who was being honored. Rick would sheepishly confess that he, there in the bar by himself, had played the song because it was his birthday. He had employed this trick many times a year in different bars, happily accepting celebratory free drinks from kind strangers on each such occasion.

"No," Rick replied to Matt's question, "I won't be playing 'Happy Birthday' at Jeers. Too many guys in there know me."

"And your devious ways," said Matt.

As they neared their cars, Rick said, "I'll meet you at Jeers in a couple of minutes. I've got to stop at the florist shop on Euclid before they close."

Matt looked at him. "My dad always said that when you see a man buying flowers, it's because of something he's done, or something he plans to do. Which is it with you?"

"None of your damn business," Rothmeyer said.

A quick two drinks it was—for Matt. He said goodbye at 7:05. Rick was lingering over the last of his drink when four of their softball-playing buddies came in, looking anxious. One of them, Jimmy Sheehan, spotted Rick. "It's poker night and we're a man short. We're going over to my place, right in the neighborhood. Beer, pizza, and some Texas Hold 'Em. How about it, Rick?"

"I'll give you an hour," Rick replied, finishing his drink. "Then I'll have to leave. Ivy's making dinner for me tonight," he said, referring to his actress-girlfriend Ivy Borchers.

Shortly before midnight, ahead more than $200, Rick attempted to pull out of the game. But Sheehan pleaded, "C'mon, man, give us a chance to get some of it back. You're killing us." At 1:15 a.m., having lost eleven straight hands and most of his profits, Rick threw the flowers for Ivy into a waste basket. His cards continued crummy: not bad enough to convince him to fold, not good enough to win more than the very occasional small pot.

After three o'clock, Rick even lost an argument over, as he put it, "why there shouldn't be some kind of American Taliban that'd ban most women from wearing those jeans or skirts that show their belly buttons. There's not one woman in thirty who looks good in those outfits. These are expanses of flesh nobody wants to be shown."

Jimmy Sheehan, however, spoke for the rest of the players at the table when he responded, "Ah, but that one."

Rick wouldn't concede. "If my Ivy is the one in thirty, okay, she looks great dressed like that." He was about to elaborate when he glanced at his watch. "Ivy!" he said. "Holy shit, I gotta get out of here."

Ivy opened the door to her apartment just after four. She was in her house coat, and in high dudgeon. Rick shrugged apologetically. Hands raised, palms out as he confronted her, Rick took a deep breath. He said, "Ivy, I hope to God you didn't pay the ransom. I finally managed to escape."

There was no hint of a smile on her face as she slammed the door in his.

Chapter Three

As Matt O'Connor rode the swift and silent elevator to the thirty-sixth floor of the Hancock Building in downtown Chicago, he wondered again about the urgency of the polite summons he had received. Moe Kellman, as Matt knew, ordinarily was the least excitable of men. A one-time teenage Marine corporal who had survived the Battle of the Chosen Reservoir, he was convinced that, from that horrendously bloody period of his life, "everything else is gravy." Moe stood five feet six inches, which was why he wound up in an armored division. "They put the short guys in the tanks," he had once told Matt. Nothing had ever seemed to bother Moe in the time Matt had known him. But he seemed to be bothered by something now.

Moe had certainly accumulated enough "gravy" in the monetary sense, Matt reflected as he was ushered into the executive suite by one of the glossy receptionists Kellman employed. The offices were one side of a floor-length corridor. On the other side was an elegantly appointed showroom for the wares Kellman sold: ultra-expensive furs for the women of Chicago's primary movers and shakers, a segment of society that PETA had failed to penetrate. Kellman's financially select clientele included wives and mistresses of the men who ran the Outfit in Chicago; indeed, it was believed that "the boys" had initially set up Kellman in the fur business when, casting about for something to try and make him dim his memories of Korea, he agreed to handle some sensitive dealings for a distant relative on his mother's side named

Meyer Lansky. If asked about this, Kellman always smiled and changed the subject.

Matt had first met Kellman four years earlier when one of Kellman's horses was named the top sprinter in thoroughbred racing for that racing season. Assigned to interview Kellman for the special *Racing Daily* issue devoted to champions, Matt agreed to a luncheon meeting at a Rush Street restaurant called Dino's. The restaurant was Kellman's choice. When Matt arrived the maître d' ushered him to a booth shielded from the loud bustle of the crowd. In the booth, Matt saw a diminutive, older man with a white, Don King-like electrification hair cut. He was issuing instructions to an attentive waiter. When he saw Matt approach, he rose to his full height and extended his hand. "Mr. O'Connor," he said, "glad to meet you. Sit down. I've ordered for us—I eat here regularly. If you don't like what you get, we can revise. Now, let's talk horses."

And that they did, for the next three hours. The excellent lunch was followed by a series of grappas so powerful that Matt had put away his notepad and just sat back to enjoy the conversation. He found Kellman to be knowledgeable about horses, vague about his past, and—surprisingly to Matt, who almost always found his interview subjects to be primarily interested only in themselves—curious about Matt's background and career.

Their lengthy, libation-rich conversation was interrupted only once, by a call Kellman took on his cell phone. He smiled warmly when he recognized the voice on the other end. Several minutes of talk followed before Kellman said "Goodbye, honey. Take care. It won't be long now."

Kellman was still smiling as he put the phone away. "That was my granddaughter, Leah. My only grandchild. She's overdue with her second baby. Getting a little anxious. So am I."

Kellman signaled for another pot of coffee. "Leah's married to a nice young lawyer, Nat Lepp. Unfortunately, she and Nat have a name already picked out for this child, which will be a boy, they know that. Ian Lepp, mind you. Their first child is a daughter they named Maeve, if you can believe that.

"They've got friends," Kellman continued, "with children named Leah Gottleib. Sinead Lieberman. Sean Applebaum. Thank God my parents didn't live to see this.

"You think they're busy over in Ireland baptizing Isadore O'Learys? Shimon Healys? Arie Donaghues?" he snorted. "I don't think so."

Matt could not control his laughter. Kellman, startled at first, quickly joined him. And a solid friendship was born that day.

◇◇◇

After Matt's lengthy profile of Kellman appeared in print, he received a call from his subject, who was both grateful and complimentary. "For an Irishman you're a real mensch," Kellman said. "How about we have lunch next week?"

As their friendship flourished, Matt consulted with one of his former journalism school classmates, Jim Draeger, a crime reporting specialist for the *Chicago Leader*.

"Moe Kellman?" Draeger said with a knowing smile. "Sharp little bastard—knows everybody. Is he mobbed up? Let's say he's connected but he's not connected, if you know what I mean. There's never been anything official tying him to the Outfit. Moe is way too smart for that. But you've always got to keep in mind that he's on very, very familiar terms with people you would never want to notice in your rearview mirror late at night. *Capice?*"

This report from his friend intrigued Matt, as did Draeger's concluding assessment of Kellman: "You can't help but like the guy. And if he likes you, he's a helluva news source for a lot of things that go on in this city."

When Matt walked into Kellman's spacious office, the little man waved a greeting while continuing a phone conversation. As usual, he was elegantly attired, white linen shirt agleam under a gray silk suit and gray tie, diamond cufflinks sparkling as he shifted the phone from one hand to another.

Kellman perched on the arm of a chair beside his desk. There was no furniture in front of the desk, for Kellman preferred doing in-person business on the enormous, soft, beige leather couch near the expanse of tall windows overlooking Lake Michigan;

from there he could easily reach over and give an encouraging pat to a customer's hand or knee.

The late afternoon sun behind Kellman served to back light and further emphasize the startling head of frizzed white hair, *like a Brillo pad*, Matt thought. Gesturing, Kellman urged O'Connor to help himself to the enormous platter of fresh fruit on the table near the couch. Responding in pantomime, Matt waved off Kellman's offer of something to drink.

This was Matt's third visit to Kellman's place of business, and he was again impressed by the prestigious Michigan avenue address, the knockout-looking female help, the impressive display of modern art gracing the walls of the tastefully furnished room.

Finally hanging up the phone, Kellman said in explanation and disgust, "Fifi Bonadio." He shook his head. "Cheapest son of a bitch in the Outfit. Every time he buys a coat from me for one of his punches, it's like negotiating the fucking Louisiana Purchase. And with all the money he's stolen and hidden…"

Crossing the room to join Matt on the couch, Kellman said, "But I didn't ask you to come in today to talk about Fifi, that tight ass." Kellman tapped a finger on a newspaper clipping that lay on the coffee table. "Matt, do you remember seeing this story back near the end of February?" The headline read *Death of an Aged Bookmaker*.

Matt said, "Yeah, I do. I remember thinking how astounding it was that the guy was still making book at what, ninety-some years old."

"Bernie Glockner was ninety-eight," Kellman said. "He was also my uncle, my mother's only brother."

"You're kidding!"

"Not in the least. And I'm also not kidding when I tell you that I don't think Bernie killed himself by jumping out of his window."

Matt sat back in the couch before responding. "Moe, let's face it, quite a few elderly people decide to check out on their own terms. And you can't blame them. Could be caused by illness, depression, loneliness…it happens."

Kellman shook his head. "I know that. But I also know this thing with Bernie doesn't compute. It's been gnawing at me. You didn't know him, or how he lived. The man was in amazing physical shape for his age. Never sick a day in his life. I talked to his personal physician after the service. He told me Bernie had had a complete physical two weeks earlier. 'He had the heart of a sixty-year-old,' the doc said, 'blood pressure and cholesterol numbers a kid would envy.'

"I know for a fact he was still engaged in an active sex life with a fifty-five-year-old widow who lived in his building. Bernie walked four miles a day and ate like a triathlete. He loved living, believe me.

"The coroner ruled it death by suicide. Bullshit. I think Bernie was overpowered and then thrown out of that window."

Kellman's eyes were bright with conviction. "And the suicide note they found was complete bullshit. Written on his own computer? Give me a break. The man never committed *anything* to paper. Not in his line of work. He stored betting records in his head. The only thing he used that computer for was to download racing results from around the country.

"People say to me, 'You got to expect this might happen with a man of that age.' But I don't. Matt, you've got to understand—Bernie was no so-called man of that age. He was a fuckin' medical marvel. We used to laugh about how he wanted to live when he 'got old.' He had a routine he loved.

"'Promise never to put me in some cut-rate codger warehouse,' he'd say, 'where I can see your Jaguar parked outside on one of your rare visits...

"'Make sure it's a place where I can do internet betting...

"'Promise to pay the attendants to clip my ear hair on a regular basis. I don't want to be slumped over in a wheelchair in some hallway with bushes growing out of my ears. That's how poor Howie Solomon looks when I visit him.'"

Kellman paused and looked out the window. "You had to laugh, listening to him. Bernie was one of those rare people that just naturally brighten you up when you talk to them. Last call

I had from him, two days before he died, he says, 'Mosey, you know how to summarize Jewish holidays?' No, I say. Bernie says, 'Here's how: They tried to kill us. We won. Let's eat.' He was still laughing when he hung up."

Noticing the skeptical expression that remained on Matt's face, Kellman pressed on. "There are things, Matt, that look to be one thing but are very much another. Just take a story in today's paper. It's about how the murder rate in the city has stayed the same for two years even while the number of serious assault cases have shot through the roof. They make this out to be a big deal.

"Know what the deal really is? Victims are getting better medical help. The paramedics, the trauma unit workers, emergency room surgeons—they've been saving the lives of people who before this would have gone right into the murder column. Now they go into the assault list—people with gaping gunshot wounds, knives sticking out of their chests. Last week at Cook County they saved the life of a guy who staggered in the front door with an ax blade in his forehead.

"So the murder *rate* may be down, but the number of jerks trying to *commit* murder hasn't dropped off any. They're just not as lucky as it as they used to be. Like I said, Matt, things often aren't what they seem. As far as I'm concerned, Bernie's death falls into that category."

Matt picked up the news story and read it again. "Moe," he said, "okay, let's say for the sake of argument that you're right about this. Let's say Uncle Bernie didn't voluntarily decide to take a flyer. So, why would someone kill him? And who?"

"Exactly," said Kellman enthusiastically, leaning forward to pat Matt's knee. "That's where you come into it. I want you to try and find out 'who' for me."

Moe went to his desk and lifted a folder out of the middle drawer. "I've made some notes on the last few conversations I had with Bernie," he said. "I had dinner with him two weeks before he died, lunch five days before it happened. Both those times, he was excited about some project he had going involving horse racing and a professor who had come to him as a 'research source,' as Bernie put it. When I asked him who the professor was, and how he came to locate him, Bernie clammed up. He wouldn't give me any details other than the fact that the professor was going to quote him in some book he was writing. Bernie was very proud of that. I don't know if you know this, but Bernie was an educated man himself. He was looking forward to the book being published. He was *excited* about it—not like a guy getting set to kill himself."

Matt said, "Moe, let's say you're right. Where do I come into it?"

"At the racetrack," Kellman replied. "I think some people tossed Bernie out that window, phonied up a suicide note, and eliminated a problem. The question is, what kind of problem could this old man pose? I've checked with a lot of people I know in this town"—he paused to let that sink in, letting Matt know that the people he checked with were people that Matt never wanted to start checking with—"and they've heard nothing. Nothing. Bernie was kind of like a hero from the old days for them, you know? He went back beyond any of them, knew guys that were local Outfit legends. If they'd heard anything, they'd tell me. But nothing.

"My thinking is that this is connected to this professor. It could be tied to horse racing, which Bernie said was the guy's big interest. I think the reason for Bernie's murder, my friend, is somewhere in your racing world. I can't think of any other place to start looking. And with your background, your contacts, you could help me on this, Matt."

Kellman leaned over to Matt, his look fiercely intent.

"You can count on this, kid," Kellman said. "I *will* find out who did Bernie. And even if God drops everything else he won't be able to help who did it when I find him. Are you in?"

Matt said yes.

Chapter Four

Bernie Glockner's death had made the news sections of Chicago's major newspapers. Television newscasts also featured the story of the "Wizard of Odds," a police spokesperson describing the note found next to Bernie's computer and then labeling the old bookie's demise as "an apparent suicide."

People who had known Bernie understood that their departed friend, who had assiduously avoided the public spotlight during his lengthy career, would have been appalled at this torrent of public notice. What his friends and acquaintances could not have known was that it was an another news story out of Chicago, dated the previous September, that led directly to Bernie's death.

CHICAGO—A federal judge here today sentenced three jockeys to five years in prison for race-fixing. Another three riders each were given two-year sentences by Judge John P. Hoban. Avoiding punishment were two fellow jockeys who were unindicted co-conspirators in this case, one of the most publicized in U. S. horse racing history.

Drawing the lengthier sentences were jockeys Jesse Wright, Bobby Walsh and Lonnie Stafford, convicted as ringleaders in the scheme to manipulate the outcome of the seventh race at downstate Devon Downs last May 1. Jockeys Pat Marchant, Basil Teague and Eduardo Lopez, who confessed to participating in the scheme, drew the lesser terms.

The six men were convicted of race-fixing under the RICO statute by a federal court jury on August 2. They were found guilty of conspiring to make their mounts finish out of the money (first three positions). A 32-1 long shot won the race, keying a $194,400 trifecta payoff—highest in Illinois horse racing history. Only three tickets were sold on the winning 3-2-8 combination. All three were cashed by confederates of the convicted riders who eventually testified against them.

Suspicions concerning the May 1 race arose immediately after its finish. Officials reviewing the videotape of the race raised questions, but issued no rulings. The scheme began to fall apart three weeks later when Wright, the alleged ringleader, purchased a luxury automobile in Belleville, IL, paying cash, and word of this transaction reached local law enforcement officials. They then alerted federal authorities. In the course of the ensuing investigation, Wright confessed to his role—his mount, the second favorite in the field of twelve horses, finished seventh—and implicated the others.

The other four jockeys who rode in the race were investigated thoroughly but none were charged with any wrongdoing, including Robby Kieckhefer, pilot of the winning horse.

Prosecutors said the case might never have been brought had it not been for an anonymous tip regarding Wright's car purchase. According to lead prosecutor Barbara Bierman, this was one of the few times in U. S. history that professional athletes received prison sentences for conspiring to fix a sporting event.

Defense attorney Bart England, who represented the men drawing the heavier sentences, argued that they acted because they were riding "at a minor track where purses are

pitifully small, where they have to struggle
to make a living."

    Judge Hoban responded by saying that the
convicted men "should have struggled harder
to make an honest living, like the majority
of their contemporaries."

    All six jockeys also were banned from ever
being licensed to ride again by the state
racing board.

One of the readers of this newspaper story sat back in his chair
in the periodicals room of the University of Wisconsin-Madison
library, a site he visited every day. Claude Bledsoe had been following the jockey scandal story with great interest. *This is like a
putsch that failed because of too many generals*, he thought. For a
moment, his gaze drifted across the large room, lingering on the
most attractive of the several female readers—"this year's crop of
lovelies," as he termed them. The forty-nine-year-old Bledsoe had
been a student using this facility for the past thirty-one years, happily enmeshed in a worry-free life of continual study and modest
but satisfactory physical comfort, some of that comfort provided
by women who had a taste for the eccentric. Now, that carefree
segment of Bledsoe's life was threatening to end, unless he did
something about it very soon. That's why Bledsoe's interest had
been drawn to the story of the crooked jockeys and their failed
attempt to get away with a big score.

    Bledsoe, who had never committed such a crime in his life, sat
in the periodicals room for the next forty-five minutes thinking
about his situation. It was apparent to him that there was money
to be made if you could figure out how to fix horse races. *But,* he
thought, *not as ineptly as that failed exercise. And not a dinky little
track like Devon Downs. I need a bigger score than that.* Later, as
he walked down the library steps into the warm welcome of an
Indian summer afternoon in Madison, he said to himself, "All
I've got to do is find a way. And I will."

    Two sophomore boys coming up the library steps turned as
they overheard Bledsoe. One of the boys smiled, then said to
the other, "You know about him? That's that weirdo who's been

going to school here forever. Everybody calls him the Professor. He's got dozens of degrees, but he never leaves." The boy added, laughing, "He was going to school here when my *mom* was here! Strange, man. I guess he's started to talk to himself, too."

◇◇◇

One week earlier Bledsoe had sat in the downtown Madison office of attorney James Altman, stunned by what he had just heard. The attorney, current head of a three-generation law firm that had handled the Bledsoe family's business for years, had just finished reading aloud a previously unrevealed codicil of the will that had been made years before her death by Claude's wealthy grandmother and benefactress, Matilda Webb Bledsoe.

Altman, a portly, vested, florid, and accurate imitation of his male forebears, was Bledsoe's age. They had met only a few times. Yet, Altman seemed to take understated relish in reading from the legal document before him. Bledsoe, listening in disbelief, restrained his urge to leap across the polished surface of the antique rosewood desk and propel this smug attorney through the window onto State Street.

Most terms in the will were very familiar to Bledsoe. As the favorite grandchild of the late pharmaceutical heiress, he was the beneficiary of an unusual gift. Grandmother Bledsoe had established a trust fund for her young relative, an odd-looking but brilliant child she had taken a liking to from the time he first began trouncing her at chess when he was four years old. Provisions of the trust stipulated that Claude's tuition, room, board, and "reasonable living and travel expenses be completely funded while he is enrolled in a degree program at the University of Wisconsin."

The product of what his first psychology professor referred to as a "profoundly damaged home," Claude had emerged from it with his considerable intelligence intact. With his IQ of one-hundred and eighty-two, he was easily able to identify a loophole in Grandma Bledsoe's bequest that he could drive an armored truck through. He would not, he realized, ever have to work a day in his life as long as he attended UW as a full-time student.

This appealed to Claude from several standpoints, not the least of which was the fact that it represented a resounding "fuck you" delivered to his father, who had unsuccessfully challenged the will in Dane County Circuit Court.

Starting when he was seventeen, Claude had taken advantage of the trust fund to earn undergraduate degrees in political science, music education, retailing, landscape architecture, English literature, food science, Native American Studies, cartography and information systems, computer science, interior design, agricultural science, French, and environmental science. He also earned an M.A. in comparative literature, and an M.S. in dairy science, and graduated from the law school (but never took the bar exam). Bledsoe had more classmates than anyone in the history of American higher education. He had planned on taking a degree in library science next year.

But now Bledsoe heard Altman saying, "Your grandmother made a major change in your trust fund shortly before she died ten years ago. That was when you were approaching age forty, and, in her concerned view, showing no signs of ever detaching yourself from student life. She was, as she phrased it, 'Concerned that Claude might not realize his immense potential without a strong motivating factor.' Her instructions were that you be apprised of this twelve months prior to your fiftieth birthday."

Altman placed the document down on the desk. He said, "With that in mind, I asked you to meet with me." To Bledsoe, it seemed the attorney took perverse pleasure in then asking, "Would your net worth currently be a million dollars or more?"

Bledsoe snorted. "Altman, as you well know I've been a full-time student. What money I made from part-time work, such as tutoring, would hardly elevate me to millionaire status. Why are you asking me this? What's this about?"

The attorney sighed. "Well, Claude," he said, tapping an index finger on the document that lay on his desk, "you seem to have a problem."

The "problem" was in the codicil. It stated, in very clear terms, that if Claude accumulated a net worth of one million dollars by the time he was fifty, he would then inherit the entire trust fund, now valued at "more than fifteen million and growing," Altman said, a trace of envy in his voice. "But," he went on, evidently liking this part better, if Claude had not managed to achieve that monetary goal, he would not only not inherit—the trust would be divided among several of Grandma Bledsoe's favorite charities—but his annual education stipend would abruptly cease.

Altman's intercom buzzed, but he ignored it. He continued, "Your grandmother wrote that she was 'very hopeful that the closure clause would never have to be invoked, that Claude will have used his great talents to reach the prescribed monetary level.'"

Altman stopped reading. He looked over the top of his glasses at Bledsoe, now slumped forward in his chair, elbows on knees. He took in Bledsoe's worn sport coat, unpressed khakis, worn cross-trainers. He could see Bledsoe was grinding his teeth, for his jaw muscles bulged as if his cheeks housed unshelled pecans.

The attorney coughed politely. He said, "I'll ask again. Have you accumulated the sum specified by your grandmother, Mr. Bledsoe?"

Bledsoe didn't bother to reply. Nor did he respond to Altman's observation that "while a million dollars today isn't what it was when your grandmother authorized the creation of this codicil, it is obvious that she had high expectations for you.

"You have a year in which to meet her challenge," Altman concluded. "Good luck." He rose and extended his hand. Bledsoe responded with a cutting look. His expression seemed to reflect a combination of surprise, regret, resentment, and rage. Spread across those broad, unattractive features, it made the attorney shudder. Bledsoe walked out of the office without saying another word.

In the elevator, Bledsoe startled a female paralegal when he said aloud, "Where the hell can I get a million that fast?" She held her files close to her breast and flattened herself against the elevator wall. Bledsoe did not notice her. He was running through his options. An obvious one would be to take a year off from his studies and play blackjack for a living in Las Vegas. He had made several lucrative forays there in the past. Bledsoe was very good at blackjack. But he knew that the casinos would eventually identify him as a card counter and consistent winner, and would then, in their unique interpretation of free enterprise, ban him from playing.

As the elevator reached one and the paralegal scurried out, Bledsoe's thoughts returned to the jockey trial story. His interest in it previously had been purely academic. Not anymore.

Chapter Five

More than anything else, what Bledsoe felt was shock and a strong sense of betrayal as he walked out of the law building and took a seat on a park bench on Capitol Square, oblivious to the foot traffic going by. And it was shock that hit him hardest, simply because he had for the most part exercised complete control over his life. Smart, strong, and ruthless, Claude from early youth had shown the ability to plan, set goals, and meet them, whether it was in school, sports, scouting, or science clubs. He'd always done it with what his admiring grandmother described as "good old Bledsoe cocksuredness," but what envious contemporaries and their parents often regarded as outright arrogance. Bledsoe abhorred surprises. Now, with the attorney Altman's revelation about the will, he felt as if he'd been kidney kicked by a two-hundred-pound karate black belt holder.

A September breeze drifted through the square in downtown Madison, rearranging the fallen leaves. One of Bledsoe's numerous former professors walked briskly past without saying hello. Bledsoe didn't notice. Against his will, he was remembering two other horrendous shocks he'd suffered, memories of which he for the most part was able to repress. Not now, though, not today. Not after learning what Grandmother Bledsoe had done to him.

Sitting on the park bench, cracking his massive knuckles, Bledsoe's earliest memory returned. On a winter night when he was just over three years old he'd been awakened in his red,

wooden junior bed by the loud sounds of one of his parents'
frequent arguments. He heard his father's baritone bellows, his
mother's shrieked responses, the sounds of glasses smashing, a
face being slapped. Then his bedroom door banged open and his
parents barged in, still screaming at each other. He could see the
reddish imprint of his father's hand on his mother's otherwise
pale face. He cowered in his bed, face turned away, hands over
his ears. But his father grabbed the back of his sleeper and jerked
Claude to his feet. The boy began to sob.

"Stand up, Claude," his father ordered. Claude struggled to
his feet, bewildered, blinking at the light that shone in from the
hallway. He looked from one grim face to the other, wondering
what he had done.

Speaking slowly, his words only slightly slurred by alcohol,
his father said, "Your Mommy and I are going to live apart from
now on. Think carefully, Claude: which one of us do you want
to go and live with?" There was no answer. *"Which one?"* his
father shouted, shaking him.

Between sobs the boy kept replying, "Don't know, don't
know," even as his father shook him again before releasing him
and turning away. The boy threw himself down on the bed,
burying his face in the pillow. He cried himself to sleep, aware
only of his mother's hand stroking his back before she left and the
verbal battle resumed behind the slammed door of his parents'
bedroom. It was a night he would dream of for years.

Bledsoe's parents never carried out their repeated threats to
separate. Claude's sister Emily was born a year later, his brother
Edward two years after that. But the parental warfare continued
sporadically. Not a night went by that Claude did not fall uneasily to sleep, fearing he'd be again awakened and confronted with
the awful choice his parents had given him. This continued until
Claude was nine years old. Until the mid-December night that
his mother drove her Volvo, doors locked, accelerator floored, off
the end of a pier leading into Lake Monona, crashing through
the ice, her two younger children securely belted in the seat
behind her. In the years that followed, Claude spent the school

year living with his embittered, alcoholic father, the summers at the home of his doting grandmother. Only once was the boy able to bring himself to ask the question that had tormented him since his mother's final night: "Why didn't Mother take me, too?" In reply, his father backhanded him across the kitchen, Claude cracking his head on the edge of the stove. He never asked again.

◇◇◇

Bledsoe got to his feet and began to walk slowly around the square. He passed food and crafts stands that were being set up for the weekend's popular farmer's market. He stepped around a man unloading pumpkins from a large wheelbarrow. All he was aware of was an overpowering sense of betrayal. How could his loving "Gram" have done this to him? He felt a rush of anger, anger of the sort he'd previously experienced just twice in his life: the lingering rage directed at his father in the wake of his mother's suicide, and, five years later, the sudden explosion of rage directed at his cousin, Greta Prather.

Walking the Madison square this late afternoon, it came back to him in a torrent of unwanted remembrance: his fourteenth summer, that long ago August when he'd been so desperately in love with Greta; their last night together swimming in the small, spring-fed lake on their widowed grandmother's estate in northeastern Wisconsin.

Claude had had a lingering, lacerating crush on Greta since he was a twelve-year-old sixth grader, the strongest and smartest boy in his private school class, possessed even then of a freakish physical strength and extraordinary intelligence that served to set him well apart from his classmates. He was an odd-looking youth that they referred to as The Weirdo—though never to his face, no, they weren't brave enough for that.

Other family members became aware of Claude's crush, especially a couple of his uncles, who kidded him frequently. For the most part Claude ignored the jibes of what he thought of as "those idiots," concentrating instead on Greta when he saw her at family gatherings three or four times a year.

In her generous fashion, Greta was invariably kind to Claude during the summer vacations and holidays when they were together. A tall, statuesque young woman who worked part time as a model while attending Wellesley, she was used to attention and accepted it gracefully. In his wallet Claude kept a photo of Greta in her high school prom dress, the face of her date for the occasion trimmed out. He wrote letters to her reporting his progress in school and sports, what music he'd recently discovered, the books he was enjoying. He never stated his feelings for her, convinced as he was that Greta was well aware of them. He knew the right time would come in which to confirm that.

That August was one of the warmest on record in Wisconsin's north woods. The rambling, old log house built by his paternal grandparents a half-century earlier had no air conditioning, and that summer, for the first time anyone could remember, even the protective stands of pines and birches could not thwart the heat, even after sunset.

Shortly after eleven o'clock that night, Claude heard light footsteps on the creaking staircase outside his bedroom. Minutes later he looked out his window and saw Greta walking across the lawn toward the pier and the lake. He quickly put on his swimsuit and moved quietly down the stairs and through the dark, silent house. He knew they would be alone at the lake, the other family members and guests long since retired after a long day of boating, swimming, then volleyball and croquet on the vast green lawn leading down to the shore.

Greta was in the water, floating on her back, when Claude walked out onto the pier. She smiled when she saw him and gave him a languid wave, face pointed toward the stars, her long black hair floating in the water. He dove in neatly and swam with powerful strokes fifty yards out into the cool water before turning back to join her.

Greta said the heat had kept her from sleeping. He told her he knew what she meant. Then she stood up in the water, which was less than three feet deep this close to the pier, and shook the moisture from her hair. Her tanned shoulders gleamed in the moonlight. Claude felt himself grow hard as he dog paddled toward her and rose to his feet. With a lunge he moved to her and put his arms around her. He cupped her face in one of his large hands and kissed her hard, his other hand on her back, pressing her to him. It was a moment he had long imagined.

To Claude's enormous surprise, Greta planted her feet and tried to push him off. Her eyes were wild as she leaned away from him, fighting to free herself. He would not let her go. He barely heard her whispered protests. He pulled the strap of her swimsuit off her shoulder and grasped her left breast. He tried to kiss her again, but she turned her face to the side, her mouth tight with fright. "Stop it," she begged. "This is a mistake. Let me go, please. We'll just forget this ever happened."

Even more excited now, he yanked down the top of her swimsuit and again thrust himself against her. "What's wrong with you?" he said harshly, his lips against her neck. "We've been heading toward this for years. Don't you know that?"

Greta fought harder. When she started to scream, he quickly covered her mouth with his hand, then looked down at her with a combination of astonishment and growing rage. How wrong he had been! How had he managed to so misread the situation, to misinterpret what he'd been sure was her returned love? Greta's was now a face he barely recognized, so full of loathing were her eyes as they burned into his.

Claude knew now that Greta would never, ever forgive him for his actions this night, that her report of what he'd done could destroy him. He could not permit that.

With a sudden move, he wrapped his left leg behind her knees and kicked her feet out from under her. She was now on her back, partly under the water, and he straddled her, one hand still covering her mouth, the other clamped on her shoulder. She thrashed beneath him. His heart pounded as he pressed her head down beneath the water. For a few moments he watched her face, contorted by pain and terror. Then he turned his face to the night sky for the minutes it took until she was at last limp beneath him.

A huge cloud momentarily covered the moon as he dragged Greta's body over to the pier. He pulled the top of her swimsuit back into place. Carefully positioning her lifeless head, he rammed it against one of the pier's stanchions. The resulting wound on her forehead was visible to him as moonlight flooded back down. It would appear that she had somehow slipped and accidentally struck her head, then fallen into the water unconscious and drowned.

Claude trotted through the shadow of the pines to the rear entrance of the old house, then slipped silently up the stairs to his room. He felt enormously tired, yet at the same time exhilarated. Yes, it was a terrible shame what Greta had forced him to do this night. But he'd at least rid himself of what he could now recognize as a ridiculously useless obsession.

The next morning Claude helped in the search once his beautiful cousin was discovered to be missing. He pretended to break down when Greta's body was discovered down the shoreline. Relatives comforted him for what they believed to his wrenching grief at this tragic loss of the love of his young life.

Whenever he looked back on that fateful August night, Bledsoe was always amazed and embarrassed. How could he have allowed his teenage hormonal seiche of love and lust to threaten his promising future? What regret he felt had nothing to do with Greta's death—there was no way he could have allowed her to live, and ruin him—but was over his stupid misperception. He vowed to never again find himself in a situation he could not completely control.

Deep in thought, Bledsoe made three complete tours of Capitol Square as he pondered his plight. Make a million dollars in a year? For him, now, it was truly all or nothing at all. He knew he'd find a way.

Glancing up at the electronic clock on a bank across State Street, Bledsoe smiled. He realized he still had time to make his three o'clock class, an elective in the physical education department that he'd really begun to enjoy. He felt better already. He quickened his pace.

Chapter Six

Later that same September afternoon in Madison, anticipation was running high at Doherty's Den, a popular saloon on University Avenue. Seated at the long mahogany bar were a couple of dozen people, mostly men, mostly students, a few townspeople sprinkled among them, all eagerly awaiting the start of Mystery Hour, during which all drinks were sold at half-price.

Many eyes were on the three television sets spaced above the back bar showing, respectively, a Cubs-Cards baseball game, an "ESPN Classic" program on Vince Lombardi's Green Bay Packers, and "Celebrity Poker." The audio had been turned off on all three sets, but the volume on the battered old radio at the end of the bar was on high. The radio carried a Milwaukee sports talk show, which today had its usual contingent of contributors: mostly lifelong bachelors, or divorced men, living in the basements of their widowed mothers' homes, all with passionate opinions on matters so slight as to hardly qualify as trivia. Two waitresses hustled food baskets from the kitchen to the worn wooden booths lining the walls of the long room. The pool table was in use, the aged pinball machine silent.

By definition, the start of Mystery Hour varied from afternoon to afternoon. It might be 1:47 or 3:21 or 5:05 or some other time, depending on the whim of the bar's owner, a mischievous import from County Meath, Ireland, named Tim Doherty. The result of this marketing practice was a clientele that tended to nurse their drinks until bargain time arrived, then began tossing them down in torrents. Many of these customers stayed on long after Mystery Hour was over, continuing to drink and spend, which was the whole idea. Doherty referred to this busy sixty-minute period as his "liquid loss leader." He signaled its beginning by loudly ringing a battered cowbell he said he'd brought over with him from "the ould sod."

At 4:59, just two minutes into that day's Mystery Hour, the front door of Doherty's Den banged open. A wide-necked, broad-shouldered man, five feet eleven, two hundred and twenty pounds, stopped just inside the threshold. With his large shaved head and steel-framed glasses, Claude Bledsoe's appearance was enough to cause a momentary hush, especially among people toward the front who could see that he was carrying an archery bow. Reaching over his shoulder, Bledsoe extracted an arrow from the quiver on his back. He carefully aimed it, then released the bow string. The arrow zoomed over the heads of the bar patrons before burying itself in the center of the dart board on the back wall some fifty feet away. Bull's-eye.

"Jesus Christ!" yelped one of the students, ducking down and covering his head with his hands, in the process knocking off his Packers ball hat.

"Nope," smiled Doherty, toweling off the moist surface on which the young man had spilled his glass of Old Style, "it's Claude Bledsoe. I guess he's taking archery this semester."

The archer hung his equipment on a coat hook before taking a seat on one of the stools at the end of the bar. Doherty drew a pint of Bass Ale and brought it to him. "Hello, Claude," he said. "How're they hanging?"

"Loose and ready, Tim. And you?"

Doherty said, "Fine, Claude." He leaned across the bar and spoke softly. "But I wish you'd leave your Robin Hood act out-side. You've scared the bejesus out of some of my customers."

Bledsoe's face darkened. Quickly, Doherty added, "Just a request, is all." He moved down the bar, his back to Bledsoe, keeping a wary eye on him in the bar mirror.

Down the bar a middle-aged man turned to the still shaken student, who was staring wide-eyed at the arrow in the middle of the dart board. "You don't know about Claude Bledsoe?" the man said. "I guess you're new on campus. He's sort of a legend around here." The student ventured a peek at Bledsoe, who was now sipping his ale and speed-reading a copy of *The Wall Street Journal*.

What the student saw was a man who looked years younger than forty-nine. He also looked different from anyone else the young man had ever seen. A weight lifter at the YMCA where Bledsoe swam laps daily once remarked that Bledsoe was built "like a hairless orangutan." That statement was made well outside of Bledsoe's hearing, for the same weight lifter had once seen Bledsoe, showing off, lift up the back end of a Volkswagon Beetle "as easy as you'd pull up your garage door."

Bledsoe's physical strength and willingness to display it were well known in downtown Madison. He had never lost an arm-wrestling match to a member of the Wisconsin football team, *any* Badger team in nearly three decades, embarrassing new recruits autumn after autumn at Doherty's Den, where their knowing teammates delivered them to be humiliated.

Bledsoe had never lifted a weight in his life. His freakish strength, like his great intelligence, sprang from a gene source not apparent in his family history. The sometimes dark nature of his character was of similarly mysterious origin.

After he'd been graduated the first few times, Bledsoe was assigned a permanent academic advisor. That man, Henry Wing, met with Bledsoe before the start of each semester and recorded the degrees earned, also noting the outside interests Bledsoe said he enjoyed: several of the martial arts, skydiving, music, moutaineering, target shooting. Wing occasionally saw Bledsoe on campus or in town in the company of a woman, but never the same one twice.

Henry Wing retired the year that Bledsoe took his degree in agricultural science, accepting the diploma while wearing Oshkosh B'Gosh overalls and a John Deere cap. In the notes he left for his successor as Bledsoe's advisor, Wing wrote, "You will

find Mr. Bledsoe to be brilliant. He has also long struck me as
being exceedingly strange, like those large men who wear dresses,
or horned helmets and breastplates, or tasseled hats and lurid
makeup, to professional football games, making one wonder
what, when the games are over and night comes, they might be
going home to."

◇◇◇

The man at the bar continued to enlighten the student, who had
now replaced his Packers cap on his head and was working on
another beer. As he understood it, the man said, Bledsoe had been
a student "here since the seventies, on some kind of permanent
scholarship from his family. I don't believe he's worked a day in
his life."

The man could not have known it, but that was not actually
the case. In the long course of his scholarship years, Bledsoe
had saved a sizeable chunk of his stipend, for he'd always lived
modestly—decent but cheap apartments, used cars, thrift shop
wardrobe, the rare gourmet dinner. But four years earlier Bledsoe,
until then an extremely conservative investor of his savings, went
completely out of character. The results were disastrous. Not long
after he'd shifted his assets, along came the economic tsunami
known as the dot com crash. Bledsoe was suddenly faced with a
new reality: he needed to replace his on-its-last-legs car, a twelve-
year-old Honda Civic that had begun flaking rust like dandruff.
But Bledsoe had no funds to finance such a purchase.

As a result, Bledsoe offered his services as a paid tutor to
the university's athletic department, a fiefdom with impressive
financial resources. With his impeccable academic record, he was
immediately accepted. He was soon assigned to tutor a talented
athlete from River Forest, Illinois, named Rocco Bonadio.

Rocco was at the university on a football scholarship. As
Bledsoe soon discovered, his brawny, amiable, dark-haired pupil
had little interest in, and even less acumen for, his studies. Rocco
was in Madison solely to block for Badger glory, drink as much
beer as possible, and screw as many coeds as he could. Bledsoe
told Harriet Okey, his girlfriend that semester, that Rocco was

"so dumb he can hardly make an 'O' with a glass. He's got a hairline that nearly coincides with his eyebrows."

After learning more about Rocco's background, Bledsoe showed more interest in him. Rocco, it turned out, was the only son of Chicago Outfit boss Fifi Bonadio, a man of such authority that, in the words of one of his lieutenants, "when he comes home at night his wife stands at attention and the parakeet and goldfish try to look busy."

Fifi Bonadio was extremely proud of Rocco's athletic exploits, but even prouder that the Bonadio clan finally had its first college student. And the mob boss was determined that Rocco emerge from Madison with a degree. Primarily as a result of Bledsoe's efforts, this happened. Bledsoe wrote all of Rocco's papers for the courses in his major, criminal justice. That was the tuck-away bin into which many scholastically challenged jocks were funneled, the irony of which, in Rocco's case, was not lost on either Fifi or Bledsoe. Because of the young man's "learning disability," Bledsoe arranged for Rocco to take all of his quizzes and tests while being monitored only by Bledsoe. He thus managed to guarantee the much desired diploma for the Bonadio family wall.

"Had Rocco ever gotten a grade higher than C in any course," Bledsoe confided to Harriet, "there would have been grounds for a full-scale NCAA investigation. I massaged him through just at the right level, work good enough to earn passing grades but not good enough to raise any red flags over the thick cranium of this dolt."

Appreciative of Bledsoe's efforts, Fifi Bonadio, during a festive dinner at an upscale Madison restaurant the night before Rocco's graduation, tapped Bledsoe on the arm. Several glasses of wine earlier, he had begun to smile benevolently at Bledsoe, who was seated beside him, addressing him fondly as Professor. "You did good with my boy," Fifi said softly, nodding toward his beaming son. "I know it wasn't easy. He's a great kid and a damned good football player. But he's got his mother's brains. Nice people, good looking, her family, but they're not much smarter than the goats they used to herd in Calabria.

"So, I toast you Mr. Bledsoe," Bonadio said, raising his wine glass. "*Salud.* And," reverting to his softer voice, he added, "I owe you. You ever need anything, any time, you call me." Bonadio slipped Bledsoe a card with a business phone number along with whopping cash bonus.

◇◇◇

Bledsoe smiled to himself whenever he thought of that night. But he never thought he would have occasion to call in the favor offered—until now, with Grandma Bledsoe's deadline looming less than a year away.

Late that same September week, two days after his meeting with lawyer Altman and two years, three months after Rocco Bonadio's graduation dinner, Bledsoe dialed Big B Construction and Paving, Cicero, Illinois, and left a message on the answering machine. Fifi Bonadio called back an hour later. "Professor, how are you? What can I do for you, my friend?"

Bledsoe said he was fine, but he needed some advice. "I'm working on a paper about horse race gambling in America," Bledsoe lied. "I'd like to talk to someone who has been involved in it, who knows a great deal about it. I don't need to use his name, I just need information he could provide. Mr. Bonadio, would you happen to know anyone like that?"

Bonadio's laughter flowed through the phone. "Are you shitting me?" he chortled. "I've got the guy for you. He worked for us for a long, long time, making our betting lines. Brilliant guy, a genius. We called him the Wizard of Odds. He could move numbers around in his head like an Einstein.

"When we finally let him retire," Bonadio continued, "he said he wanted to keep his hand in by making a little book on his own. Fine, we said. He'd earned the right. Believe it or not, Professor, that was about twenty-five years ago! He's the oldest bookmaker in town, maybe in the whole fuckin' world." Bonadio laughed. "Name's Bernie Glockner. I'll give you his address and phone number.

"Tell the Wizard I said for you to call. Tell him hello from me."

Chapter Seven

That night Matt rose from his chair as Maggie Collins walked through the terrace doorway of Chicago's North Pond Café, on her way to joining him at a table that overlooked Lincoln Park and its duck-dotted lagoon. As usual, she turned as many heads as a waiter bearing a platter of flaming saginaki.

"What are you grinning at?" she said as she slid onto the chair he was holding for her.

"Grinning? Was that what I was doing? I thought I was just gazing in awe. You look terrific. It occurred to me again today that you're really the only job-related perk I've had since I started writing about racing."

"And more than you deserve," Maggie answered, blue eyes gleaming as she patted her short-cropped black hair into place. It was said with the smile that so frequently flitted across her tanned face.

North Pond Café, with its wonderful food and exceptional view of the city, was one of their favorite restaurants, even though it was not located near either of their homes. Maggie owned a western suburb condo only minutes from Heartland Downs, where she trained her horses. Matt was an Evanston condo resident with a much longer commute to the racetrack but with nearby Lake Michigan as ample compensation. They dined at North Pond at least three times a month, usually after which Maggie spent the night at Matt's place before arising at 4 p.m. for her drive to the racetrack. It was a trek that she made in exchange for Matt staying at her place the numerous other nights each month they spent together.

Maggie and Matt had been an item for nearly three years. At thirty-six, he was three years her senior and one marriage ahead of her. He and his wife Kathy had agreed to disagree after five increasingly passionless years during which Matt repeatedly refused to leave racing journalism to join her wealthy father's media empire as a general sports columnist. Matt and Kathy realized that they had married far too impulsively, and too young, and parted on extraordinarily amicable terms, ones flavored by mutual relief.

Kathy quickly remarried—an executive in her father's company—and, from what she told Matt, was a happy woman. In his turn, Matt entered a relationship with Maggie Collins, one-time North Shore debutante, now full-time horse trainer, a person as wrapped up in her work as he was in his. They had arrived at a comfort plateau that involved time spent together on a regular but never codified basis, a rewardingly shared sex life, and no hints of a need for formal commitment on the part of either one of these very independent individuals.

As Matt confided to his friend Rick, "It's like going steady in high school, except as adults."

"Better not let Maggie hear you say that."

"Funny thing is, Rick, she feels exactly the same way I do."

Matt often thought how lucky he was, especially compared to his friend. Rick, a lifelong bachelor, had begun a volatile, sporadic relationship eight years earlier with Chicago actress Ivy Borchers. Ivy maintained she would marry Rick only if he stopped betting on horses. Rick countered that nothing less than her retirement from acting would spur him into matrimony.

After one of their regular spats, Rick explained to Matt what he deemed to be the major cause of this lengthy standoff. "Actors are dangerously devious people," Rick contended. "No doubt about it in my mind. Remember, they've been professionally trained to be somebody other than what they are. Why should I believe anything this woman says?" Matt eventually came to recognize this combative relationship for what it was: an impasse of convenience, satisfying in its strange way to both Ivy and Rick. Matt was grateful he wasn't locked up in a life like that.

Looking across the table at Maggie as she perused the list of North Pond menu specials, he smiled as he always did when thinking of how they had met. As he loved to tell the story whenever anyone inquired, "We met at third base, where she kicked me in the nuts."

This had occurred during a summer racetrack softball league game at Heartland Downs. Matt was playing third base for the Press Box team. In the first inning of this season opener against the Backstretch Bombers, Maggie had blasted the twelve-inch ball into a gap in right field. Her long legs carried her swiftly around first and then second base. As the right fielder released the ball, she sped toward third. Matt straddled the bag awaiting the throw, as he had countless times in his athletic life. The throw was a rocket, right on target. Maggie and the ball arrived simultaneously. Maggie slid in hard on her left side. Her upraised right foot accidentally caught the crouching Matt squarely in the groin, whereupon he dropped the ball, rolling across the white chalk line in agony.

Moments later, still gripped by pain, Matt looked up at the face of the base runner. It was a very attractive face, one now with an expression that appeared to combine both concern and pent-up laughter.

"Who the hell do you think you are, Ty Cobb?" he groaned, waving his treasured Brooks Robinson signature glove at her.

"Safe is safe," Maggie replied, standing over him, one foot still on the bag. Then her attempt at keeping a straight face failed. She broke into laughter that was soon echoed by the rest of the players, coaches, umpires and, finally, Matt.

"Come on, I'll help you up," she said, extending a hand.

Matt reached for her hand and slowly got to his feet. He said, "You owe me a drink. At least."

"After we finish whipping your sorry asses," Maggie responded.

"Where'd you learn to talk like that? The Marines?"

"Nope. Four older brothers," she said. "And I was the best base runner of the bunch."

They had not met before that softball evening, but Maggie and Matt knew of each other. She was a regular reader of his *Racing Daily* column and, as trainer of a successful stable, had occasionally been mentioned in it. Matt was well aware of Maggie, who was one of only three women trainers at Heartland Downs. The other two looked like Roseanne. Maggie reminded him of a taller, sturdier version of Audrey Hepburn—Hepburn with an athlete's body, the result in Maggie's case of more than twenty-five years of horsebacking.

The only daughter of prominent Lake Forest attorney Jeremy Collins, Maggie had begun riding when she was five on a pony purchased by her fond father. She grew up in the equestrian show ranks, then at sixteen talked her way onto the Heartland Downs backstretch and into the summer employ of an old Texas-born trainer named Spanky Gural. It was the most exciting season of her life. She left home each morning at five o'clock, purportedly heading for her job as a counselor at a Libertyville children's camp, but drove instead to the racetrack. There she spent long hours hot-walking, then grooming Gural's horses, until the morning he gave in to her pestering and permitted her to start galloping horses for him. Maggie soon showed she was a natural at it, so much so that Gural encouraged her to apply for an apprentice jockey's license.

Not long after that, one of Jeremy Collins' law firm colleagues, Frank Rafferty, a horse owner, was observing the workouts one morning when he looked up to see Maggie cantering past on a big chestnut gelding. He waved at Maggie, whom he had known since she was a child, but she didn't see him. When Rafferty sat down for lunch with Jeremy Collins six hours later he said, "I didn't know your Maggie was working at the racetrack." Jeremy Collins raised his eyebrows before returning his gaze to the menu. "Nor did I," he murmured.

That night he confronted his daughter. Well aware of her independent streak, Jeremy still found himself puzzled by her passionate interest in horse racing. "Can't you stay with the show horses?" he pleaded. "No," his daughter replied. "To my mind the show world doesn't compare with the racetrack. The sights and sounds of the track, the people, the best horses…it's what I want to be involved with."

Maggie walked over to her dad's chair and looked down at him. "You've got to understand," she said, "that the ribbons you win in the show world are determined by somebody's *judgment*, their opinion. At the racetrack it doesn't work like that. It's a simple question of who gets there first.

"I love the competition. But I know I'll never make it as a jockey. I'm just not *that* good a rider. But I think I'd be good at training horses. No," she amended, "I *know* I'd be good at training horses."

Jeremy Collins shook his head resignedly. He couldn't help but recognize his own relentlessly competitive nature in his beautiful, earnest daughter. "All right, honey," he said, "go for it. All I'm going to ask of you is that you finish high school and then two years of college first."

"Deal," Maggie said, smiling as she hugged him.

She spent five years apprenticing with Gural, one of the top horsemen in the sport. Then Maggie launched her own stable. Using seed money from her dad, she bought two horses. Each of them won their first race for her. She was twenty-five, and on her way. Now, eight years later, her stable had grown to thirty horses. Averaging nearly one hundred wins a year, Maggie was a solidly professional presence at Midwest tracks. And hers was now a frequently mentioned name in Matt's columns when her best horses ran in Heartland's major races.

The waiter brought their drinks, vodka and tonic for Maggie, Jack Daniels on the rocks for Matt. After ordering their dinners, he said, "I've got something I want to tell you about." He described his meeting with Moe Kellman, and Kellman's thoughts about his Uncle Bernie's sudden death. "I don't know if Moe is right," Matt said, "but his track record is pretty strong, I'm told. If he *is* right, and The World's Oldest Bookie was indeed murdered, it could be a hell of a story for me."

Maggie had listened attentively. As she finished her salad she said, "So, do I have to start calling you Sleuth instead of

Scoop?" Matt thought again how much he loved the way her eyes sparkled and her nose crinkled when she laughed, even if it was at his expense.

He said, "Are you making fun of your boon companion? You don't envision the intrepid columnist morphing into the tenacious crime solver? I am disappointed in you."

Maggie laughed again. Then she said, "Seriously, are you going to look into this?"

"Why not?" he shrugged. "It could be very interesting."

Chapter Eight

A few weeks after Claude Bledsoe began his series of educational phone conversations with Bernie Glockner, he came to understand that, eventually, the old bookmaker would have to be eliminated. He realized, too, that he could not carry out his envisioned pari-mutuel heists by himself. Reluctantly, he decided to enlist the assistance of a drinking acquaintance, Jimbo Murray. He phoned Murray at the east side Madison muffler shop where Murray now worked. They agreed to meet that evening at Doherty's Den.

Murray was a thirty-two-year-old ex-con Bledsoe had first met at his Madison YMCA, a tall, rawboned, redheaded man who, like Bledsoe, pretty much kept to himself at the workout facility.

Murray, Bledsoe learned, had entered foster care at age three and passed through a succession of non-connective care takers, bewildered by and resentful of the system the whole way. He'd been expelled from high school at sixteen for flattening his English teacher one October morning. Earlier, he had been thrown off the football team for fighting—with the head coach. The school district's two-strike policy on teacher abuse led to his immediate expulsion.

Later that year, fancying himself a fighter, Murray entered the Madison Golden Gloves tournament in the novice heavyweight division. He pawed his way to a decision over one inept opponent, drew a couple of byes, then found himself in the finals confronting a hulking ebony specimen named Leonardo

Jackson who had dispatched all of his previous opponents with awesome rapidity. In the early seconds of round one, Murray absorbed two teeth-rattling jabs, then folded like a crepe suzette. He was booed raucously as he was counted out, then hurried to the dressing room while being berated by his coach. That was the end of his boxing career.

Four years later Murray, employed as a security guard, robbed the safe of a Home Depot store on the south side of Madison—the store he was guarding. He fled to South America with $67,580 in cash. Moving from Argentina to Brazil to Costa Rica, he eluded capture for more than eight months. Then he abruptly packed up and got on a flight to Chicago. An FBI "watcher" at O'Hare Airport spotted him arriving in Terminal Five. Murray was trailed to a McDonald's outlet on the airport's lower level and arrested as he polished off a Big Mac. His backpack contained $46,226 of the stolen cash. Asked why he had returned to the country of his crime, Murray replied, "I couldn't stand the goddam beaner food." His pedestrian appetites thus led him to spend the next sixty-two months in the Taycheeda Correctional Institution outside of Fond du Lac, Wisconsin. Murray had never forgiven his cousin Norman, the family cut-up, for mailing to him at Taycheeda the "Get Out of Jail Free" card from a Monopoly game.

In their post-workout beer-drinking session, Murray had disclosed his life history to Bledsoe, finding an apparently sympathetic ear. As an ex-convict, Murray had had trouble finding well-paying work. He hated the muffler shop, where wages were weak, but was stuck there. However, he told Bledsoe, he had recently filed a lawsuit he expected would be productive.

Bledsoe said, "What kind of lawsuit?"

Murray said, "It's for these burns I got. Third-degree burns on my left arm." He rolled up the sleeve of his grease-stained blue work shirt. "You can see the scars," he said.

"I noticed that when we worked out on the big bag," Bledsoe said. "How did that happen?"

The burns came, Murray explained, as he was sitting minding his own business in Celestial Bodies, a suburban Madison "gentlemen's club," watching a nude dancer. "While I'm concentrating on the stage this other broad comes over to me and starts a lap dance, which I had not ordered," Murray said indignantly. "I've been a Catholic all my life. Plus, she was semi-chubby and full-time homely. They don't get the top girls out there in the sticks, mainly farm girls gone wrong. This was like a third-level joint, you know, and I had no business being in there except I was stoned to my toes.

"Anyway, this chick starts operating. I lean back against the table to kind of get away from her. There's a fucking candle on the table and my Packers' jacket catches fire and I'm fucking burned, man. I give the broad a swat to get her away from me. The bouncer throws a pitcher of water at me. I wind up in the goddam emergency room."

Bledsoe twirled his empty beer bottle and called to Doherty for another round. Doherty didn't hear him. He was at the other end of the long bar, attempting to referee a heated argument between two Den regulars over whether steroids should be banned from major league baseball. "I love watching five-hundred-foot homers," one shouted. "Who gives a shit if the hitter's huge with chemicals. Not me!"

After he'd finally gotten Doherty's attention, Bledsoe said to Murray, "What are you going for in the suit?"

"Big bucks," Murray exclaimed. "That's what suits are for. My lawyer says that club should have known I was in danger from the candle. Here," he said, "let me read you this."

Murray extracted a thick envelope from his jacket pocket. "I carry this along, I don't want to lose it," he explained. "This is my lawsuit that says this joint 'negligently and carelessly allowed open candles on the tables to be used for lighting, when they knew or should have known that customers would be endangered by dancers embracing and dancing in close proximity to customers.' What do you think of that? Is that strong or what?"

Bledsoe had never seen Murray exhibit such enthusiasm. He pretended to look impressed at what he had heard.

"Who's your attorney?"

Murray took a long pull at his Miller Genuine Draft. "It's kind of cool," he said. "Lady named Alberta Erlebacher. I met her years back when she was my parole officer. She was going to law school at night then. She was real nice to me. I always stayed in touch with her even when I didn't have to."

Murray shook his head. "You know," he said, "there are some real loonies doing lawsuits. Clogging up the court system."

"Is that right?" Bledsoe replied.

"Damn right," Murray said. "There's a story in the paper today about a guy got leg cramps, him and his wife, flying to Europe. London, Spain, I don't remember where. But they come up with this story that the seats on their plane didn't give them enough room for their legs.

"Well, shit, I can understand that. First time me and my girl-friend Vera took a vacation we went to Acapulco. She got a deal on a group flight, or tour, I don't know what they called it, but Claude, it was bad. Row in front of me, the guy sat back and about had his head in my lap. I had to give him a good slap to get him to straighten up. Even then it was uncomfortable as hell. We get to Mexico, I'm sore and stiff as hell when I come shuffling off the damn plane.

"So, yesterday when I read about this guy's suit against the airlines, I can, like, identify. But then I go on reading about him. Get this. He says in his lawsuit that his airline seat was so bad that five days later he's cramped up, and he trips going up the steps to some cathedral over there, and falls on his face, and busts his front teeth and his glasses. Almost a *week* later! Now he's suing the airlines for two hundred grand. Is that some major bullshit or what?

"Kind of stuff like that, man, makes my lawsuit look pretty goddam good. Am I right?"

Bledsoe signaled the bartender. "My round," he said.

Bledsoe was silent as the beers were delivered. He said, "So, your case won't be coming to trial for awhile. Am I right?"

"Right," Murray said, "they're fucking us over with the delays, all that bullshit. Fucking lawyers.

"And," he added, draining his beer, "while I'm waiting I got some major money shortages. This chick that lives with me, Vera that I mentioned, works the night shift at Oscar Mayer during the week. But when she's out on the weekends, man, she's like an ATM machine in reverse, sucking up my bread."

That had been two weeks ago. Tonight, when the two men met again at Doherty's Den, the previous conversation resumed in almost seamless fashion, Murray again complaining about his money shortage and Vera's profligate ways. "I'm crazy about that chick, but she's busting my balls with her spending," he told Bledsoe. "From the standpoint of finances, I'm in a shithole section of my life," he added morosely. "I need to get a better job, or a second bad one to go with the one I've got."

There was a silence as they drank their beers and looked up at the television set behind the bar. Murray became engrossed in the rerun of a "reality" show on which large, well-built, butch-looking women, scantily attired in fake furs, beat the crap out of muscular, equally well-oiled, but outnumbered male opponents.

At the first commercial break Bledsoe, who had remained quiet as he tried to exclude the sounds of televised mayhem, turned to Murray.

"Do you mind hurting people?" he asked.

"Claude, that's what I do best," boasted Murray, draining his beer bottle and thumping it on the bar. He smiled as he confided, "I just don't like getting hurt myself. I'm not into pain, except for giving it."

Bledsoe took another look out of the corner of his eye at the big, strong, stupid, and malleable specimen beside him. Then he said, "I think I'll have some work for you. Easy work for good money, nothing dangerous. We'll talk next week." Bledsoe got up to leave.

Murray's big red race turned an even brighter hue. "All right, brother, sounds good to me." He was still smiling after Bledsoe had gone out the door.

Bledsoe walked briskly back to his apartment. Two houses down from his building he passed the home of one of Madison's numerous resident liberals, an attorney/women's rights activist named Marcia McCollister. It was a small frame house with a huge red, white, and blue flag hanging from a second floor window. Instead of stars and stripes, the flag was emblazoned with the names of huge corporations: Exxon, Enron, GMC, Halliburton, Eli Lilly. On her front porch, facing the street, was a large blackboard, on which Marcia placed a new inscription every Monday morning. This week's read "Impeach President Pinhead, Your MisLeader."

Bledsoe passed Marcia's property without glancing at the sign. As apolitical as he was amoral, he never paid any attention to such typically Madison-like statements. His thoughts were on crimes to be committed.

Chapter Nine

Sleep never came easily to Marnie Rankin, and when it did arrive it was thick with dreams that rarely varied in their length or vividness.

Each night, after going through the laborious process of transferring herself from her wheelchair to her bed, she settled back on the pillow almost resigned to what she knew her uneasy slumber would produce. She had the same two dreams almost every night, both of them amazingly accurate replays of events in her life.

The first dream was all too short. She was ten years old, riding her saddle horse Monty through the fields of her parents' southwest Iowa farm. It was a morning in early summer, sunny, the dew glistening on the thick pasture grass, and she thrilled at the sense of speed and freedom she felt as she rode swiftly and surely in the protective envelope of her childhood. Nothing that followed in Marnie Rankin's life ever approximated the innocent exhilaration of those Iowa mornings. But this dream never lasted long enough.

In contrast, the second dream was far too long. It always began the same way, when she heard her own voice crying out:

"No…no…no room, dammit, no room."

She was standing up in the irons aboard the blocky, hard-trying horse named Royal Rascal in a race at Bayou Downs in Louisiana, hauling back hard on the reins as Royal Rascal's front hooves came dangerously close to the heels of Tucker's Dream, the runner directly in front of them on the rail. At the same time, to her immediate right, Jesus Chavez—her major rival for leading rider honors at the track—pulled even with her on the favorite, Mightily, and began edging closer to Marnie, pinning her and Royal Rascal down on the rail.

"No, no," she repeated, begging for racing room, pleas that most rival jockeys would respond to and heed. She yanked on Royal Rascal's left rein, pulling his head almost sideways. He edged closer to the rail and she felt her left leg scrape against the wood, stinging her calf muscle. Her arms ached from the effort of trying to slow down her horse and thus extricate the two of them from this moving box of peril in which they were trapped.

With an eighth of a mile to go in the race, Jesus Chavez looked over his shoulder at Marnie. He grinned malevolently. She saw him clearly, but the possibility of what he would do next never entered her mind. True, their mutual dislike was deep, and Chavez' fiercely competitive nature was well known. Even so, when Chavez first eased his mount over another two feet, Marnie screamed as much in surprise as fear. Terror tore through her as Royal Rascal clipped the heels of Tucker's Dream. As Marnie started to go down, Chavez yanked his mount's reins to the outside and, with a crack of his whip, moved away into a clear lead.

Marnie's screams of "no, no" trailed through the humid Louisiana air as she plunged off the right side of her falling horse, landing directly in the path of the trailing runners. Her first reaction was that of all good jockeys who fall—to roll, thus softening the impact of the abrupt landing from an animal going thirty-five miles an hour.

Marnie did that perfectly. When she'd come to a halt, she immediately tried to slide on her stomach underneath the rail. She realized her helmet strap had come loose, and she reached for the strap with her right hand. That was the last thing she remembered from that day.

In the next second and a half, despite their riders' frantic efforts to avoid her, Marnie was battered in quick succession by the iron-shod feet of two rapidly moving horses. The first impact shattered her left arm. The second scraped a metal horseshoe across her face, slicing open her jaw. The third broke her life in two—a crushing blow to her spine that permanently crippled her.

Breaking the surface of consciousness in her bed each night, Marnie usually found herself wet with sweat in the wake of this dream. Struggling to prop herself up against the pillow, knowing she would be awake for hours now, she wished that, if the dreams must come each night, at least their order would be reversed. But this never happened.

The action sequence that caused Marnie Rankin's injuries took seven and three-quarters seconds on the racetrack. She went from being a twenty-six-year-old athlete in peak condition to a permanently handicapped woman in the time it takes a thoroughbred to run slightly more than a sixteenth of a mile. Her subsequent hospital stays measured five months. More months of outpatient therapy followed. None of the post-fall events ever were in her dream—just the central event that decimated her body and her life forever.

Well before dawn, Marnie began her preparations for the day. She labored to transfer herself from bed to wheelchair, to roll the chair into the large bathroom of the specially constructed mobile home in which she lived, to empty her catheter, wheel herself into the shower, wash, dry, dress, turn on the coffee maker. What used to take her less than ten minutes now required more than an hour. During her riding career she had made good money and saved much of it. That is what financed construction of the trailer home, one designed specifically to meet the special needs of a physically disadvantaged person. Those savings also paid for her specially constructed Chevrolet van, with its elevator platform, swivel chair, and hand controls on the steering wheel. As independent as ever, Marnie was determined to do for herself. Those expenditures, however, had eaten up most of her savings. Now, she lived on her monthly Social Security check, a small disability pension from the Jockeys' Union, and a modest monthly check from her parents, who still lived on their Iowa farm—a place that Marnie had no desire to revisit.

Marnie guided her wheelchair to the small dressing table in her bedroom. She tied back her blond hair in a ponytail, then applied lipstick. Her face looked as drawn as it had when she was riding, for she'd not gained much weight following her accident. The long scar across the lower right of her face shone a dull white before she applied powder that partly concealed it.

"I haven't even got enough money to afford good makeup," she said bitterly into the mirror. "And I was damn pretty, once…" She sighed and tried to rub away the dark circles under her sad blue eyes. She would be having a visitor today, and she wanted to look her best.

◇◇◇

Claude Bledsoe had found Marnie Rankin in the course of his research at the UW library. After completing his telephone interviews with Bernie Glockner, Bledsoe realized that he needed a more strong tie-in to the racetrack—someone to answer the many questions he had regarding jockeys and how they lived, someone with direct knowledge. Of course, that person had to be exploited without Bledsoe revealing what he actually had in mind. Using Google as a search engine, and the library's excellent filing system, Bledsoe tracked down and read hundreds of stories and articles about jockeys in the United States. He found many of them to be enlightening. The one that excited him was about Marnie Rankin. After reading it, Bledsoe said to himself, "Maybe secrecy wouldn't be necessary." He smiled. "I'm not going to chance it by telling her anything," he said to himself, "but I doubt that this little person would mind in the least aiding and abetting crimes against her former colleagues."

The article about Marnie, headlined "Looking Back in Anger," had been written by reporter Lori Lang for *Women's Sports Journal*, a national monthly magazine. It began:

> One of America's best-known female athletes, a vivacious and attractive figure who gained success in her profession and fame outside of it, now spends her days wheelchair-bound in a self-spun web of silence, broken only occasionally by comments as embittered as her past life was joyous. This is Marnie Rankin as we find her today, a resident of Shady Acres mobile home park near Elgin, Illinois, far from the horses she rode to more than one thousand victories, far from the television cameras that

brought her smiling face into the consciousness of sports fans across the nation.

Rankin, the story continued, had never recovered, physically or emotionally, from her fall from Royal Rascal at Bayou Downs. "Thought to be near death at the time," Lang wrote, "Rankin was rushed to a nearby trauma center where physicians saved her life, but not her cherished occupation. Severe spinal injuries would confine this once super-active young woman to a wheelchair for the rest of her life."

Bledsoe read with interest the details of Rankin's background. She had begun riding horses at age five and competing in Midwestern horse shows two years later, going on to win championships all over the country. The feisty tomboy evolved into an ultra-competitive young woman whose perky, blonde good looks worked to disarm those people she didn't succeed in charming with her candor. She turned her attention to racehorses at age seventeen and, over her parents' protests, began riding professionally at Nebraska tracks the next year. She was an immediate sensation, winning races by the dozens and winning over skeptical horsemen with her ability to "get the most" from her mounts. Her photo and articles about her appeared not only in racing publications but in *People* and *Parade* and *Vanity Fair*. In defiance of her horrified parents, she posed for one of the leading men's magazines, wearing only an impish grin. She had fan clubs, vocal rooters at whatever racetrack she rode, and three years back had attracted a stalker who was apprehended and imprisoned in a much publicized case.

Unknown to people outside of racing, the story continued, was the enmity that Rankin incurred from some male rivals. "They resented the hell out of me," she told Lang, "not just because I was getting so much attention but because I could flat out-ride most of them. And I didn't take any of their crap. They had the idea they could intimidate this little girl from the equestrian shows. I showed them otherwise, and some of the guys just couldn't stand that. They hated me—especially after I had that fight with Lenny Surrico and punched him out in the winner's circle at Croft Park. That really pissed off a bunch of them," Rankin recalled with relish.

"Then," wrote Lang,

> came the fall that changed it all, an incident intentionally caused, Rankin believes, although she does not claim that the offending rider, Jesus Chavez, wanted to see her wind up a cripple. "Injured, sure, he didn't give a shit. He just wanted to keep me from winning that race by any means that he could," Rankin said bitterly. "Chavez and I had a history—I'd beaten him in about five photo finishes, and laughed in his face about a couple of them. If I'd been one of his buddies down on the inside where I was in that race, he would have made room. Because it was me, he didn't. And I guarantee you Chavez wasn't the only one of the men jocks who would have cut me off like that if he'd had the chance."

Lang described the three major operations Rankin underwent, the months of rehab and physical therapy, and the calamitous final diagnosis—that she would be permanently paralyzed from the sternum down. Her life savings had been depleted by medical costs and the purchase and expensive remodeling of her living quarters in order to make them as convenient as possible for a woman determined to make her way by herself.

So, she's not only broken but nearly broke, Bledsoe thought as he neared the end of Lang's story.

Lang concluded by quoting Marnie Rankin:

> "I was twenty-six years old. They took my life away from me. I'm struggling to exist in a damned trailer court on the edge of nowhere.
>
> "Am I bitter about those jocks that had it in for me? You're goddam right.
>
> "Could I ever forgive them? You've got to be joking. I dream about that final race every night. When I wake up

from those dreams, the first thing I think of is how much I'd love to see that bastard dead."

Bledsoe printed out the article. He re-read it, then accessed Mapquest on the computer and requested directions to the Shady Acres trailer court near Elgin.

"She is one bitter little bitch," Bledsoe said to himself, smiling as he exited the library. "This is the girl for me."

Chapter Ten

Marnie heard the knock and rolled her wheelchair to the front door of her trailer home. Standing at the top of her wheelchair ramp was a bald-headed man so broad he almost blocked her view of the trailer court yard. "Ms. Rankin?" he said. "I'm Professor Kornkven…Harlan Kornkven."

"Come in," Marnie said, swiveling her chair and preceding him into the trailer's long, narrow living room. "Have a seat."

She watched the Professor unbutton his brown tweed sport coat before he sat down on the couch. He was wearing a light tan dress shirt, dark brown tie, and brown trousers and shoes. Placing a worn-looking briefcase on the coffee table in front of him, he adjusted his steel-rimmed glasses as he regarded Marnie.

"What can I do for you, Professor?" Marnie said.

"Oh," the Professor smiled, "I think can we can do some things for each other." He removed a yellow legal pad from his briefcase and took a ballpoint pen from his coat pocket. "I'd like to make some notes as we go along," he said.

"Ms. Rankin," he continued, "as I told you in our phone conversation the other day, I'm writing a book about gambling in America. Part of it—a large part—has to do with thoroughbred horse racing. It's a subject that very few of us academics have dealt with," he said, smiling again. Marnie thought to herself that the man's smiles seemed forced. Almost involuntarily she moved her chair back a few inches from this odd-looking stranger whose presence so dominated her living room.

The Professor said, "I read with great interest that lengthy article about you in *Women's Sports Journal*. The one written by Lori Lang, with all the detail about your life after your riding accident. As I said, it was interesting, certainly, but also extremely disturbing. You've really gone through hell," he said sincerely.

Marnie looked away from him for a moment, attempting to hide the tears that had formed in her eyes. The Professor pressed on. "Would you say that story was pretty accurate?"

"About as accurate as any of them can make it," Marnie said sharply. "The only people who really know about riders are riders. But that girl did a pretty good job," she conceded. Marnie reached for her pack of Newport Lights on the coffee table. "One of the only vices I've got left," she said. "Do you smoke?" The Professor said he didn't. "Well, I do," Marnie responded. "Do you want a drink?"

"No, thank you. Too early for me."

Marnie reached under the coffee table and brought up a half-full 750ml bottle of Captain Morgan rum. "I don't pay any attention to that 'early' and 'late' shit anymore," she said as she poured the rum into a tall glass, then topped it from a can of Coca-Cola.

Bledsoe watched her intently. She must have been a real cutie, he thought, before disaster and disappointment turned her blue eyes sullen and the booze began to puff up her fine features.

Marnie took a long pull on her drink. "So you're writing something about the Sport of Kings," she said. "Sport of Bastards they should call it."

"That's what I would like to talk to you about," Bledsoe said, leaning forward with an earnest look. "And I certainly intend to reimburse you for your time and efforts, just as I mentioned on the phone. I'll pay you $300 per day for each day we talk. And they don't have to be full, eight-hour days by any means."

Marnie exhaled smoke and, eyes narrowed, looked at him speculatively. "Why are you so sure I'm going to help you?"

Bledsoe shrugged. "Well, why not?" he said. "Here you are, living on the edge of poverty, nearly immobile, bitter as hell—why shouldn't you be interested in helping me by telling me the truth about racing as you see it? There's money in it for you. You need money. All you have to do is help to enlighten me as thoroughly and completely as you can about the jockey's role in racing. You're a bright person. You're capable of doing that.

"The money isn't going to make you whole again," Bledsoe added. "But it can make things a little easier for you. Don't you think you deserve at least that much from life?"

Marnie looked at him warily. She took a long drink from her amber-colored glass. Finally, she said, "I'm not starting today. We'll start tomorrow. But you'll pay me for today."

Bledsoe smiled. "Of course," he said, "of course." He took a thick brown envelope from his briefcase, an envelope that Marnie could see was packed with $20 bills. Her eyes widened.

"What time will you be back tomorrow?" she said.

◇◇◇

That night Bledsoe stayed in one of the $35.95 per night motels just off Highway 55 west of Elgin, paying cash and registering under a false name. The "smoke free" room reeked of cigarettes. The bed sheets appeared not to have been washed, just reversed. Lying in the swale of the queen-sized bed, looking at the blotchy, water-stained ceiling, Bledsoe was restless as he thought of little Marnie Rankin and his meeting with her tomorrow. In a way, he felt sorry for her. But he knew he could not afford to harbor feelings like that. He had so much to do before next September.

◇◇◇

At mid-morning of the following day, Marnie and Bledsoe were again facing each other in the living room of her trailer. After fixing herself a drink and lighting a Newport, Marnie said, "What do you want to know?"

What Bledsoe wanted to know, he said, were the details of a jockey's life: daily routines, common likes and dislikes, habits, fears—things that would take even the most assiduous observer years to learn on his own. Bledsoe didn't have years to spend on such a project. When he had returned to Marnie's trailer that morning, he brought a long list of questions written on his yellow legal pad, answers to which he recorded on a small tape machine.

Among Bledsoe's questions was "What time in the afternoon do jockeys have to be at the track to start work?"

Marnie laughed. "Damn, you *are* green. I could probably send you out looking for the key to the quarter pole."

"What's that," Bledsoe said, looking puzzled.

"It's a joke racetrackers play on newcomers," she answered, adding, "there is no such thing."

Marnie went on to say that most jockeys arrive for work between six and seven a.m. They exercise horses for trainers in hopes they will be asked to ride those horses in races. After training hours conclude at 10 a.m., Marnie continued, they go into the jockey quarters. "We, or I should say they, call it 'the room.' That's where they wait for the races to begin three hours later." Some of them, she continued, watch television and eat light lunches, play table tennis or cards, exercise on the machines provided, get messages, take naps, or spend time in the sweat box, reducing. After twelve noon they are not permitted to go out of those quarters except to ride in races or leave the track for the day, she said.

Bledsoe asked her about the backgrounds of various jockeys. Which jockeys did she like personally? It was a short list. What kind of horses were her favorites to ride? What were the toughest challenges facing riders? What methods did they use to control their weight, which could not exceed one hundred sixteen pounds and ideally came in at one hundred ten or less? Besides the sweat box, Marnie said, which was "like a sauna and you can sit in there in a rubber suit to sweat off the pounds," there were diet pills, water reduction pills, and induced vomiting of meals just eaten. "They call that flipping," she said. "Some of the guys do it all the time, even though it's terrible for your health. But," she explained, "there just aren't that many natural lightweights. I happened to be one of them. That's what my luck was used up on, I guess," she said ruefully, reaching for another cigarette. Bledsoe encouraged her to talk as long as she wished on any of the topics that he raised or she brought up. He had carefully structured his questions so that the specific issues he was actually interested in were peppered among the generalized approach he was taking for his "book."

Each of the days they met, Bledsoe arrived at Marnie's trailer at mid-morning. Most of the trailer court residents had long before left for their low-paying jobs. The few senior citizens in residence usually devoted their days to enriching the nearby riverboat casino or staring at Oprah and then the soaps. If anyone did see Bledsoe coming or going from Marnie's trailer, they glimpsed a man moving hurriedly, his jacket collar pulled up, tweed hat pulled down, large sunglasses helping to obscure the top part of his face. Bledsoe spent five afternoons doing this over the course of a week and a half, making Marnie's total fee $1,800. He gave it to her in cash. On their fifth day of conversations he said, "I'm interested in identifying the jockeys who are the most influential in the biggest races. Jockeys that usually ride the best horses in those races. Can you help me with that?"

Marnie nodded yes. Bledsoe looked down at his legal pad. He said, "I've got a list of twenty names." He began to read them off. "David Guerin, Mark Guerin, Randy Morrison, Eddie Calvin," he began. As he read off each name, he waited for Marnie to indicate whether she ranked the man in the most elite group. When he'd finished, Bledsoe had put check marks next to eleven names. He put his pad away in his briefcase.

"This is quite a small sampling," he said. "Are the Guerins related?"

Marnie said, "The Guerins are brothers. As a matter of fact," she added, "Randy Morrison and Eddie Calvin are half-brothers. A couple of those guys on the list are brothers-in-law. When you think of it," she said, blowing a stream of smoke across the coffee table, then sitting back in her wheelchair, "it's kind of a tight-knit group."

She put her glass of rum and coke on the coffee table and reached for her Newports. She regarded Bledsoe thoughtfully through another plume of smoke she exhaled. "I wish I knew what you had in mind here, Mister Professor," she said.

Instead of responding Bledsoe excused himself, saying he wanted to use the bathroom. Marnie waved permission. Bledsoe got up from the couch and walked behind her wheelchair and down the short hallway before carefully closing the bathroom door. Three minutes later he returned, one of Marnie's powder blue bath towels in his huge hands.

Moving quickly, Bledsoe reached around from behind the wheelchair, grabbed the startled woman by the jaw, and jammed a handful of towel into her mouth. He closed her nostrils with the fingers of his other hand, cutting off all the air to her lungs.

As Bledsoe continued applying pressure, holding her head back, suffocating her, Marnie looked up at him first with astonishment, then understanding, then hatred. Her hands reached up to grip his thick wrists and she tugged at them ineffectually. Almost reluctantly, he increased the pressure. The memory of Greta's face beneath the water almost caused him to weaken. "Why must I be forced to do these things?" he whispered. But he took a deep breath and continued, though he averted his face as the life seeped from Marnie Rankin. Finally, he felt her go limp. Bledsoe was careful not to leave a mark on Marnie's face. Days later, hers would be ruled "death from natural causes" by an unsuspecting medical examiner with a caseload of more raggedly obvious homicides to deal with.

Before leaving Marnie's trailer, Bledsoe carefully replaced the powder blue towel on its rack in the bathroom. It took him three minutes to find the $1,500 he'd paid Marnie. It was in a brown Peapod grocery bag in the freezer of the trailer's refrigerator. He put the money back into the brown envelope in his briefcase. He then pushed Marnie's chair in front of the television, turned on Oprah, volume set low, and wiped his prints off every surface he had touched. After closing the trailer door behind him for the last time, he walked to his Taurus—the fifth different car he had rented from the fourth different rental agency in the past week and a half—and drove away. He'd gotten what he came for.

Chapter Eleven

Three mornings after his luncheon meeting with Moe Kellman, Matt was hailed in the Heartland Downs parking lot by his friend Tom Jaroz, the clerk who manned the pari-mutuel machine in the track's press box. They had known each other for years. "Matt, you got a minute?"

"Don't give me another of your losing tips," Matt kidded as he backed away from Jaroz.

"No, no," Jaroz said, "this is serious. I need to talk to you. Not now, I'm running late and I've got to punch in. How about after the races?"

As they walked rapidly to the clubhouse entrance, Jaroz added, "There's something screwy going on that you might want to look into for a story. *Real* screwy." Matt grimaced. "Not you, too."

◇◇◇

They met after the races at Jeers. After ordering drinks at the bar, they took a booth near the front window. Rush-hour traffic was bumper to bumper on Wilke Road. Jaroz said, "You know a guy they call Oily Ronnie? Big, dark-haired guy, mid-forties maybe? Always around the track, trying to look like he knows what he's doing?"

Matt took a drink of his Daniels and water. "You mean the guy who ran the Ponzi scheme on those Turf Club members a few years back? Paid the investors twenty percent every three months before he closed the accounts and took off with the cash?

I think they finally ran him down in Los Cabos. Some chick he stiffed down there turned him in."

Jaroz said, "That's the guy. Ronnie Schrapps—they call him Oily Ronnie. He took his friends for about four million. Got convicted and did fifty months of federal time for mail fraud, up in that Minnesota country club where they put the white collar bandits. The money was—surprise, surprise—never recovered. Ronnie claimed he blew it all on dope and horses. Lot of people think he went and recovered it from some good hiding place after he did his time. But maybe not," Jaroz said, finishing his Manhattan.

"Why 'maybe not'?"

"Because he's back running another scam. So, either he really did blow his first pile, or he just can't help himself. But he's got something going now."

"How do you know this?"

"I know this from my Aunt Sophie," Jaroz answered. "Will you do me a favor? After the races tomorrow, come with me to meet her and listen to her story. I had her tell this to a cop friend of mine, but he just shrugged it off, like she's loony. She isn't. I don't think this cop had much interest in it, some old broad with a weird story."

Matt said, "Where does she live?"

"She's in an assisted living facility in Schaumburg. And, no, she's not in the Altzheimer's wing. Just the Gullible Old Lady section," he said bitterly.

Matt tried to lighten his friend's mood. "I saw a great bumper sticker last week. It was on a car driven by a little old guy whose forehead barely reached above the steering wheel. The sticker said 'Altzheimer's: The Cure for Nostalgia.'"

"That's not all that funny," Jaroz said.

◇◇◇

The next afternoon Matt met Jaroz in the parking lot of Sunshine Meadows, the facility in which Aunt Sophie had resided for the last four years. A glass-enclosed sun porch ran across the front of the nearly block-long building. Matt glanced at its occupants:

a dozen or so white-haired ultra seniors, most of them dozing with their chins on their chests. "Heaven's Waiting Room," he commented to Jaroz as they passed this depressing scene.

After registering at the reception desk, they walked to a modest but comfortable suite, one that may have in the past overlooked a meadow, but which now fronted a paved parking lot.

Aunt Sophie was nearing her ninetieth birthday. She had inherited a sizable estate from her husband, Stanislaus, the former plumbing king of Milwaukee Avenue on Chicago's northwest side. Stanislaus had passed away eleven years earlier.

"She and Stan always liked to play the horses," Jaroz had told Matt on their ride over to Sunshine Meadows. "They were the ones that first took me to the track when I was a kid. And Stan had a solid gold connection with the mutuel clerks' union—that's what got me a track job one summer before I'd even finished high school.

"Sophie's a sweetheart," Jaroz continued. "She and Stan never had kids, but they were extra good to me. That's why I kind of look out for her. She's in great shape physically for her age, but she does get confused in her mind now and then. Goes with that age, I guess. Sometimes she'll tell me the same thing three times in ten minutes. It's sad, you know? But what can you do?

"When Sunshine Meadows took a group of their—what would you call them. Inmates? Residents?—to the races last fall, Oily Ronnie somehow glommed onto them. Fresh suckers in the pool, I guess he must have figured. Anyway, he introduced himself to the group and got to know Aunt Sophie. A week or two later, he took Sophie and a couple of her friends on another outing to the track. Then, he began to visit Sophie at Sunshine Meadows on a fairly regular basis.

"Sophie never said a word about any of this to me. I found out from the Sunshine Meadows director, who told me one day how pleased she was that Sophie had made a new, younger friend. Jesus! And it didn't take long before Oily Ronnie got around to asking Sophie how she'd like to be partners in a racehorse. Why, it was her 'lifelong dream,' she told him.

"Well, did Ronnie have a deal for her!" Tom had concluded.

After Matt and Tom had settled on her couch, and Aunt Sophie had brought out cookies and tea, Tom said, "Auntie, tell my friend Matt about how you got into the horse business."

Sophie blushed with pleasure. "Oh," she said, "it all started with this nice man I met at Heartland Downs, the racetrack, on one of our Seniors Trips from here. He looks just like that old actor Victor Mature. Very handsome. And he's as sweet as he can be," she added, leaning forward to carefully refill the teacups.

Mr. Schrapps, Aunt Sophie continued, was nice enough to even let some of her good friends in on the horse deal. "I put in $40,000," she said, "and he let Marjorie Gainer and Dorcus Rohmer get in with $25,000 apiece—even though a lot of other people wanted to join and were on the list before them, Mr. Schrapps said. They were just thrilled."

Matt said, "Exactly how did Mr. Schrapps say this partnership works?"

"Well," Sophie replied, "he said he likes to keep our syndicate kind of hush hush. He works behind the scenes in the horse business. That way he gets better horses and better prices," she said with a wink.

Sophie passed the plate of cookies. "You put your money in," she went on, "and you get to be in a group that owns several horses. When the horse wins, you get a dividend. Mr. Schrapps guarantees a return of ten per cent every month! None of my old CDs can do that!"

"And, just between us," Sophie whispered, "Mr. Schrapps says we might have next year's Triple Crown winner in our stable already!"

Matt groaned softly as Tom said, "Auntie, please show Matt the papers on the horses you own now."

She proudly proffered them. Matt looked at a faded copy of an official registration form for a thoroughbred racehorse, one issued by the sport's ruling body, The Jockey Club. The original horse's name had been crudely whited out. In its place was written the name of Birdstone, that year's Belmont and Travers Stakes winner. Other, similar papers bore the names of other currently famous American racehorses.

Sophie reached into the file and took out a money order for $4,000. "That's my payment from Mr. Schrapps," she said, "for our first month. It was a little late coming, a few weeks even I think, but that's because he had a little trouble buying one of our horses. But all the monthly payments will be right on time from now on," she smiled. "Mr. Schrapps promised that."

Matt turned to Tom. "This is pitiful," he said quietly, so that Sophie couldn't hear him. "It's got Ponzi scheme written all over it." Matt riffled through the papers again. Nowhere did Oily Ronnie's name appear. Nor was there any written contract covering the purported partnership. Just the phony registration papers, and copies of several newspaper and magazine articles heralding the joys of horse ownership.

When Sophie went into her tiny kitchen to get more tea, Tom said angrily, "Auntie and her friends all made out their checks for the partnership to cash. With nothing in writing, Ronnie can deny any involvement. All he's got to say is, 'These crazy old people are accusing me of what? Prove it.'"

Sophie returned and passed the cookie plate again. "What were you saying, Tommy?"

Tom reached over to take his aunt gently by the hand. "Auntie," he said, "will you please promise me you will never buy any more horses without telling me about it first?"

"Why, sure, Tommy," Aunt Sophie replied. She patted his hand. "I only wish Mr. Schrapps would let you in on one of these partnerships. But," she said regretfully, "he says he sets aside these great deals just for us seniors. Isn't that sweet?"

Chapter Twelve

Bledsoe drove from Madison to Baltimore in two days. He could have done it faster had he gone straight through, but he stopped three times on back roads off the turnpike to look for places to re-test his rifle. In western Pennsylvania he found what he was seeking near Livonia, adjacent to a state forest. He didn't dare go to a rifle range, where he might be remembered. He needed isolation and a target. He found both in the isolated backyard of a red brick ranch house on land abutting the woods: a ceramic deer, its brown paint flaking off, poised with one front foot up in the air in a patch of sunlight now being threatened by the advance of late afternoon shadows.

Bledsoe had purchased the Model 700 Remington from a private gun collector who lived outside Rhinelander, Wisconsin, two hundred miles north of Madison. Bledsoe found him on the internet, called for an appointment, and acquired not only the weapon but a Leopold 10x scope, a suppressor, or silencer, and a supply of seven millimeter Remington Magnum shells. He told the man he wanted to experiment with the suppressor during the next deer season. The seller accepted Bledsoe's cash and explanation without comment. Bledsoe then drove seven miles to an abandoned quarry to try out his equipment. Two hours later, having collected every one of the dozens of cartridge casings and the shredded paper targets, he drove back to Madison.

In the course of his lengthy education, Bledsoe one year had enrolled in the University of Wisconsin's ROTC program. During his training it became clear that, even as a twenty-nine-year-old novice, he was a natural-born marksman. He easily outshone his fellow cadets in every aspect of their arms training. His instructor saw so much talent and potential in Bledsoe that he urged him to consider trying to qualify for the U. S. Olympic rifle team. Bledsoe never gave the suggestion a serious thought. He just accepted the discovery of his new talent as nothing out of the ordinary—just like his ability to, without any training, bench press three hundred and sixty pounds, or do the *New York Times* Sunday crossword in nine minutes.

Lying on his belly and elbows in a copse of birch trees some two hundred yards from the statuette, Bledsoe carefully sighted the rifle. He exhaled abruptly, then was still for the instant before firing. Down the grassy slope before him, the deer's head disintegrated. Bledsoe grunted with satisfaction. He still had it. If he could hit a target that small from this far away, he would have no trouble hitting the future targets he had in mind. His body relaxed. The rifle was perfect, and so was he. For a moment or two he listened to the wind ruffle the birch leaves above him. Finally, he got to his feet and jogged up the hill toward his car.

◇◇◇

It was 12:58 p.m. as the field of skittish two-year-olds approached the starting gate. Carlos Hidalgo reached forward to stroke the neck of his mount, Alki Alley, while continuing to mutter soothing words to him. Alki Alley, like all other members of this eleven-horse field, was about to have the first official race of his life. He had joyfully raced fellow foals through green pastures in his native Kentucky, had competed in trial races both on the farm and at the racetrack, but this was different. Alki Alley was nervous, sweating, and noisily apprehensive as he was led toward the rear of the massive iron starting gate. On either side, other similarly inexperienced young horses tossed their heads, or planted their feet and balked, all the while neighing loudly.

Only two members of the field walked into their stalls in the gate without encouragement from the hard-working crew of assistant starters. It was two minutes to post-time for the first race at Pinckney Park.

An impassive expression never left Hidalgo's dark, handsome face. His slim body was almost motionless, and this sense of calm finally was transmitted to Alki Alley, who settled down and waited fairly patiently to be loaded into the gate. Carlos had always had a gift for handling young horses, since his earliest days on a farm outside of Taluca, Mexico, the farm where he had begun riding when he was four years old.

Carlos' father, Reyes, had been a prominent quarter horse jockey at the southwestern tracks in the United States Growing up, Carlos rarely saw his father, whose career finally came to a spiraling halt fueled by weight problems, alcohol, drugs, and a growing indifference to his craft. But Carlos had inherited Reyes' innate ability to horseback. After moving to the states as a teenager, he had quietly carved out a rewarding career for himself. Carlos was not cut out to be one of the sport's superstars. But he was regarded as a solid professional, winning some one hundred and fifty races each year at the Maryland and Pennsylvania tracks and thus providing a very comfortable living for his wife, Maria, and their four children.

Now thirty-six, Carlos had begun to plan seriously for his retirement. His body was increasingly beset with aches and pains from the numerous injuries he had suffered through the years (six broken collarbones, two broken legs, broken right arm and left shoulder—about normal for a jockey with twenty years of experience). Unlike his father, Carlos had saved his money. He now had nearly enough to buy a small farm near Ocala, Florida, where he could begin a new phase of his life breaking and training young horses. That, according to his calculations and those of his accountant, was perhaps a year away. He had more riding to do before that plan became reality. Today, as 1 p.m. approached, he concentrated on guiding Alki Alley into the Pinckney Park starting gate.

◇◇◇

Jimbo Murray had gone to Baltimore two weeks earlier and rented a room in a house adjacent to the Pinckney Park backstretch. He paid cash for a month's rent, telling the landlady, Katrina Schulte, he would be "in and out" during the upcoming race meeting because he was a horse van driver for a company that serviced the East Coast racetracks. Katrina had rented rooms to racetrackers for nearly forty years. Cash in hand was her primary interest.

When Murray flew back to Madison, he met with Bledsoe to give him the key to the rented room and describe the setup. The room was on the top floor of Schulte's three-story house, in the northeast corner. There were two windows that overlooked the Pinckney Park backstretch: a small bathroom window, and a large one that shed light into the combination bedroom-sitting room with its sway-backed bed, small television set with a coat hanger aerial, and three-cushion couch missing one cushion. That window offered an unobstructed view of the racetrack's backstretch, the southern portion of which was seventy-five yards away.

Bledsoe slipped up the stairs and into the rented room on Tuesday night. He looked around approvingly. It was perfect. A transient's special, no questions asked, except for "how many weeks are you paying for?" His duffel bag contained a change of clothes, some sandwiches and a thermos of coffee, and the Remington, broken down. He slept soundly that night and was up in plenty of time to observe horses working out in the gray haze of the next morning. As they galloped past, he practiced sighting the rifle. Then he went back to sleep until he heard, coming from across the track infield, the sound of a bugle calling horses to post for the first race, the one with Alki Alley, jockey Carlos Hidalgo up.

Bledsoe patiently examined the approaching field of horses through his rifle's scope. He had no trouble identifying the most visible jockey—Hidalgo, whose silks were a flaming red with white slashes. "He'll do," Bledsoe muttered as Alki Alley sidestepped and threw his head. Bledsoe smiled with satisfaction when Hidalgo, expert horseman that he was, settled the anxious colt. For a couple of seconds Hidalgo's riding helmet sat almost still in the sights of Bledsoe's silenced Remington. The time was 12:59 and twenty-seven seconds. The target was slightly less than eighty yards from the open window at which Bledsoe crouched.

Seconds later Carlos Hidalgo's head was blown apart in a blood and bone and tissue-smeared moment. Hidalgo tumbled to the dark ground, off the wheeling Alki Alley, landing amid the shocked and panicked jockeys, horses, and gate attendants. At the rail across the infield, where fans basked in sunshine, there was a sudden outcry as some noticed the unusual activity behind the starting gate. "There's a jock off his horse," a man shouted, and the news rippled along the rail. When the terrified Alki Alley bounded away from his dead rider and ran wildly down the track, the grandstand erupted with sound.

With all the rest of Katrina Schulte's renters at their jobs at the track, the rooming house was empty. Katrina was tending the rose bushes that ran along the back fence of her property. She looked up when she thought she heard the familiar sound of crowd noise. But when she glanced at her watch she saw it was 12:59. She was puzzled, because she knew it couldn't have been an exciting finish to the first race—the first race hadn't gone off yet. She shrugged and returned to her roses.

Bledsoe retrieved the shell casing that had spurted onto the floor near where he'd stood aiming the Remington. He quickly pocketed it, broke down the gun and packed it in the duffel, and took the stairs two at a time. He'd worn thin rubber gloves throughout his stay in the room, so he wasn't concerned about fingerprints. He made it to his car, two blocks away, in less than two minutes.

Driving away from the track and the sound of approaching police sirens, Bledsoe realized he was hungry as well as pumped up from what he'd done. But he decided to wait until he was a good ways west on Interstate 70, maybe even past Hagerstown, until he picked up something to eat on his way back to Madison.

That night, as he sped past Cleveland on Interstate 80, Bledsoe fought off advancing fatigue by again mentally congratulating himself on his progress thus far. Things had really been set in motion now. He'd taken giant steps in his quest for Grandma's millions.

What would he do with the $15 million? Live very, very well, for one thing. That was a given. No more secondhand cars and third-floor walkups. Then he was struck by the thought that besides elevating his standard of living, this coming bonanza could serve to buy him some immortality at the university he had long attended. A chair there—he would endow a chair at UW! Two or three of his future millions should do it.

What department should he favor with his generosity? There were so many in which he had studied over the years. Then it came to him, and he laughed aloud at the thought: the economics department, of course. The Claude Bledsoe Chair of Economics. Perfect.

Chapter Thirteen

News of Carlos Hidalgo's shocking death spread rapidly through the horse racing world and, because of its horrible and mysterious nature, well beyond. Days later, no suspect had been identified, no motive revealed, no clues unearthed. His family buried Hidalgo in his native Mexico amid an atmosphere of grief, anger, and uncertainty.

The day of the Hidalgo services, Claude Bledsoe was busy working in the office space of his Madison apartment on Mifflin Street. Using carbon paper, he carefully prepared copies of a letter on his late grandmother's old Underwood Typemaster, a mastodon of the written word that she had bequeathed to him. He typed each recipient's name in capital letters above the repeated text and addressed the envelopes on the Underwood as well. Then Bledsoe completely dismantled the old typewriter, placing its parts in a Kohl's shopping bag that he carried to his car. Fifteen minutes south of Madison on Highway 51 he arrived at Lake Waubesa. Finding an isolated and empty short pier, he hurled the typewriter remnants far out into the lake. When he got back to Madison later that afternoon, he sent Jimbo Murray to a Mail Box outlet sixty miles away in Whitewater that handled UPS deliveries.

He'd set everything in motion now. Carlos Hidalgo's death had sent a message, these letters would emphasize it. With three months to go in which to meet Grandma Bledsoe's deadline, Bledsoe glowed with confidence as he headed down Mifflin for an early evening drink or two at Doherty's Den.

◇◇◇

Randy Morrison's letter bearing its fictitious return address was delivered by UPS the next morning, addressed to Morrison in care of the Racing Secretary's office, Dell Park, San Diego, CA. One of the junior clerks from that office brought the letter to the Dell Park jockeys' room at 11 a.m. and placed it on the bench in front of Morrison's locker, along with the rest of his mail. Morrison regularly received requests for his autograph and other forms of fan mail. He was the leading rider at the Dell Park meeting, a twenty-seven-year-old rising star. Making the junior clerk's day was Morrison's muttered, "Thanks, buddy."

Morrison, a five-foot-four, one-hundred-and-twelve pound bundle of muscle and sinew, had just showered off the residue of his morning exertions, including exercising two stakes horses for top trainer Wayne Calabrese. He decided to open his mail before sitting down for his daily session of racetrack rummy with his fellow riders. He picked up the brown envelope from the bench. He read:

> *Randy Morrison,*
> *You don't know me. You never will.*
> *I am the person who killed Carlos Hidalgo. It is very much in my power to do the same to you IF YOU DO NOT DO WHAT I SAY.*
> *You must intentionally LOSE on three horses of my choosing in the next month. You will be told which horse on the day of the race.*
> *You must make these losses look legitimate. I don't want to have you suspended and unavailable for the second and third races. You can figure out how to do that.*
> *If you do not do as you are told in Race Number One, someone CLOSE TO YOU will die as Carlos Hidalgo did.*
> *If you do not do as you are told in Race Number Two and Three, you will die.*
> *IT IS AS SIMPLE AS THAT.*

There was no signature on this plain piece of paper.

Randy Morrison read the letter again. Then he snorted, crumpled it up, and tossed it into a nearby wastebasket. "What a bunch of crap," he said. He remembered notes from other crazies he'd received in the past. There had been many. Like most prominent professional athletes, Morrison drew unwanted attention from a frothing fringe group of fans. They included the seventy-four-year-old woman threatening him with a paternity suit if he didn't agree to begin dating her, and the man who identified himself as "Master Winslow" and said he had laid a powerful voodoo curse on Morrison for having cost him a big daily double.

"What are you talking about?" asked Gene Wishman, who was carefully polishing Morrison's riding boots. Wishman served as Morrison's valet. In every jockeys' room in America, Wishman's occupation was pronounced "val-let," not the familiar "val-lay" in keeping with the word's French origin. These men performed personal services for their jockey-employers: laundering their riding clothes, inspecting their whips for wear and tear, insuring that the correct amount of lead weight was placed in the saddles before each race. Those saddles were then transported by the valets to the paddock for placement on the horse. Like many of the men who worked as valets, Wishman was a former rider and therefore very comfortable in the milieu all of them referred to as "the room."

Morrison shook his head as he finished pulling a clean white tee shirt over his impressively muscled torso. "Another crackpot threat is all," he said. "C'mon, let's go play cards."

Five days later, at 9:47 in the morning, a jockeys' room attendant at Dell Park answered his phone, then called out to Randy Morrison. "Phone for you, Randy."

"Yeah," Morrison said into the phone.

"I'm the letter writer," said an obviously disguised voice in a whisper. "Listen carefully. Lose with your mount in the eighth race today. The four horse in the eighth race. Or I'll do what I said I would." Before Morrison could reply, the phone went dead.

Morrison kept thinking of the phone call that afternoon as he dressed in the blue and yellow silks of Tom and Evie

Knutson, owners of Bailey's Babe, horse number four in the featured eighth race, and the strong favorite to win. Morrison was uncharacteristically reserved as he met the Knutsons in the paddock before the race. He barely heard the riding instructions given by trainer Leon Leving. As Bailey's Babe left the paddock and walked through the tunnel leading to the track, Morrison muttered to himself, "This is bullshit." Minutes later, he crossed the wire first with Bailey's Babe and smiled broadly at the jubilant Knutsons, who eagerly awaited him in the winner's circle.

Chapter Fourteen

Bledsoe entered the Addison Hotel, located just west of the first turn of Indianola Park outside of Indianapolis, through an open loading dock on the building's east side. The morning sun was at his back. He wore a gray jumpsuit that he'd commissioned from a Madison seamstress who specialized in costumes for the university's theater department. On its back the inscription read "Corrigan Plumbing and Heating." He carried a brown duffel bag in his right hand. A plain blue baseball cap was pulled down low on his forehead, almost touching the top of his dark sunglasses. He walked through the service door with a nod to a hotel maintenance worker who was dumping trash. "Emergency call," Bledsoe grunted as he passed the man and headed for the freight elevator. He rode it to the top floor of the hotel and climbed the interior stairway to the roof. It was 5:33 a.m.

Bledsoe had done his homework. He had accessed the Jockeys' Union internet web site and carefully studied the photos available there of Eddie Calvin, Randy Morrison's older half-brother. On the second to last day he'd spent with her, Marnie Rankin had finessed her way into an informative phone chat with an old friend of hers, trainer Danny Hiller, eliciting the information that Eddie Calvin was riding first-string for him at Indianola Park. "Eddie comes out every morning to work horses for me. He's been great to work with for several years now," the normally reticent Hiller enthused.

At 6:01, just as the morning haze had almost completely dissipated, Bledsoe peered through his binoculars from his rooftop perch overlooking the first turn of the Indianola Park racing strip, two hundred and ten yards away. He saw a momentary break in the procession of horses heading from their barns to the track. He put down the binoculars, reached into the duffel bag, and then began to assemble the Remington.

◇◇◇

Eddie Calvin had kissed his wife Lucy goodbye at 5:30 that morning. It was a kiss on her forehead that, as deep in sleep as she was, she may not have noticed, for she was accustomed to his early departures and rarely awakened before he went off to work. Their two young daughters also slept soundly in their room in the Calvins' Indianapolis townhouse.

Dressed in jeans, boots and a blue tee-shirt worn under his black protective riding jacket, Eddie carried his riding helmet to his red Ford pickup. Dew lingered on the carefully trimmed grass lining the driveway. As Eddie buckled his seat belt, he glanced at the simple wooden cross that dangled from the Ford's rearview mirror, then tapped it for good luck. It was a gift from his oldest daughter, Ashleigh, age eight, who had made it in her bible class.

As he drove to Indianola Park, Eddie made a mental note to give his brother Randy a call that night; Randy's birthday was the next day. Eddie never looked at the wooden cross, or touched the St. Christopher medal he wore on a chain around his neck, or read his bible each evening, without thinking of his older half-brother. It was Randy who had "helped pave the way," as he put it, for Eddie's turnaround—the salvaging of a promising riding career and what Eddie now firmly believed was his immortal soul. Both had been threatened by a potentially lethal combination of substance abuse and pride.

Six years earlier, after two straight sensational seasons in which he had earned hundreds of thousands of dollars, Eddie Calvin had fallen deeply into drugs and, finally, despair. The quality of his riding declined sharply. His marriage teetered. He knew what was happening to him. He was convinced he couldn't do a damned thing about it.

Aware of Eddie's deepening troubles, Randy had several times flown in from the coast to attempt to counsel his brother, urging him to enter a substance abuse program, as he himself had done four years earlier. Randy also pleaded with Eddie to attend meetings of the Racetrack Chaplaincy—as he himself regularly did. The half-brothers were products of hard-working, hard-drinking parents who had struggled to make a modest living on a small Arkansas farm. The boys had seen firsthand the ravages of alcohol excess. Still, both had taken to drinking on a regular basis early in their teenage years. During these visits, Eddie always listened respectfully to Randy, vowed to reform, but soon reverted to his destructive ways.

One autumn weekend Eddie traveled to Woodburn Racetrack on the outskirts of Toronto to ride in two stakes races for an old trainer friend of his, a man who was not then aware that Eddie's life and livelihood were in jeopardy because of drugs. Eddie didn't arrive at his hotel until late the night before the races. He promptly fell asleep, but awakened less than thirty minutes later feeling, as he often later recounted, "as if all of a sudden I was not alone."

Energized, restless, Eddie reached for the remote control and turned on the television. Appearing on the screen was a famous television evangelist. Eddie found himself listening intently as the man implored his audience to "come to Christ." Suddenly, Eddie found himself weeping. An enormous sense of peace, an almost physical release, swept over him. As he later would tell the many treatment groups he addressed, "I just knew all of a sudden that Jesus was with me and that I needed to accept him into my life. I had found what I'd been missing."

Starting that night, Eddie Calvin's addictions were a thing of the past. He never touched drugs or alcohol again. The following afternoon, he won both the stakes races for his old trainer friend. When he returned home, he told his amazed and delighted wife that their old life was "dead and gone." Eddie became an active spokesman for, and heavy financial contributor to, the racetrack substance abuse agency, and a very vocal advocate of the "power and love of Jesus." His riding career took off again, too.

Five minutes from his home this rainy morning, Eddie hit the drive-through window at the Dunkin' Donuts for a large black coffee, then continued on the three miles to the back-stretch entrance of Indianola Park. It was 5:57 when he parked his truck outside of Barn Nine. Walking to the barn office to say good morning to trainer Hiller, Eddie heard the familiar sounds of banging feed tubs, pitchforks scraping stall floors, radios tuned to Spanish-speaking stations, horses nickering as they were bathed. The sharp smell of horse manure, horse urine, horse sweat, liniment, and hay made him smile, as always. It was an aural and odorous wrap-around experience he thought he would never tire of.

"Need you to gallop five horses and work one, Eddie," said Hiller as he glanced at the morning's schedule. Eddie nodded, sipping his coffee as his first mount, a big bay filly named Asbury Julie, was tacked up and brought to him outside the barn. "She's an easy one," Hiller said. "Take her around twice." Hiller returned to his office as Eddie steered Asbury Julie onto the dirt riding path that led to the racetrack a quarter of a mile away. The jockey's shoulders bobbed in rhythm with the filly as she bounced along. He could tell that she felt good. He did, too. The morning sky had begun to brighten.

Eddie brought Asbury Julie onto the racetrack at 6:08. Bledsoe, who had been scanning the arrivals through his bin-oculars, easily identified Eddie from the photos he had studied in the *Jockey News*. Eddie was grinning as he said something to the clockers at the rail.

A tall, lean woman on an outrider's pony approached Eddie and took hold of Asbury Julie's bridle. Bledsoe watched as Eddie waved her away, indicating that he did not require her assistance. He said something to her and Bledsoe, now observing the scene through his rifle's scope, saw her throw her head back and laugh before moving away from Eddie.

Eddie looked back over his shoulder and grinned at the woman. The bullet from Bledsoe's rifle smashed down through the back of his head and through the center of that grin. Eddie's riding helmet seemed to slightly elevate in a gush of blood and matter, some of which spewed onto the woman's pony. That terrified beast wheeled and tossed the woman to the ground. She landed within a yard of where Eddie had fallen. She frantically turned away from his shattered face and continued to scream as track workers rushed forward.

Before the track ambulance arrived on the scene, Bledsoe had already pressed the "lower level" button in the otherwise empty freight elevator. By the time the elevator car had descended the twelve floors, he had removed his plumber's coveralls and blue cap. He put his dark glasses on before he stepped off the elevator on level one, a broad, bald man in a blue business suit carrying a brown duffel bag.

Chapter Fifteen

The day Eddie Calvin was to be buried, Matt finished his morning run on the Evanston path bordering Lake Michigan just as the rim of the emerging sun climbed into view.

He'd gotten up earlier than usual because he, Maggie and Rick were scheduled to begin their drive to Indiana by 6 a.m. Eddie Calvin had ridden for Maggie some years before, and she was going to pay her respects. Matt and Rick had both been assigned to cover the event for their respective papers.

After checking his watch, Matt sprinted the last two blocks to his Hinman Avenue condo, pounded up the back stairway, and hit the shower right after activating the coffee maker. Twenty minutes later, dressed as formally as most racing writers ever get—shirt, tie, sport coat, pressed slacks—he sipped his coffee as he watched out the front window for Maggie's black GMC Denali. When it pulled up in front of his building, he went immediately down the stairs and out the door, hair combed but still damp from his hurried shower. As he approached the curb, Rick got out of the passenger seat. He said, "You sit with Maggie. This is way too early for me, man. I want to stretch out in back get a little more sleep."

"Help yourself," Matt said. He kissed Maggie on the cheek as she began to pull away from the curb. She was wearing an expensive-looking black dress. Her broad-brimmed black hat lay on the console between their seats.

"Let me give you one tip before I go to sleep," Rick said as he settled into the broad second seat. "Maggie, keep going straight south once you're on the Outer Drive. It's old Highway 41 and it'll take you down along the lake to 90 before you hook up with 65 to go south. That way you'll miss the Skyway tolls."

"I'll pay the tolls," Maggie said, eyes on the mirror in which she could see Rick. "No time for the old scenic route this morning. We're in a hurry."

◇◇◇

Three hours later Rick awakened just as Maggie turned off Highway 65 at Lebanon, Indiana, and headed east to Carmel, where Eddie Calvin's funeral would be held. "Lebanon," Rick said sleepily, "home of Rick Mount, the greatest shooter in the history of college basketball."

Matt said, "You aren't that old to have seen him. Mount played for Purdue in the sixties."

"My dad graduated from Purdue," Rick said. "He used to show me all the old films of Mount, over and over. That cat could flat out shoot."

Nearing their destination, Matt thought that it was with this kind of small talk that people tried to avoid confronting the sad scenes awaiting them. Matt had been lucky, he knew, having attended very few funerals thus far in his life, his parents and both siblings all alive, most of his other relatives, too. The lone major loss he'd experienced had been the car crash death of a high school baseball teammate, Hank Wiggins, killed at seventeen in a head-on collision with a truck driven by a multiple DUI offender.

Matt was one of Wiggins' friends who, a month or so later, received a copy of a poem written by the dead boy's sister, Mary Anne, a devout Catholic whose faith turned out to be another victim of that horrible accident. The poem described the funeral home visitation for her brother. It ended with words Matt had never forgotten.

I saw God and Evil there
Dancing on a lily's bloom.

I believed in them, oh
Yes. And left the room.

Maggie had used Mapquest, and they found the funeral home in Carmel without any trouble. Its parking lot was jammed with cars belonging to Calvin's fellow jockeys, horse owners and trainers, friends of the family, and some racing fans. Efficiently managing the traffic flow was a team of neatly dressed funeral home staffers wearing the kind of solemn, concerned expressions only they have mastered.

"Well, at least attention is being paid," Matt said softly as they parked. He was thinking of the tirade he'd heard from Tyree Powell the previous afternoon. The Jockeys' Union rep had phoned Matt in the press box. He was steaming. "Naturally, your paper has been writing about the jockey murders," he said, "but what about writers on the dailies, for God's sake? If some madman were knocking off lunkhead linemen from the NFL, or bumping off some of baseball's steroids boys, they'd be all over the story. But two of my guys have been killed and hardly anybody outside of racing seems to give a damn. I am seriously pissed off about this," Powell concluded.

Maggie, Rick and Matt got in line to sign the register in the foyer of the funeral home, nodding to people they recognized. There were quite a few other racetrackers from Chicago. Inside the large room with the bronze coffin at its far end, dozens of chairs were occupied. Eddie Calvin's widow stood to the right of the closed coffin. Next to her stood Reverend Dave Cruikshank, the well-known "backstretch minister." Lucy was wan, her eyes red from weeping. Her two young daughters sat quietly with relatives in the front as mourners filed past to pay their respects. The minister looked to be even more in shock than Lucy, responding automatically to the expressions of concern and condolence uttered by people in the line.

Waiting alongside Maggie for the line to move forward, Matt heard Rick say from behind him, "I can't use my old sidling move in here."

"What are you talking about?" Matt whispered.

Answering in a hushed voice, Rick said, "Usually at these things I make one very quick appearance. I sign the registry book, make sure the principal mourners have noted my presence, hurriedly shake a few hands, and get the hell out of there. I hate these things. Thank God they went with a closed coffin."

"I don't think they had much choice," Matt said.

The coffin was flanked by dozens of impressive floral arrangements. One was in the shape of a horseshoe, its "U" facing down. Rick nudged Matt. "Somebody should have told the florist about that mistake. The 'U' should always be pointing upward. That's how all the horseshoes hang in racetrack tack rooms. If the horseshoe is pointed down, they think it means luck is running out."

Matt said, "Doesn't make any difference now. Poor Eddie's luck has already run out."

Later, leaving the cemetery on this gray-skied, humid, late June afternoon, Matt putt an arm around Maggie as they walked to her car. She had wept softly at the funeral home after embracing Lucy Calvin, and now her tears began to flow again. "Eddie rode the first winner I ever saddled," Maggie said. "I've known him and his family for years. I can't even imagine how much Lucy must be hurting right now. Once he'd gotten himself straightened out, they had a great life together. That poor woman. Those poor children."

"And for what?" Matt said. "That's what I don't get. Either with Eddie Calvin or Carlos Hidalgo before him. Who would want them dead. Why?"

Opening the back door of the Denali, Rick gestured toward the car containing the bereaved family. "I'll give the widow and Randy Morrison a lot of credit for their restraint. They kept the TV vultures completely out of the picture. Pun intended. No weepy interviews, no sappy statements about tragic loss from assholes who can't wait to get in front of the cameras. People like that make me sick," he said, slamming the door shut.

The drive back to Chicago seemed twice as long as their trip down to Carmel. Gloom prevailed. The three of them spoke rarely, Maggie concentrating on driving, Matt sitting with his head back and eyes closed, trying to make some sense of it all. The only sound out of Rick until they approached Gary, Indiana, was a succession of piercing snores that Matt was able to interrupt only by reaching between the seats and slapping his friend's leg. Rick finally awakened as Maggie drove onto the arching toll bridge leading to Chicago.

Rick yawned, stretched and began drumming his fingers on his knees. Then he attempted to change the mood in the car.

"Driver," he said, half smiling, "I have a question for you."

Maggie glanced at him in the mirror. "Yes?"

"Did you hear the joke about the old horseplayer who had a heart attack right after the first race one afternoon?"

She shook her head no. Rick said, "The track doctor rushes to the scene and examines the poor guy. After checking for vital signs, the doc reaches into the old man's shirt pocket and pulls out a mutuel ticket.

"'How is he, Doc?' a bystander asks. 'Is he alive?'

"The doctor looks down at the mutuel ticket in his hand, then shakes his head sadly. 'Only in the double,' he says."

Rick hooted with laughter. Maggie gave him a weak smile. Matt grimaced. He said, "That joke has been around since Seabiscuit was a yearling."

Rick looked hurt. "It has? I'll be damned. A guy just told it to me last week.

"Oh, well," he added, "I was just trying to lighten you guys up a little bit."

Pulling up at the toll taker's booth Maggie said, "Thanks for trying, Rick."

◇◇◇

Four days later, when Randy Morrison had returned to California after helping to escort his half-brother's remains back to Arkansas where their parents were buried, he received a phone call in the Dell Park jockeys' room. Randy's shoulders slumped dejectedly as he listened to the now familiar whispered voice.

"You should have done what I said. But you didn't. I warned you after I killed Carlos Hidalgo that you had better obey. He was an example I chose at random to prove to you what I could do. But you didn't listen to me. And Eddie Calvin died as a result.

"If you don't lose with the next two horses I tell you to lose with—and that's all there will be, I promise you—you will die. I promise you that, too. Do you understand?"

There was silence. Then the whispering voice commanded, "Answer me."

"I'll do it, you bastard," Randy Morrison replied. "I'll do it."

"Yes, you will. You have no choice. This call is untraceable. The letter I sent you is untraceable. The killer of your half-brother is untraceable. Your next instructions from me will be untraceable. Neither you nor the police or FBI will ever know who I am. That's why you will do what I say."

There was a pause before the voice said, "You'll be hearing from me soon."

The phone went dead.

Bledsoe rose from the chair in his Madison apartment and stretched. He smiled, feeling pumped up in the best sort of way. The groundwork had been laid. His plan was unfolding right on schedule. It would not be long before he started really picking up momentum, and money, on his way toward what he'd begun thinking of as "Grandma's millions."

Chapter Sixteen

Randy Morrison heard the boos. They were loud and clear and persistent. No way he could have missed them. The torrent of abusive sound seemed to increase as he strode rapidly through the tunnel leading from the racetrack to the jockeys' room. He had been the target of angrily shouted comments in the past—what professional athlete hadn't?—but never at this high level of furor.

"Morrison, you little bum, you should hang your head in shame...Worst ride I've ever seen...Wake up, you runt, what's the matter with you?...How much did they pay you to do that, you thieving pinhead?" These were the more genteel critiques.

On and on it went from the gauntlet of horse players lining his path. Finally, Morrison burst through the jockeys' room door and into sanctuary. Yanking off his helmet, he hurled it into the bottom of his locker. His valet, Gene Wishman, looked at him in puzzlement. The other riders in the room studiously avoided looking at him at all as he angrily tore off his silks. "Gene," he said, "call the stewards and take me off those last two mounts today. Tell them I'm sick."

Minutes later, standing beneath a hot shower, Morrison did indeed feel sick—as if there was a cold chunk of shame lodged in his stomach, weighing him down, rendering him almost immobile. He stood under the shower for nearly ten minutes, going over and over in his mind what had happened in the recently concluded Dell Park Derby.

Morrison had received the phone call in the Dell Park jockeys' room that morning. The disguised voice said, "Eighth race today. Lose with Lord's Heir. Or else you'll be dead within the week. Just like your brother." The phone clicked off. Morrison dropped the receiver and leaned against the wall, feeling faint. It was what he had dreaded: being instructed to intentionally lose on one of the best three-year-old colts in the country, in the final leg of a National Pick Four, on national television. His bowels began churning and he hurried to the bathroom, where he remained seated in a stall, head in his hands, for many minutes. He finally emerged after the concerned Wishman called out, "Randy, you okay?" *No,* Morrison thought bitterly, *I'm never going to be "okay" ever again.*

Four hours later, Randy Morrison did what he'd been ordered to do. When the gates sprang open at the start of the Dell Park Derby, Morrison tugged hard on the left rein, causing Lord's Heir to soundly bump the horse next to him, ridden by Morrison's friend Jesse Bartlett. Jesse looked over at Morrison in amazement. Randy heard him say, "What the hell?"

In the collision both horses were knocked briefly off stride, and Lord's Heir, the three-to-five favorite, was shuffled back to sixth place. Impatiently, Lord's Heir threw his head and pulled against the tightly held reins. Ordinarily, Lord's Heir was on or near the lead from start to finish of his races. That was his preferred running style. But Randy reined him in, for there was nowhere to go at that point, what with five horses bunched up in front of them. Lord's Heir tossed his head resentfully at this restraint and began to fight against his rider, thereby losing even more lengths.

It got worse after that for Lord's Heir and his thousands of backers, at Dell Park and at hundreds of simulcast locations around North America. When an opening seemed to occur nearing the far turn of the Derby, Morrison opted to go outside and around horses. This cost Lord's Heir additional lengths—more than enough of them to keep him from hitting the board. Coming back to unsaddle, Morrison—one of the sport's more popular jockeys—felt the crowd's anger hit him like a giant

fist. Even Lord's Heir, once Randy had dismounted, seemed to
regard him irritably. Morrison brushed past Lord's Heir's red-
faced trainer, mumbling, "Just didn't have it today." The furious
trainer hurled his track program at Randy's retreating back.

After showering, Randy dressed hurriedly. He ignored
Wishman's attempts at conversation and headed out the jockeys'
room door. Randy could hear the track announcer describing
the ninth race action as he jogged to his pickup truck. The horse
he'd been taken off of was winning. That hurt, but not as much
as what had come before. Randy Morrison had never felt this
bad on any day at any racetrack. He had betrayed the sport he
loved, the sport that had made him wealthy far beyond any of
the farm boy dreams he'd had back in Arkansas.

Randy felt a strong need for something to assuage his enormous sense of loss, of self-betrayal. An almost overpowering
desire for alcohol swept over him, making him shiver despite
the warm air pouring in his truck's windows as he sped down
the highway toward his home.

But "almost" was as overwhelming as he let it get. Pulling
into the driveway of his townhouse, he saw his daughters wave
at him from the backyard's raised swimming pool. He shivered
again. Then he said, "I just can't go down that road again. Lord
Jesus, help me not to. Help me not to."

◇◇◇

SAN DIEGO—One of the largest payoffs of
the thoroughbred racing season occurred yesterday, spurred by the shocking result of the
Derby here at Dell Park. When huge favorite
Lord's Heir finished out of the money in the
$500,000 race, two lucky bettors collected on
their winning National Pick Four tickets.

One of the winning tickets was sold at
Heartland Downs near Chicago. The other was
purchased at a Wyoming off-track betting
parlor.

The four winning horses were Jo Jo's Dream
($17.80) at Cantering Downs, Dreary Petunia
($9.80) at Hellas Park, Judy's Nightmare

($18.80) at Golden Gateway, and Chuck A Lot
($48.40) in the Dell Park Derby. The winning
numbers were 3-2-8-2.

The Dell Park Derby produced the biggest
surprise of the day as Lord's Heir, under
regular rider Randy Morrison, ran the worst
race of his career. A winner of five straight
going into the Derby, Lord's Heir's loss
ruined thousands of National Pick Four tickets across North America since he had been
confidently "singled" on many of them. It
was just the second loss suffered by Lord's
Heir in his ten-race career. He had a very
troubled trip yesterday, checking in fourth
after finally shaking loose from traffic and
closing belatedly.

Claude Bledsoe had viewed the televised running of the Dell
Park Derby on one of the sets in Doherty's Den. He watched
Randy Morrison's artful ruination of Lord's Heir's chances as
impassively as he could. But as he told Jimbo Murray that night,
"I felt a kind of rush in my chest and a major vibration in my
balls. It was fucking great."

The televised racing show had started late (delayed by the
completion of a log-rolling contest from northern Minnesota)
and run so late that it concluded abruptly. To Bledsoe's surprise, the broadcast crew made no mention of the payoff in the
National Pick Four. So Claude hurried from Doherty's Den to
the UW library just a few blocks away, booted up a computer,
and logged on to the *Racing Daily* web site. He read: "Two winning National Pick Four tickets, each worth $460,000, one in
Chicago, one in Wyoming."

Bledsoe laughed, so loudly that a Pakistani med student
jumped in his seat at a nearby computer monitor.

"Wyoming," Bledsoe said. "Must have been somebody's
grandma in Cheyenne betting her license plate and piggy-
backing our train. More power to her," he added benevolently.
"If we'd had the *only* winning ticket, it might have looked kind
of suspicious."

Chapter Seventeen

Matt turned on his computer after rolling out of bed, then shaved and showered while his coffee percolated. Dressed, coffee cup in hand, he sat down in front of the computer screen to peruse the general and sports news from overnight. The first item he saw on the *Racing Daily* website made him sit up straight in his chair.

ANOTHER JOCKEY MURDERED

NEW ORLEANS——Jockey Mark Guerin was shot to death here Wednesday night in the parking lot of Randolph's restaurant on the city's west side. The twenty-nine-year-old rider died instantly from a single rifle bullet to the head fired by an unknown gunman who apparently fled the scene immediately. Guerin was standing with his wife, Charlene, and a group of friends shortly after 8:30 p.m., saying his goodnights after dinner, when the shot struck. None of the other six people were injured. With the exception of Charlene Guerin, who refused to leave her husband's side, all in the group ran back into the restaurant to seek shelter and summon help.

Randolph's is a popular gathering place for racetrack workers and racing fans, located some two miles from the Far Grounds Race Track. Guerin and his wife were regular patrons. Charlene Guerin was standing alongside her husband when he was shot. She was eventually taken to Tulane University Medical Center and treated for shock.

According to police sources, the fatal shot was apparently fired from a point some eighty yards west of the restaurant parking lot. The trajectory of the bullet suggests the shooter was above ground level when he fired, perhaps on the steps of a water tower on the adjacent property. After Guerin was hit, three or four more shots were fired. Evidently they were fired into the air, intended to frighten the bystanders, who dashed into the restaurant or took refuge on the other side of the one-story building. One of the bystanders reported hearing an automobile rapidly driving away moments after the incident. There has been no description of the car given.

Guerin, a fixture on the Louisiana racing circuit, is the third United States jockey to die of a rifle wound in the last two months. Other such incidents occurred in Maryland and Indiana. No arrests have been made in any of the cases, all of which continue to baffle law enforcement officials. It has been confirmed that the same rifle was used in the first two killings. Ballistic tests on the bullet that killed Guerin were to be conducted today. In each instance, only one shot was fired directly at the victim by an obviously extremely efficient marksman. Each of those direct shots proved instantly fatal.

Members of the racing community and his fellow riders expressed shock and sorrow at Guerin's death. "He was a good rider and an even better man," said his younger brother, David, currently the leading rider at Elmont Park in New York. "I can't believe this," he added.

Matt stared at the computer screen. "Damn it," he said. "I can't believe it either."

◇◇◇

That afternoon Matt waved a greeting to Harry Schwartz, the elderly Heartland Downs paddock security guard, then crossed the rubber-bricked walking ring and walked across the carefully trimmed lawn to stall number two. He could just see Maggie's wide-brimmed hat beside a gleaming dark bay colt whose halter was being held by groom Bobby Mendez. Maggie, dressed in a tasteful beige pants suit, was bent down, cinching the girth on the young horse, which stood passively. On either side of him, horses were pawing the ground, neighing nervously, shifting their bodies from side to side, rolling their eyes and sweating in anticipation of what was to be the first career race for each of them. In contrast, Maggie's entrant, Kenosha Kid, was a model of decorum.

"He looks like he's about to fall asleep," Matt said as he approached the stall. Maggie grinned up at him. "Wait till they ring the bell. He'll wake up then. This baby can scoot."

Cinch on tight and saddle secured, Maggie stood up and introduced Matt to Kenosha Kid's owners, Lou Romano Senior and Junior, a middle-aged man and his twenty-something son. Matt could almost hear their nerves jangling. They were new owners, and Kenosha Kid was their first horse. Maggie, whose training acumen was matched by her sense of public relations, assured the Romanos that "He'll run well. Try to relax and enjoy this experience," she urged, before turning to greet Kenosha Kid's rider, Dean Kristufek.

Matt stood silently with the Romanos as the horses paraded around the walking ring with their riders up, then turned into the tunnel beneath the grandstand that led to the track. He looked up at the dozens of fans on the grandstand balcony that faced the spacious paddock, at the hundreds more ringing the paddock fence. A slight breeze ruffled the leaves of the old elm trees that divided the flower beds from the lawn. The sun bounced off the dappled coats of the neophyte racers. "What a day to be alive and at the racetrack," Matt said. The lovely scene served to temporarily take Matt's thoughts off Mark Guerin's death. The senior Romano smiled briefly and nodded in agreement. His son anxiously twisted his racing program into a sweat-stained cylinder.

Matt's thoughts went back to a similar summer day, two years earlier, when he had visited the paddock to see Maggie about setting up an interview with her. Maggie's career was taking off. Matt wanted to give it a proper boost—both because he was interested in getting to know her as a person after their memorable meeting at third base, and because he prided himself on recognizing early on the talents of young, upcoming trainers and jockeys, then beating his competition in bringing those talents to the racing public's attention.

After agreeing to meet the following morning at Maggie's barn following training hours, they continued talking. It was several minutes before the brightly clad jockeys would arrive to take their perches atop the horses. Trainers chatted up their owners, meanwhile keeping observant eyes on their equine starters and opponents. Horse people, Matt knew, were always eager to assess the competition. They were also ever on the alert when in the vicinity of these thousand-pound creatures. As one old horseman had pointed out to Matt years before, "They can hurt you without even trying."

While Maggie and Matt were talking that afternoon, a stumpy gray gelding was being led around the walking ring toward where they stood. "That's the favorite in this race, old Fleet Argo," Maggie said. "Doesn't look like much, does he? He's nine years old, but he's still tough. Now," she said, "watch this," as she stared at the oncoming horse. As Fleet Argo walked past, he turned his head and looked at Maggie. In turn, Maggie looked the horse directly in the eye. Moving on, the old gelding looked back over his shoulder at Maggie.

"What's that about?" Matt asked.

"Oh, it's just kind of a game I play sometimes," Maggie answered. "I learned early on that horses here are kind of used to being dismissed. Somebody leads them into the paddock, slaps a saddle and a jock on them, and then sends them out to the racetrack. Most of the time, nobody interacts with them. It's almost as if they're pieces of furniture.

"Awhile back," she continued, "I discovered I could make horses look me in the eye just by standing here in the paddock, not moving, but looking intently at them. I would pick one out and concentrate on him as he went around the walking ring, making eye contact. Not moving my hands or raising my voice, just *looking* at him. The horse would look back at me as if he was amazed by the attention I was giving him. Next time around, he'd be looking for me. He'd start to walk past and then look back over his shoulder to see if I was still watching him—just like Fleet Argo just did. This happened almost all the time. It makes you wonder what horses think of us," Maggie had said pensively.

Matt's reverie was interrupted when he heard the paddock judge call out "Riders up," the signal for the jockeys to get aboard their mounts. Lou Romano Senior said, "We want to go and bet our horse." Maggie instructed them how to find her box located above the finish line. She told the father and son that she and Matt would meet them before the race started.

As the Romanos moved away, Matt said, "You seem to handle these two greenhorns very deftly. Just as you do your horses. It makes me marvel even more at you, and what you do," he smiled, putting an arm around her waist, thinking back to that paddock talk they'd had two years earlier, grateful it had led to this life they enjoyed today.

Maggie quickly but gently removed his hand. "Please," she said as they exited the paddock, "I'm a professional horsewoman engaged in the work of my profession. Can't be fooling with the likes of you while I'm on the job."

◇◇◇

It wasn't until forty-five minutes after Kenosha Kid's race that Matt had a chance to talk to Maggie about the jockey deaths. As Maggie had said, Kenosha Kid "could scoot," and scoot he did to a three-length win for the delighted Romanos. They reacted as if they'd just won the Kentucky Derby, ordering champagne to be delivered to Maggie's box, insisting that Matt stay and share it with them. Finally, after politely declining an invitation from the departing Romanos to join them for dinner at one of Chicago's most expensive restaurants, Maggie and Matt were left alone in the box. The retreat of the late afternoon sun was beginning to lay shadows across the grandstand as the horses came out for the final race of the day.

"So, Mister O'Connor," Maggie said, "I get the impression you have something on your mind." When Matt told her what it was, all of Maggie's playfulness and post-victory jubilation quickly evaporated.

"I'm sure you heard about Mark Guerin getting killed last night," Matt began. She nodded yes.

"Well, I'm wondering if Mark Guerin's death is connected to the deaths of the two other riders who were shot to death recently. And I'd like your help in trying to find out."

Maggie gave him a puzzled look. "What could I do?"

"I'd like you to let me know what the jocks here are saying about this. You know these guys better than I do—you work with them, you hire them, you hear things in the stable area that I never could."

Maggie said, "Nobody *really* knows jockeys, Matt, except other jockeys. Don't kid yourself about that."

"Okay, okay. But what I'm saying is you have a much closer relationship with them than I ever will. What do they think is going on here? They must be talking about these murders."

Maggie took a small sip of her champagne. "Everybody's talking about the killings. But none of the riders I know here seem to have any clue as to why these murders are happening. One of them—Sam Scollay, I probably have more dealings with him than any of them because he rides the majority of my horses—says that the rumor is some riders at other tracks have been pressured by some mystery phone caller. That's what some of the valets have told me, too. The riders involved aren't saying anything, according to Sam."

Matt said, "Pressured to do what?"

"Nobody knows. And it could be just one of those wild race-track rumors. They sprout up like mushrooms in horse manure, you know that."

Matt took out his notebook and pen. "I just can't see any common thread here. Carlos Hidalgo, killed for no known reason in Maryland. Same thing for Eddie Calvin in Indiana and Mark Guerin in Louisiana. Did these guys piss somebody off? Or did their friends or relatives? What the hell could it have been?" He absentmindedly started tapping the notebook with his pen. "I've got a call in to David Guerin in New York. I've known him since he first came on the racetrack. I'd like to see if he's got any theories about his brother dying like that. It's pretty rare that there's two top athletes in the same profession who are brothers, and one gets killed under circumstances like these."

Maggie frowned before saying, "No, maybe not as rare as you think."

"What do you mean?"

"Let's go back to poor Eddie Calvin."

"What about him?"

"You know Randy Morrison? One of the leading jocks out in California?"

"Yes."

"Well," Maggie said, "a lot of people aren't aware of it, but he is Eddie Calvin's half-brother. Their mother was widowed after she had Randy. She later remarried a man named Calvin and had Eddie by that man. Randy just kept his real father's name. Those boys were raised together. I was surprised we didn't see Randy at Eddie Calvin's wake. As I understand it, he couldn't make a plane connection in time to be there that day. I heard he arrived late that night, then accompanied his brother's body back to Arkansas the next day."

"I'll be damned," Matt said, drumming the pen on his pad. "So two of the three murdered jocks were related to very prominent riders."

Maggie said, "Yes, but what about the other guy? Carlos Hidalgo? He's evidently an isolated case."

"Not if Hidalgo was used as an example—a warning that maybe wasn't heeded. Which, because it wasn't, led to the deaths of the other two."

Maggie stood and stretched. "It's been a long day. I've got to get back to the barn for feeding time. But I'll be happy to hash this out further with you over an early dinner."

As they exited the box Matt said, "Dinner it'll be. But no more talk about these murders today. I need to get my mind around something else for a couple of hours."

Maggie smiled up at him as she stepped onto the escalator. "Let's make it a couple of hours for dinner, followed by a couple of hours of adult gratification of a carnal nature."

"I wouldn't complain," Matt grinned.

◇◇◇

While Maggie and Matt were departing Heartland Downs that afternoon, David Guerin emerged from the showers in the jockeys' room at Elmont Park in New York. He'd received word of his brother's death early that morning. Still stunned, he nevertheless called his agent to say he would honor his riding assignments that afternoon, then leave for New Orleans in the evening. He had calls on promising horses from two prominent trainers and he didn't want to risk losing his assignment on either of those mounts in the future.

Minutes earlier Guerin had won the final race of the day aboard Higgins Hideaway. He was rapidly toweling himself off when he heard the voice of his agent, Ray Krantz. Ray was sitting on the bench in front of Guerin's locker, reading the jockey's mail. It was a function he performed daily, weeding out the junk and setting aside the pertinent missives and requests for autographs and personal appearances for his celebrated client. David Guerin was a New York favorite, receiving dozens of letters and postcards each day.

"Davie," Krantz said, "come over here."

Guerin finished carefully combing his blond hair with one of his small, strong hands, slipped into his briefs, jeans, and tee-shirt, and walked to where Krantz was seated. There was a stricken look on Krantz' usually cheery face. "I don't want anybody hearing this," Krantz said in a low voice, "but there's a telegram here you better look at right away."

"Who from?" said the puzzled jockey.

"Some guy signs himself Professor. That's all. Damned if I know who he is," Krantz said. "But whoever he is, he claims he killed your brother."

Chapter Eighteen

On a Saturday afternoon two weeks after jockey Mark Guerin's funeral, Jimbo Murray looked up from his large, leather-bound menu, then placed it on the linen-covered table in the Heartland Downs Turf Club. There was a look of disgust on his face. Vera Klinder continued to read her menu, pausing occasionally to sip from her cranberry-flavored vodka cocktail and look around the beautifully appointed room, crowded with well-dressed patrons who were eating, drinking and discussing how they might wager on the next race.

Jimbo shook his head. "Damn," he said, "I didn't know we were coming to a place where they charge you thirteen bucks for a damn hamburger."

Vera reached across the table to pat his hand.

"Honey, we should be able to splurge a little. If things work out in this race, we'll be taking home a bunch of money." She nodded toward the twelve-inch television set, a standard feature on every table in the upscale Turf Club. The set was tuned to Elmont Park in New York, where horses were approaching the starting gate for the final leg of that day's National Pick Four. There were nine of them, but to the bettors, both at Elmont and at the hundreds of simulcast sites around the nation, only one seemed to matter: Number Five, Sena Sena, winner of his last five races and favored today at 2-5.

The Elmont track announcer, commenting when the camera concentrated on the prancing, gleaming-coated Sena Sena and his rider, David Guerin, referred to the horse as "the prohibitive favorite."

Jimbo said, "I don't get it. They're calling this horse the prohibatable favorite, or whatever. That's like prohibition, when they outlawed booze, right? But it don't look like anybody's been prohibited from betting on this son of a bitch. Look at those little odds on him." He smiled as he re-examined the Pick Four ticket in his hand. "He's not on our ticket," Jimbo said. "And I'm pretty goddam sure there's a reason for that." He clinked his Budweiser bottle against Vera's upraised cocktail glass. Then he motioned for the waiter and ordered the $13 hamburger. Vera opted for the fruit plate, "and an order of French fries on the side."

◇◇◇

Some forty minutes later, Oily Ronnie Schrapps sauntered up to the $50 window on the third floor clubhouse side of Heartland Downs. He was feeling relaxed on what was a "day off" for him—no old broads to snooker, no naïve prospects to impress, just a regular day at the races, trying to make some money with his bets.

With fifteen minutes to post time for the ninth and final race on the program, Oily Ronnie had plenty of time to bet. He knew what horse he was going with, one he had followed for weeks, so he had time to schmooze with Toby Mullins, the veteran mutuel clerk who had manned this $50 window for as long as Ronnie could remember.

"One race to go, Toby," Ronnie said. "Give me two hundred win and place on the five horse."

Mullins adroitly punched out the ticket. Then he leaned forward across the counter and beckoned Ronnie closer to him. "See that redheaded guy over there with the duffel bag?" he whispered.

Ronnie turned to his right. He spotted a redheaded man who was talking on one of the public phones on the west wall. There was a maroon duffel bag at his feet, a large beer in one hand, and a broad smile on his freckled face.

"What about him?" Ronnie said.

Mullins said, "Guy came to me with a winning ticket on the National Pick Four. One of only ten in the country."

Ronnie's eyebrows raised. "That had to be a good score," he said. "What'd it pay? Nearly $200,000, right? I sure as hell didn't have it," he added, "not when Sena Sena flopped in the final leg at Elmont. I was only alive on my ticket to that pig."

"That Pick Four paid just over $245,000," Mullins said, "but that's not the interesting part. The guy insisted on cash, no check, all $20 bills. Couldn't be talked out of it. That's the second time this summer that's happened. Some broad hit the National Pick Four awhile back for well over four hundred grand. She wouldn't take anything but cash, either."

Schrapps frowned. "That's got to be a hell of a big bundle of money, right?"

Mullins reached for a pen and applied it to a piece of scrap paper. "No, not all that heavy," he said after finishing his calculations. "Each bill, like every piece of U.S. currency, weighs one gram. There are 454 grams in a pound. So, this guy was only lugging a little under twenty-seven pounds."

"They tell me that when the broad cashed in the 460 grand and took cash, she had a couple of security guards carry it out in shopping bags to a car in the parking lot. Know what she tipped the guards? Two bucks apiece. That was it," Mullins said disgustedly.

"For this redheaded guy," Mullins continued, "Terry Dart, the mutuel manager, spent ten minutes counting out the money for the guy down in his office. Very unusual," the clerk added. "Most people naturally want a check. Who wants to be walking around carrying that kind of bread on him? And the guy refused an escort from track security, just like the woman before."

"You know this guy?"

"Never saw him before today. He won that bet with a pretty small ticket. And he left the big favorite, Sena Sena, completely off it, if you can fathom that. I guess I'd better keep my eyes open for him next time, see who he's betting," Mullins added with a laugh.

The two watched as the redheaded man replaced the phone on its hook. He hefted the duffel bag to his shoulder. It appeared to be heavy, evidently bulging with currency, but he carried it easily. He drained his beer cup before moving toward the escalators.

Oily Ronnie said, "See you later, Toby. Got to head out. If I win the ninth you can cash me out tomorrow." He put his mutuel tickets in his wallet, then hurriedly followed the redheaded man down the escalator.

Many people—especially parents with children, patrons who had come in groups, and tapped-out losers—were leaving before the final Heartland Downs race of the afternoon as Ronnie followed the redheaded man through the clubhouse door and toward the parking lot. It was a noisy, crowded scene, the valet parkers scurrying to retrieve cars, senior citizens walking slowly to their buses, children chattering to parents deflated by defeat of their horses, and Ronnie had to hustle and sidestep to keep his target in sight. In Section C of the vast parking lot, he saw the redheaded man approach a blue Toyota, open the passenger side door, then enter. There was a woman behind the wheel, and another figure in the back seat that Ronnie could not see clearly.

As the blue Toyota backed out of its slot toward him, Ronnie raised his binoculars. When the car had straightened out and began driving off, he read its license plate, which was mud-spattered but not so badly that its numbers were illegible. He quickly said to himself, "Wisconsin 869-1121," and knew he'd locked it into his memory. Looking up from the license plate to the back seat, Ronnie saw another pair of binoculars, aimed at him. They were in the hands of a broad-shouldered, bald man. Ronnie could not see the eyes behind those glasses. But as the blue Toyota receded in the distance and he lowered his binoculars, Ronnie felt a chill, as if the gaze aimed at him had contained a strain of invisible, but very tangible, menace.

Ronnie shook off his feeling of concern, concentrating on the bag of money he'd just seen leave the track. "I've got to

keep an eye out for these people," he said to himself. "If they
hit again and are this dumb, I know the boys that'll take that
cash off them."

Opening the door to his gray BMW, Ronnie heard the track
announcer call the finish of the ninth race. His horse finished
third. Ronnie reached for his wallet, extracted the $400 worth
of worthless tickets, and scattered them across the tarmac before
getting behind the wheel.

"Damn," he said, "I thought that horse was a cinch." He was
parked directly beneath one of the overhead television cameras
monitoring the lot, but he carefully looked around to make sure
he was not being observed by any people walking to nearby cars.
Ronnie cautiously reached below the dashboard and extracted
the cigarette lighter, which had been hollowed out and contained
his portable drug stash. Leaning sideways in the seat and keeping his head down, he poured coke into a crisp, tubed $50 bill,
snorted twice, and replaced the lighter.

He sat back up behind the wheel, then momentarily leaned
back against the cushioned head rest, feeling better already. Then
he started the BMW and drove off, singing to himself:

"You take Mary, I'll take Sue,
"Ain't much difference 'twixt the two,
"Cocaine…run all 'round my brain."

Chapter Nineteen

Matt started his work day by interviewing Moss Tilton, the man in charge of starting the races at Heartland Downs, who was about to celebrate his thirtieth year on the job. Tilton, a hard-bitten old Texan, allowed as how he had "watched more horses' asses in full flight than any man in America outside of the U. S. Congress."

That scheduled interview had been followed by an impromptu and unwanted session with Leon the elevator operator. Leon held the car at floor level and wouldn't open the doors until he had described in excruciating detail the small fortune he'd "just missed in yesterday's fifth race. For about the thousandth time, I play a trifecta that comes in 1-2-4. If they would invent a bet like that, I'd hit it so often I'd retire in a week," Leon lamented.

"Yeah, and if they wrote races at six furlongs and one jump, I'd be living on an estate on a Caribbean island," Matt replied, finally escaping Leon's clutches.

A few minutes later Matt had just poured his second cup of coffee of the morning when his phone rang in the Heartland Downs press box. There was no greeting when he picked up the receiver, just a question barked out by his chronically impatient editor, Harry Cobabe: "How many jocks have died in strange ways that you know about?"

Matt shifted the phone to his left ear, the one farthest from colleague Rick Rothmeyer, who was arguing loudly on his phone with his girlfriend, then saying to her, "Ivy, let me tell you something. Some day, you'll find yourself. And you'll be really, really bummed." Rick put down the phone, a satisfied grin on his face. Matt resumed talking to Cobabe.

"Why are you asking me?" Matt said. "'You've got a crack research department down there at the main office, don't you? Or why don't you put some of your copy desk gerbils on it, so they'd stop fiddling with the prose I send them?"

Matt enjoyed sparring with Cobabe, who two years earlier had replaced an editor Matt despised, Hugo Hamilton, dismissed because of increasing ineptitude. Hamilton later talked himself into the sports editor's job on a small paper in southern Ohio, where he was fired again, this time for an act that entered journalism lore. A terrible writer who was obliged to provide one sports page column per week, Hamilton faced a deadline one day with a blank computer screen before him. Desperate, he went to the internet and downloaded a column from a major Cleveland paper. It was a piece that sharply criticized the Ohio State University football program. Without reading it, Hamilton deleted the byline of its writer, Bill Livingston, and hurriedly put his own byline on it. The controversial column ran that night. The next morning, Hamilton got a phone call from an irate reader and OSU alum who lambasted him for "such a dumb, scurrilous, vicious column." After listening for a minute or two, Hamilton angrily interrupted the caller. "Listen, jerkoff," he shouted into the phone, "go shove that column up your ass. *I* didn't write the goddam thing."

Cobabe ignored Matt's remark about the copy desk. He said, "I am asking you in order to determine whether you retain any shred of the acuity that occasionally has appeared in your work during my time here."

Matt laughed in acknowledgment of this jibe. He took a sip of coffee. "Well," he began, "there was Citation's rider Al Snider back in the 1940s—he disappeared while fishing off the Florida Keys. There was an ex-jock named McKeever and another named Miller, back in the '80s. They died off the other coast of Florida, evidently in a boating accident that no one saw. How am I doing?"

"Since then. Let's talk more recent," Cobabe said.

"Mike Hole. Suicide, but under suspicious circumstances. Eric Walsh. Murdered by persons unknown. Then there was that Cajun bug boy down in Louisiana a few years back. His death was ruled a suicide—even though he'd been shot in the back. Ah, Louisiana. How's that?"

Cobabe admitted, "Not bad. Evidently you haven't sacrificed all your brain cells to Jack Daniels. I find this encouraging. Sometimes, you know, I tend to give up hope for your generation, so many of them walking around yapping on cell phones, or listening to crap music on their headsets, going down the street and refusing to make eye contact with anyone except themselves in the store window reflections. They make Narcissus look like an amateur at self-absorption. But don't get me started on that."

"You started," Matt said.

"Never mind, let's get back to the subject at hand," Cobabe said. "Those deaths you mentioned were spread over many years. Did you know that this year alone there've been three of these midgets murdered in the last two months?"

Matt put the phone down on his desk and took a deep breath. "Midgets." What a term to describe the most amazing athletes Matt had ever observed. Somehow, sometimes, his acerbic editor could catch Matt with his defenses down and thoroughly appall him with his callousness.

"Yes, of course I know that," Matt finally answered. "There was Eddie Calvin over in Indiana. Before him, that Mexican rider, Carlos Hidalgo in Maryland. And Mark Guerin in New Orleans. Who could forget?" he said softly.

Cobabe, barking orders to a staff member in the office, evidently didn't hear Matt's response. Or at least he resumed talking without any acknowledgment of it.

"On top of that," Cobabe said, "there have been upsets in two of our major races and huge gimmick payoffs as a result. My question is: what's happening here? Jocks murdered. Handicapping form falling apart. What the hell's going on in American racing?"

Cobabe paused, then sighed into the phone for effect. "Am I being too demanding, like the tyrant my troops believe me to be, if I ask: 'Don't I smell a major story here? One that my ace Chicago columnist should be poking his sizeable proboscis into?'"

"That's a redundancy. Besides, no one even knows what proboscis means anymore, Harry."

There was a sigh at the other end. Then Cobabe said, "All right, tell me what you're working on now."

"I'm doing a long feature for Saturday on a trainer here, Mark Kaplan, young guy in his first year out of Minnesota, off to a great start. I'll file that Racing Board wrap-up I told you about this afternoon. I've got to cover a Horsemen's Association meeting tomorrow night, they're electing officers and there are some wild-eyed nut cases challenging the current incumbents. Should be lively."

"And," Matt said softly into the phone, "I'm looking into rumors of a guy here running an investment scam involving racehorses. Nobody else knows about this, Harry, this is a case in progress. So, I'm keeping this quiet."

Another silence. Then Cobabe conceded, "Okay, I know you're busy, Matt. But this jock thing could be hot. As soon as you can, next week at the latest, I want you to move this to your front burner. Get it?"

Matt finished his coffee. Then he said, "Fax the clippings on all three of those jocks who were killed this year. Hidalgo, Calvin and Guerin. I already know about the two races you're talking about—those payoffs had everybody flapping. I'll start thinking about this."

"Think hard," Cobabe answered. "Think fast."

Matt went over the clipping file late Sunday night. When he was finished, just before midnight, he called Cobabe at home. This was akin to interrupting the Pope during his rosary, and very much discouraged by the editor, but Matt dialed anyway.

"This better be good," Cobabe growled.

Matt said, "I need to go to Vegas. I'll be away one, maybe two days. You'd better send one of your deskmen out to Heartland to cover for me while I'm gone."

There was a silence on the other end before Cobabe repeated himself. "This better be good."

"It could be. I need to talk to a friend of mine about these 'unusual races.' If something's not kosher about them, he'll know."

Cobabe said, "Matt, I'm tired. It's late. Make the trip. I trust your judgment on this. Call me if you need anything." Then he hung up.

Matt dialed Maggie's number. The phone rang six times before she came on to sleepily say, "This better be good."

"You know, that's exactly what Harry Cobabe said to me about fifteen minutes ago. Imagine, you and my esteemed editor sharing speech patterns."

Maggie sighed as she sat up in bed. She waited him out. With less than four hours to go before her alarm clock went off, she was conserving energy.

He said, "I hate to call you at this hour, but I just wanted to let you know I'm going out of town early tomorrow. I'll be gone a couple of days."

"Okay," Maggie said, "where?"

"I am going to Vegas to consult with the most expert source I know concerning all matters related to horse race gambling."

Maggie yawned, then said, "Okay. Just be careful. Call me from out there tomorrow night. And say hello to The Fount for me. Love you," she added before hanging up and clicking off her light.

Chapter Twenty

"Darlene, bring me a couple of corned beef on rye. Two pastramis on onion rolls. Sides of potato salad, cole slaw. A jumbo shrimp cocktail, the big fruit salad. And another pitcher of margaritas. No salt, right? Thanks, darling," smiled David Zimmer, otherwise known as The Fount, as he settled himself into a poolside chair at Las Vegas' Delano Tower Hotel.

The order he'd placed was the first full meal of the day for The Fount, a six-foot-three, one-hundred-and-thirty-eight pound metabolic marvel who ate relentlessly in such quantities without gaining an ounce. Darlene, the waitperson who often served The Fount, gritted her teeth as she wrote down the order. So depressed at missing the cut at Hooters that she had subsequently packed on fifteen pounds but still affected a version of the well-known costume, Darlene nearly split her shorts as she pivoted away from The Fount's table. It was 7 a.m. under a bright blue Nevada sky, the temperature reaching for eighty degrees. While taking the order from this thirty-five-year-old beanpole, Darlene never blinked, for she had waited on The Fount many times before and seen him demolish portions usually seen only on National Football League training tables. "This freak eats like that five or six times a day," Darlene told friends. "He's like a human landfill. He's a good tipper, though. And he's supposed to be the smartest guy in town."

As the sun began to create steam from small poolside puddles left by the hoses of the janitorial crew, The Fount spread his

Racing Daily on his umbrella-sheltered table. Then he opened his briefcase and laid out a thick sheaf of sheets containing his figures for the day's horses races scheduled at tracks across the U. S. and Canada. After his usual ten hours of preliminary work handicapping the numerous cards, Fount had arrived at the tipping point of his day, when he would make his final decisions on which horses to bet, for how much, and in what combinations in events that would be conducted, as he liked to put, "on both sides of the Continental Divide." He smiled in anticipation of the early morning "lunch" he had just ordered. He had breakfasted four hours earlier in his Delano Tower suite, and he was ravenous. Dinner for him would be at noon. The Fount labored primarily at night, made his bets in mid-morning, slept four hours, then reviewed the race results he'd videotaped on his twelve big-screen television sets and began to calculate the next set of figures. It was a seven-day-per-week work routine designed to grind most mortals into sawdust. The Fount thrived on it.

Years earlier, as a sixteen-year-old sophomore at MIT, he had read A. J. Liebling's book *The Earl of Louisiana*, about one-time Louisiana Governor Earl Long, one of the more colorful politicians in a state wonderfully notorious for producing them. Long loved playing the horses and, each morning on a long table in his state house office, would lay out side-by-side various editions of the *Racing Daily* containing the records of horses running everywhere in the country. After making numerous picks, Long would call his bookies and bet. "If he's betting a bookie in Louisiana," Liebling quoted one of the governor's staffers, Long "puts it on the tab…But if he wins he has a state trooper over at the bookie's joint within a half-hour to collect."

This, wrote Liebling, "was the life I had always wanted to live."

That line of Liebling's made The Fount chuckle whenever he thought of it. He had managed to achieve an existence reminiscent of the one-time Louisiana governor's. He stretched expansively as he thought of the day ahead. He would never govern any state, but as the widely recognized kingpin of race book betting in the world's gambling capital, The Fount had found the life he'd always wanted to lead. He lived at a "comped" rate in a first-class hotel only twenty floors above his "office," the room created for him by the hotel's owners, who also rebated a goodly chunk of his wagering because of its huge volume. This wasn't Earl Long's Louisiana, but it was about as good as it got for a horse player in America. The Fount was convinced that Liebling would have approved.

Dave Zimmer had been tagged The Fount—as in Fount of Information—in grade school when, as a six-year-old advanced to third grade, he had first revealed an amazing ability to answer even the most trivial of trivia questions. Facts, obvious or arcane, seemed to permanently attach themselves to his active brain. Eventually, he had chosen to aim his formidable mental arsenal at betting on horses.

This decision by The Fount came after he had graduated summa cum laude from MIT with a double major (mathematics and modern European literature), then spent three and a half lucrative but increasingly boring years working as a stock analyst for a major New York City brokerage house. The Fount was introduced to horse racing at Aqueduct and Belmont by Jeff Henry, a fellow stock analyst whose father owned horses.

The Fount found himself to be intrigued by racing—not only by the beauty of the athletic events unspooling before him on those weekend afternoons at the New York tracks, but by the challenge of deducing how to identify and wager on winners. After months of intensive study of racing history, including its voluminous literature devoted to "how to beat the races," he spent more months watching and re-watching thousands of videotaped races. Then The Fount constructed his own system of betting, based primarily on "speed figures" of his own devising plus such elements as the type of shoes worn by horses, wind factors, and a sophisticated deconstruction of trainer patterns.

The Fount realized he was onto something after his first two weekends of betting following his intensive study. Two more months of daily plays confirmed that initial impression and bolstered his bank account resoundingly. This was going so well he began to feel constrained by his brokerage house job, which allowed him to be in action only an hour or so per day at a nearby off-track betting shop. Finally, Zimmer announced to his astounded parents, Dr. Nate Zimmer and Naomi, that their only child was going to become a full-time horse player based in Las Vegas. "No, I'm not going to be a full-time *gambler*," he patiently explained. "Gambling is for dummies cemented in front of slot machines, or howling around roulette wheels, where eventually they leave what money they brought. I'm going to make a living as professional horse player. There's a difference."

That was a dozen years earlier, and The Fount had never regretted his decision. So proficient had he proved to be at picking winners that the Delano Tower management set up a special private room complete with television sets and his own personal mutuel clerk. Because the Vegas casinos no longer operated as independent bookies handling horses races, having chosen to send all monies bet with them into the common pools at the racetracks, the casino managers loved all horse bettors, winners or losers, since—like the racetracks—they received a percentage of each dollar bet. The bettors were all competing against each other, not against the casinos, which simply provided the mechanism for their action while taking a nice layer of cream directly off the top. The bigger the bettor, the larger the casino's total share. Since The Fount bet thousands of dollars each day, the owners of the Delano Towers treated him royally. The fact that he had chosen to set up shop at their place gave them a healthy publicity boost among the knowing players who trekked to, or lived in, what author Tom Wolfe once termed "middle-class America's Versailles."

With his betting research laid out on the poolside table, The Fount sipped at his margarita. Then he sat back in his chair for a few moments, relishing the feel of the morning sun on his face, the challenge of the day to come. He was a happy man.

When his cell phone rang a few minutes later, The Fount checked its caller ID. Clicking on the phone he said, "Matt, my man. What's up?"

Matt O'Connor replied, "I've got one for you. Ready? Baseball trivia. Who was the only man to die as a result of an injury suffered in a major league baseball game?"

Said The Fount dismissively, "Are you kidding me? Ray Chapman, hit in the head by a fastball. August 16, 1920. He was a shortstop for the Cleveland Indians."

Matt said, "I'm not done yet. Who threw the pitch that killed Chapman?"

The Fount sighed again. "Carl Mays. Come on, Matt, who do you think you're dealing with here?"

"I'm not done," Matt repeated. "After poor Chapman was carted off the field, Mr. Smart Guy, who did they put in the game to run for him?"

The Fount smiled appreciatively before saying, "Not bad. Not bad. Harry Lunte ran for Chapman. How's *that*?"

"You son of a gun," Matt said admiringly.

"Now," Matt continued, "let's talk about why I'm calling. I need to come and see you for some advice and counsel."

"I'll vacuum the welcome mat, Matt. Are you bringing Maggie?"

"Nobody—not even me, whom she justifiably adores and reveres—*brings* Ms. Maggie Collins anywhere. I *invited* her to accompany me. She declined—she's got a string of horses to train."

"So I'll vacuum half the welcome mat. How long you staying?"

"One day—most of which I need to spend with you."

"You can use the guest bedroom at Chez Zimmer. I hope you've got some good Chi Town stories for me."

◇◇◇

Matt had first met Dave Zimmer at a Las Vegas handicapping "world championship" that he was covering for the *Racing Daily* in the summer of 2000.

Not being involved as a contestant, Matt found himself bored in this sea of seriousness: hundreds of dedicated horse players lured from all over the country by the chance at a $100,000 contest winner's share. By the end of the first day, as Matt told Maggie on the phone that night, he was "convinced they could run J-Lo naked up and down the aisles here and these guys wouldn't take their eyes off the fifth at Far Grounds."

After three days the contest winner was declared: Dave Zimmer, aka The Fount. Matt's post-contest interview with Zimmer had gotten off to a rocky start. The two men were in the casino's private hospitality room. A waitress asked for their drink orders.

"Jack Daniels on the rocks with a splash," Matt answered.

Zimmer said, "I'll have a Daniels and Coke."

Matt's distaste for The Fount's drink order was evident. "Daniels and Coke," he snapped. "That's a disgrace. Like mixing Moet champagne and Mountain Dew."

The Fount's face flushed. "I'm not the only guy who likes Daniels and Coke," he said defensively. "I first heard about it when I was reading a magazine article about Roy Hofheinz, the guy who built the Astrodome. He drank Daniels and Coke."

Matt said, "I don't care if Roy Hofheinz, or Roy Rogers, or Trigger drank that mix. It's crap. It's a desecration.

"This," he continued, tapping his half-empty glass, "is booze that deserves respect." He took a long, respectful swallow.

"You ever hear of Bing Crosby's bandleader?" Matt continued. "Phil Harris? A major league drinker."

"Married to Alice Faye," The Fount shot back. "My mother was a big fan of hers."

"Right. Now, I'm going to tell you a story about this good bourbon. One time Crosby had a concert date in New Orleans. The local paper sent out a rookie feature writer, a young woman, recent j-school grad, to interview him in his hotel suite. It goes well—Crosby's shot a good round of golf that morning, he's in a fine mood. As the interview concludes and the young reporter is preparing to leave, she says, 'By the way, Mr. Crosby, where is Mr. Harris? I understand he's not in town yet.'

"'True, true,' says Crosby, playing it straight. "'Phil can't get here until tomorrow. Coming down from New York, he made a little detour into Tennessee. Said he had something very important to do there.'

"Naturally, the reporter's curiosity is piqued. 'That's interesting,' she says, 'do you have any idea what he was doing in Tennessee?'

"'Oh, yes, my dear,' says Crosby, 'I know exactly what Phil was doing in Tennessee. He went to Lynchburg—to lay a wreath on Jack Daniels' grave.'

"This poor girl bought this fable," Matt laughed. "It got right past her editor and was in the paper the next day. And even though what Crosby said Harris was doing was apocryphal, it emphasizes my previous point—Jack Daniels deserves to be treated with utmost respect. Not with Coke." He emptied his glass for emphasis.

"Why are you taking up my time with this?" said The Fount impatiently. "What do you want?"

"I want your story for my paper—your background, how you got started handicapping horses, your lifestyle. But first I've got to ask you something else. My paper carries countless tout ads from people offering to sell their selections for money. As sharp as you must be—you know, to win a contest like this—why haven't you started your own tout service?"

The Fount clunked his empty glass down on the table. "Why," he asked, "should I tell anybody what I know when I'm the only one who knows it?"

Matt looked at him with new respect. "I can understand that," he said. "I once asked one of these tout sheet kingpins that same question. Know what bullshit he came back with? Said he was dying of cancer, had just months to live, and therefore wouldn't have enough time left to make all the winning bets he needed to make in order to finish paying for his grandchildren's college educations. He looked me straight in the eye when he was telling me this. That was nearly eight years ago. He's still in business, as healthy and crooked as ever."

A grimace appeared on the Fount's long, thin face. "I know the old bastard you're talking about," he said. "He'd steal a homeless cripple's only blanket."

"Exactly," Matt said, laughing with him.

More Jack Daniels had followed that night in Las Vegas, and a friendship was formed. When The Fount came to Chicago for a big race, he always called Matt and they met for dinner. Matt, in turn, recognized The Fount as a valuable source to have on the Las Vegas scene, and he consulted him often.

This morning, after telling Matt he'd have him picked up by a driver at the airport the next morning, The Fount hung up the phone. He again stretched his lanky frame. His food order arrived, courtesy of two busboys being supervised by Darlene. Once the spread was laid out before him, he fell to with a vengeance.

Chapter Twenty-One

"Flight okay?"

The Fount asked Matt the question without taking his eyes off of the computer screen before him. Matt closed the door behind him and entered The Fount's Delano Towers work room. He nodded at the only other person in the medium-sized, carpeted, and functionally furnished space that contained the dozen television sets, two couches, a dining table with four chairs, a pari-mutuel machine, and a huge desk with a swivel chair behind it in which sat The Fount, hard at work.

The other person in the room was Wally Jensen, a longtime employee of the Delano Tower race book who now served as The Fount's personal attendant. Wally sat on a stool behind the pari-mutuel machine, which was located back of a wooden counter at the room's north wall. Near Jensen in that area was a refrigerator stocked with beer, sodas, three bottles of champagne and a huge deli tray, half emptied. Wally also had access to a house phone, which he was using to order The Fount's lunch.

"...No mayo on the smoked turkey sandwiches...double Cobb salad...four bean burritos...large anchovy-pepperoni pizza with double cheese...Yeah, that'll be it for now. I'll talk to you again in a few hours. Thanks."

The Fount called out, "Pimlico, sixth race. Two thousand to win on the seven. Hit it, Wally, they're going into the gate."

Wally quickly punched in the numbers. The machine kicked out a ticket, which Wally carefully placed atop a pile that had grown to nearly four inches high since his work day began. The Fount had thus far bet about three-quarters of his normal daily action—around $40,000.

Matt set his travel bag down and stretched out on the couch. He rubbed his eyes. He was worn out. He'd risen early and written that day's column, then pounded out another one for the next day before driving to O'Hare for his flight to Vegas. He hadn't had time to see Maggie in two days and felt bad when all he could do was leave a final message on her voice mail. "Duty calls, Scoop-Sleuth answers," he had said jokingly. "Be back tomorrow night." He hoped she thought it was funny.

The Fount said, "Matt, why don't you go up to my suite and take a break. I've got to stay here through the third at Bay Meadows. There's a two-year-old in there I want to see. After that we can talk."

When there was no answer, he looked over at his friend, who was already asleep beneath the bank of TVs that carried the Midwestern night tracks. He turned his attention back to the television set showing the sixth race at Pimlico. Number seven was crossing the finish line nearly four lengths clear of his nearest rival. The Fount smiled.

◇◇◇

Ninety minutes later the two men were seated at the dining room table. Matt was now refreshed, while The Fount appeared fatigued. "I've been working fourteen hours, so excuse me for being kind of out of it," he said. "I've got just about two hours for you. Then I've got to grab some sleep before I start working on tomorrow's races." When The Fount was working—which was twenty-four/seven for forty-eight weeks a year—nothing could make him deviate from his iron-clad schedule. A few weeks earlier his mother had begged him to return home for his Uncle Morris' funeral. "Ma," he had told her, "I can't do it. I'll visit his grave on my vacation in December. He'll still be there."

"This is an amazing existence you've carved out for yourself. Who could ask for anything more?" Matt said ironically. "You live in a hotel. You work eighteen hours a day, watching races, making figures, calculating odds, busting your brain. You have no social life. Wally is probably the person you say the most words to each day." Matt shook his head.

"Who could ask for anything more?" replied The Fount happily. "Pass me those tortilla chips and the dip bowl, will you? Then tell me why you're here."

Matt began by describing the death of Bernie the bookie, then told The Fount about his relationship with Bernie's nephew Moe. The Fount's eyebrows went up when he heard the name Moe Kellman. "Moe I've heard of," he said. "I'm impressed. His name still means something to the old Vegas guys."

"Look," Matt said, "I'm not here just on Moe Kellman's behalf. I think there could be a hell of a story for me—if I can figure out what the hell the story is."

The Fount said, "What are you looking for?"

"I'm looking for your expertise. There isn't a man in America who watches and bets more races a day, or a year, than you. What I'm asking is this: have there been any kinky races that you've noticed the last few months? You know what I mean—strange reversals of form, hard-to-explain upsets. Anything along those lines?"

The Fount gave Matt a long look. Then he hit a mute button that silenced all twelve TVs. He signaled over his shoulder for Wally to end his shift. Wally left slowly, ears wide open as he neared the doorway. Like most longtime Vegas residents, Wally knew information was currency, and he would have liked to glean some here. He closed the door reluctantly. Horses dashed about in silence on eleven of the TV sets. The Fount went up to the set in the middle of the wall and inserted a videotape in the VCR.

"It's not funny you should ask, Matt. I'm just kind of surprised that nobody else has. Take a look at this."

The tape was of the Dell Park Derby. The announcer calling the race seemed astounded at what he was describing: "And here they come down the stretch. It's longshot Chuck A Lot leading the way by two, now three lengths. Grisham's Dream is second,

Wing Warrior third…and the overwhelming favorite Lord's Heir is not doing enough…he's beaten today, folks!"

The Fount hit the pause button. He said, "Well?"

"Well what?" Matt answered. "I saw the result of that race last month. It was a big upset. Lord's Heir, the heavy chalk, finished out of the money. That happens."

"Yes, he did," said The Fount. "The chalk, Lord's Heir, huge favorite, ran out. Let's run this race back in slow motion, okay? Then you'll see why the 'overwhelming favorite' Lord's Heir flopped through no fault of his own. Watch this closely."

◇◇◇

On board his return flight to Chicago the next morning, Matt reviewed what he'd learned the previous night while watching two significant races with The Fount, who had first concentrated on the Dell Park Derby and Lord's Heir.

"Take a close look as they come out of the gate," The Fount said. "Lord's Heir breaks inward just enough to lose about two lengths. The jock, Randy Morrison, is pulling hard on the left rein, just for an instant, just enough to get the horse off course. This horse runs his best races on the lead. But after this kind of start, he can't get to the front like he usually does."

The Fount was silent as he and Matt watched the field go around the first turn and then down the backstretch, Lord's Heir buried in the middle of the pack and stuck down on the rail. "Okay," The Fount said, "now they're going into the far turn and Morrison's still got him down inside with nowhere to go. He's waiting for an opening—or, he *seems* to be waiting for an opening. Look right there! The opening comes when the five horse drifts out, but Morrison doesn't go through. He pulls Lord's Heir to the right and goes around two horses instead of zipping up the rail when it was clear. It looks like a bad decision, and it was. When Lord's Heir finally gets rolling in the stretch, he's got too much ground to make up. He doesn't hit the board, although he only misses third by a length. The winner pays $48.40. Payoff on the National Pick Four is $460,000 for $1. Two winning tickets."

The Fount hit the mute button and turned to Matt. He said, "Randy Morrison is one of the top five riders in the country. He's been ranked up that high for several years and for good reason. He's terrific. I've watched him in hundreds and hundreds of races. And he just doesn't *make* mistakes like that. What he has done here is very cleverly, very subtly, stiff his horse. Lord's Heir didn't lose that race. Randy Morrison lost it for him."

The Fount extracted the tape from the VCR and inserted another. Before hitting the play button, he went to the refrigerator and got a quart of Ben and Jerry's Cherry Garcia. Matt declined his offer to share the ice cream. The Fount began polishing it off out of the container, accompanying the ice cream with a plate of chocolate chip cookies. "Haven't eaten in a while," he explained. Between bites he started the videotape and resumed his lecture.

"Now here's the Gorham Stakes from New York two weeks ago. Another heavy favorite—Sena Sena. He's ridden by another top jock, David Guerin. On paper, Sena Sena stands out in this field. Pure class. He'd won his last five in a row. Horse is a stone cold closer—usually comes from way back with a big rush in the stretch and wins going away. Not many sprinters run like that, but he does, and he's a big crowd favorite because of it, as you know. Watch this."

Matt saw Sena Sena come shooting out of the gate as if there was a flame thrower scorching his rump. The horse's ears were back and he looked startled as Guerin whipped him hard right-handed while urging him forward. Sena Sena got the message. He dug in and sped to the front, opening up by two lengths, three, then five as the field went down the backstretch. The fractions were torrid. Guerin kept his hands moving on the horse's neck and Sena Sena entered the turn nearly seven lengths in the lead. Then the gas started to go out of Sena Sena. At the eighth pole this exhausted leader was passed by four horses. He staggered across the finish line seventh. Matt saw Sena Sena's trainer, red-faced and steaming, give Guerin hell. Guerin didn't even look at the trainer after he dismounted, just hurried away to the jockeys' room, his face averted.

The Fount stopped the tape. "That winner paid $34.60," he said. "The National Pick Four that day returned $245,000."

The Fount tossed the empty ice cream container into a wastebasket. He shook his head as he looked at Matt, his expression serious. "This is very weird stuff, man—two front rank riders evidently doing everything they could do to get their horses beat in a National Pick Four finale.

"In the thousands of races I've watched over the years," The Fount continued, "I've seen a few examples of bad jocks trying to lose. But those examples were very obvious, to me and any other racing expert." The Fount laughed. "One guy at one of the minor tracks last year pulled his horse so hard the horse's head was turned sideways. The horse was looking at himself on the infield television screen as they came down the lane. They got beat in a photo. The stewards suspended the jock six months for 'insufficient effort.'

"But a top jock wouldn't do it that way. They're smarter, they'd be way more subtle. They'd get themselves boxed in, and stay there. Or get carried wide and then go wider. Maybe drop the whip if they're desperate. Look like they're going to run up on the heels of a horse in front of them, when they're really not, and stand straight up in the saddle pulling back on the reins. You lose valuable lengths that way, enough to get beat.

"They can also miss the start, losing ground there. Or fall off at the start. Nobody wants to fall off going thirty-five miles an hour. But if you take a little tumble when the horse comes out of the gate, you're probably not going to get badly hurt. Remember, these guys are terrific athletes. When they were in high school they were gymnasts or wrestlers. Ever watch them play table tennis in the jocks' room? Their reflexes are off the charts."

The Fount stopped and took a gigantic bite out of a triple deck club sandwich he'd just removed from the refrigerator. Then he said, "The stuff I've shown you today falls into the subtle category. That's for sure. These are two expert riders intentionally losing races in ways so that they can't be accused by the stewards of wrongdoing. I heard that when the stews called Guerin on the carpet after the Gorham, he gave them some song and dance about 'experimenting with new tactics' with Sena Sena. Randy Morrison in California wasn't even questioned officially about his performance on Lord's Heir. After that race he told the press the 'race just didn't unfold' the way he'd anticipated. Bullshit. But there's no way for the officials to prove otherwise. What Morrison did, what Guerin did, these were masterful exercises in deceit, carried out by two of the finest jockeys in the world. The question, of course, is why?"

Matt said, "You can't believe that money is the motive, not with what these guys earn. Come on."

"No," The Fount replied, "I don't see it that way. Randy Morrison and David Guerin and each grossed over a million bucks in earnings last year. And for years before that. What would entice them to jeopardize lucrative careers like that? It can't be money."

"Well, then, what *could* it be?"

"Matt, I've got no idea. Why don't you ask them?"

◇◇◇

When Matt arrived at his apartment early that evening, he went to his PC and pulled up the *Racing Daily* charts of the two races The Fount had showed him. He read each one carefully. Besides the fact that the favorite had flopped what stood out, of course, were the National Pick Four payoffs—the largest of the year by far. On the Dell Park Derby, the chart reported, there were two winning tickets sold nationwide following Randy Morrison's machinations. There had been ten winning tickets cashed on the Gorham Stakes, the outcome of which had been orchestrated by David Guerin.

Matt unpacked his traveling bag, made himself a sandwich. He shuddered as he remembered The Fount at dinner last night, demolishing three prime rib plates, a whole sea bass, and a platter of roasted chicken. Then he reached for his Rolodex and flipped to the phone number of the Professional Jockeys' Union. When the phone was answered, he said, "Tyree Powell, please."

Chapter Twenty-Two

At Heartland Downs the following morning, Matt stopped at Maggie's barn to say hello. It was a busy place. Grooms were walking horses that had just exercised around the interior of the long wooden building, cooling them out as feed buckets banged amid the sound of pitchforks scraping. Other workers were cleaning stalls empty of everything but horse manure that had to be removed, then laying fresh straw over the floor before the animals were returned to the stalls in which they stayed for more than twenty hours each day. Spanish-language music played loudly from a radio placed at the center of the barn. One of the young Mexican-American women grooms was watering the geranium-filled flower baskets that hung every ten yards down the shedrow. An elderly countryman of hers carefully raked the dirt pathway beneath the flowers into the familiar herringbone pattern favored by meticulous trainers, such as Maggie. Matt stepped to the side of the walking path as two exercise riders guided their mounts toward the main track for workouts.

Maggie was about to pony a nervous filly to the training track and had time only to smile a greeting to Matt before saying "See you tonight." Then he heard her say, "Pedro, are you using the same brush on all three horses you groom?" There was a muffled answer. Maggie said, "Well, don't. No wonder all three have got skin infections. One had it, and you've given it to the other two. Throw that brush away. Go into my office and get three new brushes out of the trunk behind the door. Keep one for each of those three horses. *Comprende?*"

Matt heard "Si, senorita" as he began walking away from the barn to the Heartland Downs track kitchen. It was a bustling place with a long cafeteria steam table, three pool tables, and dozens of Formica-topped tables populated by trainers, exercise riders, grooms, and a few owners, all breakfasting under a canopy of cigarette smoke. The crowd was some eighty-five percent male, thirty percent Anglo, seventy percent Hispanic, with a very small scattering of African-Americans. Among the latter segment, sitting alone at a table in the rear of the large room, reading the *Wall Street Journal*, was Tyree Powell, the man Matt had come to see.

Powell was a couple of years older than Matt and, at five foot five, considerably shorter. His handsome, dark brown face was marred only by a thumb-size scar on his right temple, souvenir of having been kicked by a two-year-old behind the starting gate one long ago morning at Lincoln Downs. With his blue blazer, gray slacks, white shirt and muted red tie, Powell looked as if he could be sitting at a vice president's desk in a major metropolitan bank.

Matt bought coffee and two Krispy Kreme doughnuts, then stepped between the tables, saying hello to the many people he recognized. He smiled at Maggie's stable foreman, Ramon Martinez, who was using his work break to concentrate on a plate of huevos rancheros. "Buenos dias," Matt said. "Hi, Matt," Martinez replied with a friendly wave.

Before picking up a fork, Matt noticed, Martinez took off his ball cap and blessed himself. He bowed his head while making the sign of the cross. Observing Martinez, and then others of the large Mexican-American contingent at the track kitchen tables, Matt smiled as he remembered a comment made a few weeks before by Rick Rothmeyer. "How many bald Mexican men do you know or have you ever seen? I'll bet not two in your life. It's amazing when you think about it," Rick had insisted.

Tyree Powell nodded hello as Matt sat down at the table. He raised an index finger, indicating he wished to finish the newspaper story he was reading. Still silent and concentrating on the newspaper, Powell took one of the doughnuts that Matt offered.

Sipping coffee, Matt looked at Powell, recalling their first meeting eight years before, when Powell became the first black jockey to ride regularly in Chicago in some twenty years. It had come after the jockey's biggest career win, in the $250,000 Heartland Downs Handicap. Powell had driven a rather nondescript bay horse named Took Over up the rail in the late stretch to score a shocking nose victory over a heavily favored invader from New York. Took Over had paid $152.20. What had made Took Over's triumph even more noteworthy was the fact that he was owned and trained by another African-American, Manfred Stuart. On his way down to the winner's circle from the press box that afternoon, Matt noticed that the very short lines of people waiting to cash tickets on Took Over were comprised almost exclusively of black men and women. There was hardly a white face in this jubilant collection. Matt smiled, realizing that he had never before seen so many blacks at a racetrack. They'd evidently come out to bet on Took Over, and Manfred Stuart and Tyree Powell were their heroes that afternoon.

Powell enjoyed some other success, too, but a combination of ingrained racial prejudice and increasing weight finally compromised his career. For years he had struggled to "make" one hundred sixteen pounds on a frame much more suited to the one hundred and forty that he carried today. The physical toll involved in that for a relatively large-framed man was extraordinary. It involved one-thousand calorie per day diets, sweating weight off in a hot box, running while wearing a rubber shirt, taking diuretic pills to force liquid out of the system. A few riders regularly resorted to "flipping," which meant they ate and then forced themselves to immediately vomit up that intake. Some became so proficient at this they were legendary. Matt had heard stories about a Florida rider who, his first year in Miami, each night for a week visited an all-you-can-eat, $7.95 buffet. He'd go through the line, pile his plate with food, down it, then repair to the washroom and regurgitate. He was doing this three or four times an evening before management caught on and barred him permanently.

Finally, after years of growing frustration from battling weight and being denied opportunities his talent warranted, Tyree retired from riding, earned a business degree from a local college, and went to work for the Jockeys' Union, the organization that represented him when he was riding and that today was the major labor group for the nation's seventeen hundred active riders. Powell served as the organization's Midwest representative.

Matt had once written in his *Racing Daily* column that Powell was "not only one of the strongest and coolest under pressure members of the local jockey colony but also one of the smartest. Powell seems to perceive race patterns before they unfold. Put this man on the best horse, and that horse wins."

Powell had been grateful for Matt's endorsement and the two became nodding acquaintances. But Matt was under no illusion that today's conversation would be easy for either of them. Powell was a cool customer and, like most from that little world of small people who rode horses for a living, was fiercely protective of the group ethos, particularly when it came to privacy. Because of their size, and what they did, these men and women regarded each other with understanding, and looked warily at most of the rest of the world. Once a rider, always a rider, is how Matt had heard one old-timer put it.

Powell finished reading and folded the newspaper. He smiled at Matt and reached across the table to shake his hand. "How you doing, Matt?"

Matt said, "Tyree, you may not be smiling when you hear what I have to say."

Over the next twenty-five minutes, Matt laid out his reasons for believing that two of the most prominent members of Powell's organization, Randy Morrison and David Guerin, had intentionally lost their two recent National Pick Four races. At first Powell listened quietly, eyebrows raised. As Matt detailed his suspicions, Powell's expression turned cold and he folded his arms across his chest. As Matt continued, the expression on Powell's face changed from concern to shock to incredulity and, finally, anger. Still, he said nothing until Matt had finished, saying, "Believe me, Tyree, I wish I was wrong about this, but I don't think I am. I need you to help me get to the bottom of this. If we don't, this sport could be destroyed."

Powell took a deep breath before responding. "You know, this year already has the making of one of the worst in our history. There've been three riders shot to death at various places around the country, all three murders still unsolved. Not a one of them. Then, you've got the sudden death of Marnie Rankin, which didn't make sense to a lot of people. Now you're talking about accusations, the most serious kind you can make about a rider? I can hardly believe this."

He glanced around the room. "First things first," Tyree said in a low voice. "I don't think for a minute that Randy Morrison or David Guerin would do what you say they did. I know both of those boys. They're squeaky clean, for God's sake, always have been."

Powell leaned forward, arms on the table, exasperated, his eyes drilling into Matt's. "Do you have any idea what you're talking about here, Matt? Crimes being committed by men who make more money in two years than you and I will make in half our working lives? That's so off the wall, it's...hell, it's out of the ballpark."

Powell stopped drumming his fingers on the table long enough to look around the room. Then he again leaned forward, speaking softly but forcefully.

"You know what I went through as a rider, the battles I fought just trying to make a living. You even wrote about that. And I appreciated it.

"Now I've got this great job, doing work that I like and that I'm good at. It wasn't easy for me to *get* the job. There were still a few good ole boys on the Union's board of directors who didn't want to hire some upstart nigger. But they got voted down.

"This job means everything to me, Matt. I don't intend to mess it up. If I'm seen being involved with you when you're poking around asking personal—no, insulting—questions about two of our leading Union members, this job could be taken away from me. You see where I'm coming from?"

Matt nodded. "Yeah, Tyree, I see where you're coming from. But you'd better consider this: if something lousy *is* going on, the truth will come out eventually. It always does. How's it going to go for you if it appears you completely turned your back on the situation?

"The results of these Pick Fours, with just a handful of winners each time, the result of amazing reversals of form, just don't compute. There's something going on. I'm sure of it."

Matt paused and looked around the track kitchen before speaking. He said, "You ever hear of a New York newspaperman named Jimmy Breslin? Wrote some good novels, too."

Tyree shook his head no. "Well," Matt went on, "Breslin was great. He was the source of a lot of classic lines. One of my favorites was when he wrote 'Figures, of course, are notorious liars, which is why accountants have more fun than people think.'"

Tyree smiled slightly before Matt continued. "These figures, these payoffs on these races, Tyree, they don't lie to me. And they're sure as hell not funny. I'm no accountant. But I can count. They say, 'Something rotten is going on.' They say it loud and clear."

Matt crumpled his coffee cup and got to his feet. He said, "Tyree, I don't want the image or reputation of the Jockeys' Union damaged any more than you do." Matt continued, "And I'm not after some sensational bullshit story that ruins reputations.

"I'd just like to find out for sure what happened in those two big races. You should want to find that out, too."

Powell stood up abruptly, the cartilage in his knees making the audible popping sound familiar to retired jockeys and ex-football players. Matt thought Powell was going to walk out of the room. Instead, he went over to the water cooler and drank, said hello to some trainers playing cards at a table near the south window, then returned to where Matt was still standing.

Tyree said, "You're right in the sense that this has to be looked into. I'll see what I can find out—very quietly, very unofficially.

Then I'll get back to you. I owe you that." He picked up his newspaper and walked out the door.

◇◇◇

In Madison that same morning, Claude Bledsoe was about to go out his apartment door to his Chaucer seminar when the phone rang. He pivoted, picked it up, and heard a woman's voice say, "Mr. Altman calling for Mr. Bledsoe please." Bledsoe put his briefcase on the kitchen table and sat down. "This is Bledsoe," he said. "Please hold a moment," the woman said.

It turned out to be nearly three minutes before Bledsoe heard attorney James Altman say, "Good morning, Claude. Do you have a minute?"

"That's what I've got."

There was a pause. Altman said, "Well, then, I shall be brief. I've given quite a bit of thought to your situation since we had our talk concerning your grandmother's codicil. Finally, I must admit, my curiosity got the best of me." Altman chuckled. "I'm just calling to inquire about your progress in acquiring the needed million dollars."

Bledsoe was sure that he then heard muffled laughter on the line. He got up, phone in hand, and walked over to the window. He attempted to calm himself by looking down into the yard next door, where one of Madison's organic gardening specialists, Gayla Hilton, was busy weeding an impressively disciplined congregation of vegetation, her broad-brimmed hat almost sideways on her head, padded knees in the soil.

Altman broke the silence. "Mr. Bledsoe. Are you still there?"

"Keep cool," Bledsoe told himself. "When I dump my pile of cash on this little prick's desk, Altman will soil his pleated lawyer pants. I'll save my gloating for then."

Forcing himself to speak in calm, polite tones, Bledsoe said, "I would have to say that I'm on track, Altman. Be assured, I am on track."

He crashed the phone down and went out the door. He didn't want to be late for class.

Chapter Twenty-Three

As usual, Dino's Ristorante was wall-to-wall with loudly talkative diners. In the crowded foyer, an impatient throng waited in line for tables, or at least for access to the jam-packed bar. And, also as usual, as soon as he said the magic words "Moe Kellman" to the harried hostess, Matt was whisked past the crowd and conducted immediately to the booth in the rear of the dining room.

Kellman sat in his regular booth against the back wall, beneath an enormous black and white photo of owner Dino Nigro with Frank Sinatra. Photos of other show business luminaries covered most of the wall space in the restaurant, but Sinatra's was the largest by far. Photos of Dino with one ex-president of the United States and two former Illinois governors were far more modest in size and placement.

Kellman placed his cell phone on the table as he greeted O'Connor. "Matt, good to see you, kid. Let's have a drink." He tapped his nearly empty Negroni glass and a waiter hurried forward. Matt ordered a Jack Daniels on the rocks. He was tired from his long day at the track and long drive into the Chicago Loop. He hoped the most famous product of Lynchburg, Tennessee, would have its usual salutary effect on him. "I don't have time for dinner, Moe," he said. "But there are some matters I want to go over with you."

The first subject was Bernie Glockner, and Matt had to admit that the old bookie's death remained a mystery. "There are some weird things going on in racing," Matt said, "but I can't see how they tie to Bernie's murder."

"What are they?" Kellman asked. He sat back in the booth and shoved his cell phone to one side before taking a drink of his crimson-colored cocktail.

Matt began with his suspicions that the recent deaths of three American jockeys—by rifle shots, fired by an unknown gunman or gunmen—were somehow linked. "I don't know what the hell is actually going on, and neither do the police," Matt said. "But I do know that two of the dead jocks have relatives in the sport—one has a brother who is an active jockey, another has a half-brother who is one. Both very good riders, too, although they sure as hell haven't looked like it in a couple recent major races.

"Then," Matt continued, "there is the case of one Oily Ronnie."

"Schrapps?" Moe said sharply. "I thought that bastard was still doing time. He took an old friend of mine for about $300,000—all she had. What's he up to now?"

"Same cheating game, just a different chapter." Matt described Oily Ronnie's preying on gullible oldsters such as Tom Jaroz' Aunt Sophie. The problem, Matt said, was obtaining solid proof of what Ronnie was doing.

"There's got to be a way to set this guy up, Moe. God knows he's got it coming. But I don't know where to go with this. And I'd like to work with, or through, somebody who'd promise that I get first crack at publishing the story. It'd be a big one for me. I figured you might know somebody helpful."

Moe finished his Negroni before answering. He said, "I got a guy."

Matt nodded, in recognition of what he thought of as the "Chicago Syndrome." It involved a surprisingly large percentage of people he knew who, when confronted with problems, major or minor, "had a guy" to guide them safely through the shoals of local vicissitudes. He thought of parking tickets fixed, liquor licenses miraculously restored, jury duties ducked, premier concert or sporting event tickets scored, reduced-price Bar Mitzvah and First Communion celebrations. It was a mantra woven into the soul of the city's sharpies, the movers and shakers…Moe's world.

"Guy's name," Moe continued, "is William Popp. He's a Sheriff's Department detective. He and I go back a long way. Good guy."

Matt looked doubtful. Kellman picked up on it. He chuckled before taking a swallow of his newly delivered drink. "I can't tell you how good this makes me feel," he smiled, "getting Oily Ronnie in our sights. I'd love to see that bastard nailed. But I can see something's bothering you. Let's hear it."

Matt, trying to be as diplomatic as possible, hesitated before saying, "I thought that your sphere of, well, influence, was more on the other side of the law. Not with a Cook County Sheriff's detective."

Kellman laughed so hard his Don King-like hairstyle shook. When he'd finally finished, he smiled at Matt and said, "Matt, my boy, you might be surprised at what you refer to as my 'sphere of influence.' It's fairly wide.

"And I suppose, kid, that you might be wondering whether an old cocker like me still has juice, right? Up in my seventies now, working up in my Hancock suite, way off the street. You've got your doubts about how much heft I've got left, right? Be honest. Am I right?"

Matt nodded sheepishly. In return, he got another broad smile from the little man across the table. Moe leaned forward. "You've put me in a good mood," he said. "Let me tell you a story that a guy told me once.

"Years ago there was this young couple here in Chicago, deep in love, struggling through the Depression but wanting to get married. So they do. They've got no money for a real honeymoon—he's a hotel desk clerk going to law school at night, she's a third grade teacher—so after the wedding, and their little reception just with their immediate families, they take a train north up the lake shore to this little resort town in Wisconsin. Their honeymoon haven! There's a short main street, a dozen stores, three gas stations, two hotels. They check into one of the hotels, the cheapest one, all they could afford, late in the afternoon.

"They take to the nuptial bed, later order sandwiches from the lone bellhop, and a few hours later the bridegroom takes a look out of their window and says, 'Darling, there's a theater lit up across the street. They're advertising an act called The Great Zambini. What do you think? Shall we go?' His bride says, 'Why not?'"

Moe paused to sip his drink. Matt declined Moe's offer of "a fresh one." Then Moe continued his story.

"This was back when theaters still had live acts between movies. The newlyweds pay a modest admission fee and enter the theater. Pretty soon the theater owner comes onstage and announces, 'Now, the featured act of the evening, the one and only Great Zambini.' The theater is packed and excitement is running high.

"The curtains part to show a table in the center of the stage. On the table are three walnuts. The spotlight shines upon them. Then out from the wings comes a short, well-built, good-looking young man with a bushy black mustache. He's wearing a tall red turban and a long red robe. He bows to the audience. Then he walks over to the table. He opens his robe. The crowd gasps—he's not wearing anything under the robe, and he's hung like a horse. There's a drum roll from the pit band. The Great Zambini takes his big schlong in one hand, steps up to the table, and cracks the walnuts open, one by one. Then he closes his robe, bows modestly, and walks off stage. The crowd goes wild cheering him."

Moe took another sip of his drink. Matt watched him, bemused—he had never before heard the little man tell a joke.

"Now," Moe resumed, "shift forward fifty years. That young couple I described is now about to celebrate their golden wedding anniversary. He is a very successful but now semi-retired attorney, she's raised their four children. They can afford to celebrate anywhere they want in the world. How will they mark this grand occasion? In a sentimental mood, they decide to return to the little town where they spent their joyous honeymoon.

"To their delight and surprise, the same hotel is still there in that little Wisconsin town. They check into the same room they had all those years ago. The man looks out the window. There, across the street, is not only the same theater, but on its marquee in huge letters is the notice 'The Great Zambini Appears Tonight.' The couple is amazed. It can't be him! They laugh, the woman saying this is like something out of the Twilight Zone. But they can't resist. After dinner that night, they go across the street to the theater.

"After a preliminary act there's a drum roll announcing the featured attraction. The curtains part. Out comes this little, wizened-up guy wearing a red turban and a red robe. His bushy mustache is white, but the man and his wife look at each other in astonishment—it's definitely him, The Great Zambini, from fifty years ago.

"There is another roll of the drums. The Great Zambini walks up to the table that's placed at midstage. On it are three coconuts. With a flourish, he opens his robe, takes out his big schlong, and cracks open the coconuts. The crowd goes wild.

"The couple can't resist. They go backstage to his dressing room and introduce themselves to The Great Zambini, who receives them graciously. They tell him about first seeing him a half-century ago on their honeymoon weekend.

"Then the husband says, 'One question, if you don't mind: why did you switch from cracking walnuts in your act to cracking coconuts?'

"Replies The Great Zambini softly, 'To tell you the truth, my eyesight isn't what it used to be.'"

Matt broke up, his laughter startling the customers in the next booth. Moe smiled and took another drink of his Negroni.

"Anyway," Moe said, obviously pleased at Matt's reaction, "the moral of my story is this: I'm no Great Zambini. But even at my age, kid, I know how to get things done. I'll have my old friend Detective Popp call you in a day or two."

After signaling the waiter for the check, Moe looked at Matt. The smile was off his face now. He said, "Oily Ronnie has made a big mistake. He may not know it yet, but he has. He's a bad thief and an egomaniac to boot, and he's going to pay.

"Like the old wiseguys used to say, 'If you eat steak, you shit blood.'"

Chapter Twenty-Four

Vera Klinder walked rapidly through the Oscar Mayer Company employee parking lot, past the famous Weinermobile, stopping only to light a cigarette on the way to her Ford Falcon, a faded green vehicle riddled with dents and creases. It was just after 6 a.m. Vera finished her first Pall Mall of the last eight hours as she slid her tall, lanky form behind the wheel, then immediately fired up another as she pulled out of the lot on this early Wednesday morning in Madison. Smoking was not permitted inside the giant meat packing plant. It wasn't until she'd driven around the state capitol square that she cranked open a car window. Even after three years in the bologna packaging division of the huge facility, Vera hadn't gotten used to the powerful odor of processed meat that pervaded the neighborhood near the Mayer factory.

Vera was tired. She never wore makeup at work, or did much more to her straight, dirty blond hair than just pin it up so it would fit under the plastic caps the Oscar Mayer workers were required to wear. Fatigue showed on her face, the result of a couple of sleepless afternoons—her normal bed time—and the strain of the fight she'd had last night with Jimbo Murray. Ordinarily after work she'd head home to shower, change clothes, and go out for something to eat. But as she watched the sun rise in her rearview mirror—one of the few aspects of her factory night shift that she appreciated—she altered her normal routine.

Instead of going straight to the Dahle Street apartment she shared with Jimbo, Vera stopped at a 7-Eleven for coffee and a breakfast burrito. Then she drove west to the Curtis parking lot of Madison's famed Arboretum. She took her coffee, burrito, and cigarettes to a picnic bench that overlooked the Nakoma Golf Course. Wiping dew off the bench, she sat down to review the list of things that concerned her. Jimbo and Claude Bledsoe led the list.

As Vera's gaze wandered over the lush golf links, her mind returned to the previous weekend's argumentative exchange with Jimbo. It was an unusual conflict for them, since Jimbo normally acquiesced to just about anything Vera asked of him. That was one of his qualities she found so attractive. The two husbands she'd divorced had been abusive drunks. In contrast, ex-convict Jimbo was one of the most even-tempered people she'd ever known. That's why their argument had so stunned her, leaving her thinking about it days later.

They had just finished their evening meal—Jimbo's dinner after his shift at the muffler shop, her light lunch before they caught an early movie and she headed for Oscar Mayer and the ten to six shift. It had begun with what Vera thought was an innocent question: "Jimbo, why are we getting so little money out of this stuff you're doing with Bledsoe? Don't you hate to be taken advantage of?"

Jimbo looked at Vera in disbelief. He got up from the table and stomped around the room. Then he erupted. "Are you crazy?" he shouted. "The man pays us almost a hundred and fifty grand for cashing a couple of goddam mutuel tickets? A hundred and fifty? And you're bitching? I can't believe you."

He had stalked to the apartment door, but then reversed himself, pulled back by the tether of her pleading voice saying, "Jimbo, can't we at least talk about this? C'mon back, baby." He plunked down on the opposite end of the couch, before reaching for the remote control and muting the taped rerun of a recent NASCAR race.

So they had talked, Vera reiterating her belief that Jimbo was being "played for a sucker. If this is such a simple and safe thing to do, cashing these tickets, well then why isn't your friend

Mr. Bledsoe doing it himself? And if it *isn't* such a simple and safe thing to do, how do you figure what he's been giving you is enough?"

Vera lit a cigarette and took a slip of paper from her jeans pocket. "I did some numbers," she said. "That Pick Four ticket we cashed at Heartland Downs that you signed for, it came to $460,000 after they took out the tax. The one I signed for paid $245,000 after taxes. Claude gave us a total of $140,000 for the two tickets. Now, hell, that's only twenty-five percent when you total them up and do your damn division. Doesn't seem like enough to me," she said, looking at Jimbo from behind a haze of exhaled smoke.

Jimbo knew the numbers well. Following Bledsoe's instructions, he had asked the Heartland mutuels manager for payment in cash just as Vera had. The manager, Terry Dart, had congratulated him on his win but warned him about his choice of payment form. "Taking payment in a check is safer and easier on everybody," Dart had said. "We had a young woman in here a few weeks back that I gave the same advice to," he went on, but Jimbo left the office without listening to any more.

The Monday after the race, Bledsoe deposited most of the money in a safe deposit box, rented under a fictitious name, in a Sun Prairie, Wisconsin, bank. Two days later he met with Jimbo and Vera at their apartment and gave Jimbo and Vera their share.

"We're not going to do it this way again," Bledsoe said, after he had counted out the money.

"Why not?" Jimbo asked.

"Because we can't have the same person signing for these payouts. Vera signed for the first one, you did the next one. We need somebody else for the third one, which is coming up soon. We have to go a different route with that one."

"Why?"

"Because," Bledsoe said impatiently, "we don't want the same faces showing every time we cash. Too risky. I don't want to spend the money to fly the two of you to another track. Heartland Downs works fine for us, both as a place to put down our bets and to collect them. But we don't want that mutuels boss down there getting too familiar with either one of you. We've got to hire some outside help we can trust."

Vera had been pretending to watch "Survivor" from the living room couch of the apartment, but she had turned down the sound in order to better monitor their conversation. Then she heard Jimbo say, "Vera, can you come in here?"

As Vera took a seat at the kitchen table, Bledsoe said, "I understand you have a grandmother living near LaCrosse. Jimbo says she's quite a character."

"Well," Vera replied, "Grandma Vi is eighty-four but she can still drink any of those river rats up there under the table. She's a tough one."

Bledsoe smiled. "My kind of woman," he said. "I have a proposal for her, one that can make her some money."

He explained that he would like Grandma Vi to cash one winning Pick Four ticket on a date to be determined. "We'd cover all of her expenses. She'd have to go down to Chicago, but we'd pay her a generous fee for her services. Think she'd be interested?"

"Hell," Vera replied, "Vi's game for about anything. Most of her old girlfriends have passed on. About the only thing she looks forward to now is visiting me, or her trips to the Indian casino near where she lives. She still drives," Vera added, lighting another Pall Mall. "Her car's got a bumper sticker on it that says 'Custer Had It Coming.' Vi thinks the Indians treat her nicer at the casino because of that.

"And," Vera continued, "Grandma Vi goes to Vegas at least once a year to bet horses. Spends about a week. They don't have horse rooms at those Indian casinos in Wisconsin. So, I'm pretty sure she'd be game to do what you want. But let me call her tomorrow."

When Vera phoned her the next day, Grandma Vi was eager to cooperate. "I'm always looking for some excitement, honey," she told Vera, promising to be ready to travel whenever she was needed.

It was this plan that prompted Vera to begin thinking about gross receipts from Pick Four tickets. "Maybe there's more money to be had from Bledsoe. Why shouldn't we at least talk to him about it," she had said to Jimbo, thus sparking their bitter exchange. That was when Jimbo hit the ceiling.

◇◇◇

After stomping around their apartment for ten minutes or so, hollering about what an "ingrateful bitch" she'd revealed herself to be, Jimbo finally cooled off enough to take a seat next to Vera on the couch. "Maybe you forgot something here," he said, "the fact that Claude has cut me in for more money than I can make in five years slapping on mufflers, or any other sort of shit job an ex-con like me can get.

"You've got to understand," Jimbo continued, "that Claude runs this whole show. He's the mastermind, the idea guy. I don't agree with everything he does," Jimbo admitted, momentarily recalling Bernie Glockner's fatal fall—something he had never told Vera about—"but I go along. Because, to tell you the truth, he'd have no more regret about booting me out if I complained about our cut than, well, he just wouldn't have any regret, that's all.

"And it might just piss him off. You wouldn't want to see that happen, Vera, I guarantee you."

"What do you mean?" Vera said.

Jimbo hesitated before saying, "Just take my word for it."

Vera thought that over before pressing on. "Has he ever killed anybody?"

Jimbo jumped as if he'd been cattle-prodded. "Jesus, Vera," he said, "don't talk about shit like that. Just don't talk about it."

The morning dew was disappearing from the lush golf course grass as Vera finished her coffee and lighted another cigarette. She remained deep in thought as a couple of elderly duffers flailed away in a nearby sand trap, alternating miss-hits. One finally threw his ball onto the green. The other just pocketed his ball and stomped over to their golf cart and drove it to the next tee.

Jimbo's fear of Bledsoe was very real, Vera could see that. She had to keep that in mind. At the same time, it angered her to see her man being shortchanged, not to mention herself. Vera frowned, knowing she'd have to give some more thought to this aggravating situation. She walked back to her car and used the burrito bag to wipe the dew that had accumulated on the back window.

Chapter Twenty-Five

Matt was certain that his day could not get any worse—until he drove up to Maggie's barn on the Heartland Downs backstretch.

He'd walked out of his apartment shortly after 6 a.m. to find his Geo Prizm sandwiched between a gray SUV and a black SUV in its parking place on Hinman Street. When he had struggled unsuccessfully to extricate his compact car from between these two vehicular mastodons, he'd accidentally bumped the one in front hard enough to set off its alarm. The sound shrieked down the quiet Evanston street like a London blitz siren. After nearly ten irritating minutes had gone by, a young, blond-haired woman in a black designer sweat suit came charging out of a house four doors down across the street. She was screaming at Matt, "What are you doing to my car?" on her way to turn off the alarm.

Matt rolled his window down and gestured at her SUV. "You parked in here after I did," he said, "and jammed me in. I've got to get out. I have to go to work. Move that thing."

His angry expression served to silence the yelping woman, who reluctantly got behind the wheel, perching like a child on the high seat, and awkwardly eased her SUV forward so Matt could extricate his car. In his rearview mirror as he headed north on Hinman to Dempster, Matt could see her giving him the finger with one hand and holding a cell phone in the other. She must have been steering with her knees. All the way to the racetrack as he surged through early morning traffic, his stomach roiled.

The third race that afternoon was, on paper, a forgettable affair—a claiming race for horses valued at $5,000. Among them was Maxwell F., a one-time stakes runner who, as a ten-year-old gelding with bad ankles, had dropped down the class ladder to Heartland Downs' lowest level. Maxwell F. was a fan favorite, for he tried his very best every time he set foot on the track, even though his talents had been severely compromised by physical decline.

As the field approached the starting gate Matt rose, stretched, and decided to watch the race from the press box porch. Heading to the door, he could hear Rick on the phone, obviously talking to Ivy the actress.

"I heard Lemon Tree Theater has scheduled 'The Taming of the Shrew' for next fall. They tell me the female lead is yours for the asking." Rick slammed the phone down without waiting for a reply and said to Matt, grinning, "She loves it when I talk to her like that."

Matt and Rick were both watching the race with their binoculars when Maxwell F. came around the stretch turn leading by two lengths. Then, in an instant, horror unfolded. The old horse snapped his left foreleg and nearly fell. His jockey, Zoe Crozier, went over his left shoulder, landing with a thud. But she sat up immediately, apparently shaken but not seriously hurt, as Maxwell F. limped up the stretch toward the finish line, his broken limb waving like an empty sock. Matt could see the terror in the old gelding's eyes. He shuddered. Rick said, "Damn, that is ugly."

Zoe Crozier got to her feet and started to run after Maxwell F. She caught the horse by his dangling reins and managed to get him to stop moving. She cradled Maxwell F.'s head in her arms as track attendants came to her aid. The horse ambulance arrived soon afterwards, as did the track veterinarian. A large screen was set up behind the ambulance, shielding from the grandstand any view of the horse. Matt knew the vet was administering a lethal injection. The horse's body would then be loaded on the ambulance, all of this taking place out of sight of the fans.

Matt walked back into the press box and sat down. "This is the worst part of this sport, of this job," he said. Even Rick, ever the cynic, was noticeably affected. "I hate to see that, too," Rick said softly. "That old horse ran his eyeballs out every time. Maybe it's best that he died doing what he loved to do. Maybe."

After the last race, Matt drove to the barn area. He had arranged to pick up Maggie and take her out for an early dinner. Usually, she was dressed and ready to go, seated in a camp chair on the lawn outside her barn, reading the *Racing Daily* or chatting with the night watchman she employed at her stable. Not this evening. Instead, Matt found Maggie in her small, cramped office. When he knocked and opened the door, she silently looked out the window. She didn't turn to him at first. He admired the profile that he cherished before he noticed her tears. When he walked around her desk and reached for her, he saw that her eyes were red from weeping. He didn't say anything at first, just took her in his arms. Her arms went around his neck as she began sobbing.

Minutes later, Maggie lifted her head from Matt's chest. She looked up into his face with a wry smile. "Well, Scoop," she said, "I imagine that you want to know what has reduced your favorite trainer to emotional rubble." Matt smiled and kissed her gently and said, "Let's have it, babe. Sit down and tell me about it." He took her by the hand and led her over to the battered couch and swept a brown barn cat off it, along with a pile of racing magazines. "Start at the top."

What had happened was that—without warning—Maggie had been fired as a trainer of the horses owned by the Romanos, the father and son team Matt had met weeks before in the paddock. Lou Senior had called Maggie at her barn early that morning to announce that he and his son had decided to "take another path" with the eight horses they had in training with her. Yes, they said, their stable had been in the black under Maggie's guidance, and, yes, they had won more races this year than they had anticipated. "But we want to try another fellow," Lou said, naming the leading trainer at Heartland Downs, Archie

Winkleman, known as "The Vulture" for his habit of stealing owners away from other trainers.

Maggie wiped her tear-stained face with a tissue. "Mr. Romano said to me, 'It's nothing personal.'"

"Nothing personal! What could be more personal than to get dismissed just like that—and with all of his horses doing so well here! And some nice horses, with promise, like Kenosha Kid." She threw the dampened tissue in a nearby wastebasket.

Matt was not just sympathizing, he was also curious when he asked, "Well, what's he thinking? What's going on with this guy?"

Maggie shook her head, a knowing look on her face.

She sat down on the old brown couch, elbows on her knees, face in her hands. "Same old story," she said.

"What old story?"

Maggie's shoulders slumped as she replied, "Oh, I'm sure Mr. Romano got pressure from his wife to drop me as their trainer. I've met her. Middle-aged lady, heavy set, expensive clothes, suspicious eyes. She's one of those women who feel very threatened by a female training their husband's horses. I know it. I've seen it before. I've gone through this before. It's just a part of this business for me—unfortunately."

Matt sat down beside her, stroking her cheek, thinking how they had frequently discussed this sorry subject in the past: the fact that women, although comprising nearly half of the backstretch work force, were so rarely entrusted with good training jobs. Old prejudices die hard everywhere, he knew, but they were particularly hard to kill in the tradition-bound, singular world of horse racing.

"There are some wives who are very supportive of women trainers," Maggie continued, "but I've got to say that from what I've seen, most are not. I tried to be friendly with Mrs. Romano. I invited her to the barn. I sat with her at the races. I was polite to her, just like I try to be with everybody. But I'm not about to be her best buddy—or her husband's. I've got a job to do. I train race horses."

She sighed. "Maybe Mr. Romano said to her one time that he thought I was pretty, or smart, or something else positive. That might have been enough. But if she thought I had designs on her fat old husband..." Maggie began to laugh. "That man," she said, "with his nose hairs almost tangled in his damn mustache...and dandruff drifts on his suit coats...Well, what the hell!"

Maggie stood up and wiped away a lingering tear as she smiled. Her laughter was full-throated now, a release, an acknowledgment that this career setback could be overcome, if not forgotten. Matt got to his feet and she hugged him hard. Looking up at him, her smile widening, she said, "My Aunt Florence, I think of her at times like this. She was a typical Irish spinster schoolteacher. Whenever something bad happened to any of us in our family, Auntie Flo would just reach for her rosary beads and say, very positively, 'Remember, every knock's a boost.' I never understood what that meant when I was a kid."

"But now you do," Matt murmured, holding Maggie tight once again.

Chapter Twenty-Six

"It's better if I don't meet you at the track," Matt said into the phone. "This guy Oily Ronnie has got elephant ears. I'm told that he seems to know everything about everybody out here. Why don't you pick another spot? Late afternoon, after the races, is good for me."

Miles away in his office, the man Matt was addressing tugged at his right ear, a reflective action he'd often repeated since childhood, when the nuns at St. Gabriel's would yank at his lobes attempting to kickstart his attention. Detective William Popp, a twenty-seven-year veteran of the Cook County Sheriff's Department, said, "How about Max's Deli, over on Palatine Road?" They agreed on a time, for the next day, and hung up.

Matt had no difficulty recognizing the detective when Popp entered the restaurant. He was wearing a rumpled gray suit, white shirt open at the collar with the gray tie loosened, and scuffed, brown shoes. He moved deliberately, his paunch slightly protruding from his unbuttoned suit coat, holstered pistol visible under his left arm. Popp wore a blue-banded, short-brimmed straw hat back on his head. Branding "Cop" on his forehead could hardly have made him any more identifiable. Popp walked directly over to the booth where Matt sat. "I've seen the picture that runs with your column," the detective said, offering his hand. "I follow the races a little bit."

Popp was in his late fifties, a big man with a big head, most of it revealed to be bald once he had removed the straw hat.

What hair remained on the fringes was a dark shade of red now turning gray. Matt couldn't help thinking, *This guy's got ears bigger than Lyndon Johnson's.* Popp's eyes seemed to inventory the entire restaurant before he lowered himself carefully onto the booth seat across from Matt. "Piles been killing me," he explained with a sigh.

Matt, wondering if Moe Kellman knew what he was doing when he recommended William Popp to him, said, "Can I buy you a beer? That's all they serve here for alcohol."

"Naw," replied Popp, "coffee's fine. So, tell me what you've got. Moe Kellman says you know something I should know. He's usually right about these things."

Matt felt Popp's eyes boring into him as he began his story of Oily Ronnie scamming the old ladies in the retirement home. He told it with the conciseness demanded of him by the first good editor he'd worked for, a mad genius named Ted Moffett, who always emphasized to his reporters, "The nuts, I want to know the nuts of it, you assholes."

When Matt finished, Popp sat back in the booth. From his inside right coat pocket he extracted a black leather notebook so worn and tattered it could have been the cover of his First Communion missal from St. Gabriel's. With a nub of a yellow pencil, he dashed down two quick notes before returning the notebook to his pocket.

"Well," he said, a wide grin crinkling his face for the first time since he'd arrived, "maybe we've got something here. I remember this guy Ronnie from the first time he went down, for the stock scam. Busted out some of his best friends in that one. A real prince of a guy.

"Actually," the detective went on, "I was about to nail the son of a bitch back then for running a prostitution ring before the feds stepped in and got him for mail fraud. Yeah, before he got the Ponzi scam going, Ronnie had a mobile 'dating service.' Called it 'Dial a Maid.' Word got around pretty quick that it was more 'Dial and Get Laid.' He had these good-looking Croatian girls, fresh off the plane, dressed up in house cleaning outfits.

They'd come to your home and fuck for a fee. He promised he was banking part of their fees for them and just paid them a flat daily rate no matter how many so-called dates they had. He ran that business for about a year. Sent most of those poor green card girls packing without a cent of the money they had coming. The man is scum. Always will be."

Popp finished his coffee and picked up his straw hat from the booth's seat. "Let me check out a couple of things," he said, "then I'll get back to you. It'll be some time later this week. I think I've got a way to lure this rat into a trap that'll hold him. Thanks for the coffee." Popp stopped on his way to the door and turned back to look at Matt. "Like anything tomorrow?"

"You might bet Cilio's Hope in the feature. Looks to me like he's sitting on a win."

Popp said thanks and left.

◇◇◇

Late Friday afternoon, Detective Popp called Matt in the Heartland Downs press box. The first thing he said was, "That was nice, $18.60 on Cilio's Hope. Me and a bunch of the boys had him. Thanks."

"Once in awhile they'll run like they should," Matt said. After some more small talk regarding racing, the two men agreed to meet after the races back at Max's Deli.

When Matt arrived the detective was already seated in the back booth, reading the *Racing Daily*. They shook hands. Popp had a coffee cup in front of him. Matt ordered an iced coffee. Then Popp said, "I've figured out what we're going to do with Oily Ronnie."

"What?"

"We're going to throw another fish into his pond," Popp replied. "Only this one will be wearing a wire. I already did the paperwork for permission on this."

It was usually difficult to find octogenarian informants, Popp continued, but he knew "a great one. She lives in the addition my wife and I put on our house. It's my mother-in-law. Her name is Martha Ensworth.

"That name," Popp continued, "won't mean anything to you. You're too young. But Martha was a pretty famous radio actress on serials back in the 1940s. She retired from show business when she got married. She looks like Grandma Goody Two Shoes today, but she's razor sharp still. You play her gin rummy, you better ask for a line of credit."

"Would she do something like this?"

Popp said, "Are you kidding? She's been bored to death since her husband died five years ago. She's worked her way through the bingo and casino stages. Martha's looking for action. She'll be perfect for this."

The following Wednesday, when Tom Jaroz' Aunt Sophie and her group from Sunshine Meadows made their monthly visit to Heartland Downs, they had a new addition, Detective Popp having planted Martha Ensworth in their midst before their bus departed late that morning. Popp had arranged for this with the Sunshine Meadows director, Miles Renfrow, who explained to the aged race goers that "Mrs. Ensworth is considering moving into our facility and wants to meet some of you residents." Martha, barely five feet tall and less than a hundred pounds, was a bright, outgoing individual who quickly began chatting up her new acquaintants. "Your voice sounds *so* familiar," two of the women said to the ex-actress.

Matt and Tom had gone to see Aunt Sophie the previous afternoon to tell her about "a new friend" she would be making the next day. "That's wonderful, dear," Aunt Sophie said to Tom. "Maybe Mrs. Ensworth will get to meet Mr. Schrapps and learn about horse ownership," she added sweetly. Tom and Matt looked at each other. "I sure hope so, Auntie," Tom said.

Detective Popp strolled into the press box a little after 3 p.m. From the east window he and Matt could see the Sunshine Meadows group, nine well-dressed, broad-hatted, energetic members of the geriatric set seated in two adjacent boxes near the Heartland Downs finish line. They had been sipping bloody marys and diet sodas, eating from nachos and cheese plates, and placing small bets on every race, cheering their choices with enthusiasm. Minutes earlier, this all-female gathering had been joined by Oily Ronnie, who was now sitting in their midst, conversing with three attentive seniors. Ronnie was resplendent in a white sport coat, dark blue shirt unbuttoned to sternum level, blue slacks, white loafers, and dark glasses. His mousse-saturated hair glistened in the afternoon sun.

Popp, getting a close-up look through Matt's binoculars, said, "This guy must jingle like a Budweiser Clydesdale when he walks, all the body jewelry he's got on." That moment, Popp saw Martha turn away from Oily Ronnie for a second to look in the direction of the press box. She gave a thumbs-up sign before turning back toward Ronnie. Popp grinned. "Way to go, Martha," he said.

Matt's concentration on the scene in Martha's box was interrupted by Rick's voice. "Matt, damn it, pay attention, the phone's for you," he heard.

"Take the number," Matt said. "I'm tied up here right now. Tell them I'll call back in a few minutes."

Rick said, "It's your editor. Says he's got to talk to you right now. Period."

Matt sighed as he walked back to his desk, leaving Detective Popp still staring out the window.

"What is it, Harry? I've got something going on here now."

"Where the hell's your Saturday column?"

"So much for social niceties, eh Harry?" Matt replied, adding, "Look in your damn story queue. I filed it before eight o'clock this morning."

There was a silence before Harry responded, in a subdued tone, "Well, the gremlins must have hit again. We can't find it. Somebody must have mistakenly purged it. Can you send it again?"

Matt said, "Give me ten minutes and I will."

"Matt, please, we're on deadline for the first edition. It'll just take you a minute. I'm sorry about this."

Matt sat at his desk, pulled up the column on his computer, typed a quick message "Dear Copy Desk, please get your heads out of your asses and don't lose this transmission," and hit Send.

When he was finished, he looked up to see that Detective Popp had left the press box. When Matt looked over at the box where Martha and Oily Ronnie had been sitting, it was empty.

◇◇◇

It wasn't until after eight that night that Matt heard from Detective Popp. "Sorry I couldn't call sooner, Matt, but I've been busy at headquarters."

"Fill me in."

Popp said, "My little mother-in-law got some great stuff on tape," he said. "Ronnie gave her his big pitch about buying into a horse just like Aunt Sophie and the other women had done. Martha played right along. They agreed to meet at the track again on Sunday. Ronnie said he wanted to talk to Martha alone—didn't want the 'rest of the girls to know' what a great deal he was going to give her on a hot prospect that was 'ready to race.' Martha promised him she'd be there. I'll make sure she is. The hook is set pretty good now," Popp said with satisfaction.

At almost the same time Sunday night, Matt heard again from the detective. Matt and Maggie had just walked into Matt's condo when the phone rang. She went into the kitchen as he picked it up. Matt thought that he had never before heard anyone chortle, but that these sounds emanating from Popp probably qualified.

"This," said Popp with considerable relish, "is how it went down. Martha, wired up again, brought along a money order I'd had prepared for her in the amount of $20,000. She tells Ronnie, 'That's all I can spare now, but I could probably get some more later this summer. Would that be all right, Mr. Schrapps?'

"'That's fine,' Ronnie tells her, 'that will buy you part owner-ship in a very pretty horse that'll probably race next week.' Right after he tucks away the money order, Martha takes off her hat, which is the signal for two of my deputies to grab this bum.

"When I get to the box, just to be cautious, I say to her, 'Mother, did he take the money order? And was the wire in place?' Martha says, 'Billy, I've never missed a cue in my life. I *certainly* was not about to start this afternoon.'

"You should have seen Oily Ronnie," the detective continued. "He's looking at Martha with his jaw dropped near his Guccis. Then he turns to me and says, 'This is so fucking sick, that I gotta start body-searching eighty-five-year-old broads in order to protect myself.'

"The boys cuff him, but Martha is hot. She gives Ronnie a couple of bangs on his chest with her purse. She's mad as hell. 'I was only eighty a month ago, you thieving brute,' she says to him. Thieving brute? You got to love it.

"The DA says he's going to ask for no bail, considering Ronnie's past performance lines. He's pretty sure that's how it will go.

"We've got the bastard good this time," Popp said. "Thanks for your help, Matt."

After Popp had hung up the phone, Matt called his editor at home. Harry Cobabe's answering machine clicked on. "Harry," Matt said, "save me room on page one tomorrow. I've got a story no one else has. It should go right up on our website, too.

"And Harry, please see to it that your copy-editing gerbils down there don't lose it or screw it up, okay?" He was grinning when he put the phone down and walked into the kitchen to tell Maggie.

Chapter Twenty-Seven

Rick Rothmeyer concentrated on one of the half-dozen Heartland Downs press box television screens, a series of emotions flitting across his face. In order, these emotions were: worry, concern, and much deeper concern.

Prior to this moment it had been a typical Saturday afternoon in the press box. Racing writers from the two Chicago dailies worked on stories or talked on phones. Correspondents from two racing weeklies, in from out of town to cover that day's featured race, the $200,000 Heartlands Dash, had settled into the desk slots reserved for visitors in the long, air-conditioned, carpeted room. Half of the press corps, which also included talent from a local television station and one radio reporter, reserved at least some time for placing bets with press box pari-mutuel clerk Tom Jaroz and grazing at the lavish free buffet provided each weekend by Heartland Downs management.

Trainers, horse owners, and track officials drifted in to say hello, some stopping at the large popcorn machine on the first level to take a bag of freshly popped product. Among the latter group was Heartland Downs President Robert L. Duncan. It was on Duncan's orders that the popcorn machine had been purchased and installed several years earlier, and it was at his direction that it was scrupulously maintained. Duncan loved popcorn and, as with everything else he could control in his ultra-successful business life, demanded that it be "the best anyone can do."

Popcorn bag in hand, Duncan walked up behind Matt, who was writing the ad lead to his *Racing Daily* story for that afternoon's edition. Duncan placed a hand on Matt's shoulder, saying, "How goes it, Matt?"

Matt frowned at the interruption, but smiled when he turned and saw Duncan. "Tension is building, Bob," he said, pointing toward where Rick stood in front of a television set. Rick's arms were down, one hand clenched in a fist, the other tightening on a rolled-up copy of the day's track program. "Rick's alive in what could be a good-sized National Pick Four," Matt explained. He got to his feet. "C'mon, let's watch this last race with him." The two men walked over and flanked Rick, whose gaze never left the screen containing the telecast of the Prairie Schooner Handicap from Des Moines Downs in Iowa. Five of the starters had entered the gate, with another three to go, when Duncan asked, "What have you got going here, Rick?"

"The beginning of a bonanza," Rick replied confidently. Never taking his eyes off the screen, he quickly told Duncan that he had scored with two "bombs" in the first two legs of the Pick Two: a $22 winner to begin with, a $52 horse in the second leg, followed by a favorite that had returned $6.60. He had played four horses in leg one, five in the second, two in the third. In this final leg of his $80 ticket he had played the two main contenders. "It looks like a match race between these two to me," Rick said confidently. "I've got Tashkin's Baba and Rim Shot. New York's top jock, David Guerin, went out there to Iowa to ride Tashkin's Baba. And Randy Morrison came in from California to ride Rim Shot. How about that, two of the top jocks in the country going to Iowa to ride. Of course, it is a big purse, $400,000. But these two horses are two standouts in this field. And I don't care which one wins," he grinned.

Morrison and Guerin, Matt thought, Guerin and Morrison. And in a National Pick Four. "They still got to run around the track. Don't count your winnings yet," he murmured as Tashkin's Baba strode into his stall in the starting gate. Rick heard him, but shrugged off the admonition. "Not to worry, men," he said. "God put me on earth to bet horses like these." Matt rolled his eyes as he looked at Duncan. "They showed the possible Pick Four payoffs a couple of minutes ago," he whispered to the track president. "Rick's ticket will be worth either $21,000 or $28,000 if one of his two horses win, depending on which one. Either way, the biggest score of his life. He's pumped."

A minute and fifty seconds later the field for the Prairie Schooner Handicap had flashed across the finish line and all of Rick's concern had been replaced by disappointment and anger. Rick hurled his copy of the track program into a nearby wastebasket. He then began to kick the basket across the carpet toward the press box door, bellowing "God *damn* those idiot little son of a bitch pinheads." A lengthier stream of expletives would have followed had not Rick suddenly realized that Duncan, a man who despised public displays of emotion and abhorred curses, and had fired or barred from his track dozens of people guilty of engaging in the former or uttering the latter, was glaring at him, his face red. Rick quickly turned and went to his desk. He sat down. He put his head down on the desk, forehead first, and began thumping it against the surface.

The official order of finish of the Prairie Schooner Stakes appeared on the television screen. First—Mark Madness. Second—Justakisser. Third—Tashkin's Baba. Fourth—Rim Shot. Mark Madness, a 19-to-1 shot, returned $40 to win. Minutes later, the Pick Four payoff appeared on the screen: $350,000.

Matt sighed as he looked at his stricken friend. He knew he'd better stay out of Rick's pain-wracked personal orbit for the rest of the day. Turning back to the television, Matt heard Tashkin's Baba's rider, David Guerin, say softly to the interviewer, "Don't know what happened to him out there today. Horse just didn't seem to have it," he added, eyes averted.

The interviewer, Carol Conti, pressed on. "David," she said, "your horse was seemingly such a standout in this field that I have to ask you a little more. Was he rank early? Is that why you went to the lead right away? We were all surprised, since that sure hasn't been Tashkin's Baba's style."

Guerin, usually one of the more accommodating and articulate of jockey interviewees, startled Conti when he abruptly turned and walked off. Startled, Conti quickly composed herself and faced the camera head on. "I guess he's taking this loss pretty hard," she managed. Then she added kindly, as if to further explain the jockey's uncharacteristic rudeness, "Of course, David is still dealing with the terrible shock of the recent death in New Orleans of his brother and fellow rider, Mark. They were very, very close."

Conti turned to Tashkin's Baba's trainer, who was standing nearby. Jon Voelkner, a fixture on the national racing scene for many years, was grim-faced. As Conti asked, "What do you think happened out there, Jonny?" the trainer's lips tightened. He shook his head. "Sorry, Carol," he answered, "I can't tell you. I don't know what the hell happened out there today. My horse never had a chance to run his race the way he was ridden today. That's all I've got to say."

Conti shrugged her shoulders as she faced the camera. "I tried to get Randy Morrison, rider of the other big disappointment in the race, to come on camera. But he declined. That's it from trackside. Back to you, Chris," she said to the television show's host. A commercial quickly followed before the program's fadeout began. Behind the list of sponsors and technical staff members being shown came the replay of the race. Matt watched it carefully, wanting to confirm his initial conclusion: that David Guerin and Randy Morrison had both ridden to lose. He watched Tashkin's Baba being taken out of his game plan by Guerin. In the second replay, Matt concentrated on Morrison. "This is amazing," he said softly. "Morrison had this horse in every pocket but mine. Rim Shot had *no* shot with that ride."

With the replay now in its final seconds, Matt was joined by Rick in front of the screen. "I don't think I can watch this again," said the anguished Rick. "What in hell were those riders thinking? *They* cost me the race, not the damn horses." He walked over to the press box refrigerator and yanked out a Heineken.

"What was Guerin thinking?" Matt said to Rick. "I think he was thinking, 'I'm going to get this sucker beat today.' That's what I think he was thinking." Disgusted, he turned away from the television and went back to his desk.

After sitting silently for nearly ten minutes, reviewing what he had just witnessed, Matt picked up the phone and dialed Las Vegas. When his call was answered, he heard loud voices, the sound of water being splashed about, and music blaring in the background. Then he heard The Fount's voice, saying "I thought you'd call. Hold it a second. I'm down at the pool, it's noisy as hell. Let me go inside."

Matt waited a minute or two before he heard his friend resume talking. "You're calling about the Iowa race, right? What a fucking joke," The Fount said. "Matt, do you remember when you were out here last and I showed you the tape of the Gorham Stakes in New York?"

"Yes, I remember."

"Well, it's the same damned scenario," The Fount continued. "Today Guerin takes a stone cold closer completely out of his game and gets him beat. And in the last leg of a National Pick Four for the second time! Then you've got Morrison on the other favorite, giving him no chance whatsoever to run a winning race. I can hardly believe these guys are pulling this crap. Believe me, I thought they were two of the straightest shooters in the game."

"So did I," said Matt. He didn't know Morrison well, but he readily remembered the day nine years earlier when he had first met David Guerin, then a sixteen-year-old apprentice jockey already recognized as the latest in a long line of terrific riders to emerge from Louisiana's Cajun country. After two sensational months at Evangeline Park in his home state, David had been brought to Chicago by Tom Morgan, one of the Midwest's top jockey agents. Guerin won 348 races during his first full year of competition, easily leading the country's apprentice riders and finishing third in the overall standings. His career had kept on a steadily rising curve since then. Until now, Matt thought.

In the first story he'd done about the fresh-faced riding sensation, Matt wrote that "David Guerin looks like he should be sitting on somebody's knee, not somebody's horse." Matt had been impressed by the kid's good manners and his career objectives. "All I want to do," young Guerin had earnestly stated, "is ride horses and win with them and save enough money to buy my folks a decent house and get my little brother started as a rider, too." Nine years later the flush of idealistic youth was gone along with, as far as Matt was concerned, Guerin's reputation for professional integrity.

Would there be repercussions from this race? Matt thought not. The Des Moines Downs stewards might call Guerin and Morrison on the carpet, but they would just contend that their horses had been "too rank for me today," or that "he just got away from me." So talented were these two that they could easily disguise their intent to lose. Besides that, Matt knew, there was no way for the officials to prove malfeasance even if they were convinced it existed.

"But why in hell are these boys doing this stuff?" Matt said. Rick didn't respond. His head was down on his desk, hands covering his ears.

◇◇◇

Matt met Maggie after the races at Radigan's, a popular steakhouse near the track, for an early dinner. Most of their conversation concerned the Iowa race, which Maggie had not seen, but which Matt glumly described in detail. After dessert and coffee, both declared themselves to be tired. They decided to make it an early evening and head for their respective homes.

Standing beside her car as Maggie hooked on her seatbelt Matt said, "I'll be better company tomorrow, I promise." Maggie smiled up at him as she inserted the key into the ignition. "Don't let this thing eat you up, Matt. I know it's a big deal, and potentially a big story, but you shouldn't let it dominate your life. Our lives, for that matter," she added. He leaned down to kiss her, then watched as she drove out of the parking lot.

In his Evanston condominium forty-five minutes later, Matt clicked on his computer. According to the *Racing Daily*'s website, there had been eight winning tickets at racetracks and off-track betting facilities around the country sold on that afternoon's National Pick Four. Besides Mark Madness at Des Moines Downs, the other three winners of Pick Four races were Over at Lisa's at Elmont Park, Graustark's Memory at Flader Race Course, and Dim Donny at Green Valley. One of the eight $350,000 tickets had been sold at Heartland Downs, marking the third time this season that the big bet had been hit by someone at that track.

Matt sat back in his chair, staring at the computer screen. Then he revolved his old Rolodex to the Js and found Tom Jaroz's home phone number.

"Tom," he said, when the phone was picked up, "it's Matt. Sorry to bother you at home. You got a minute?"

"For you, Matt, after you helped get Oily Ronnie's claws out of my Aunt Sophie and her pals? Anything, buddy, anything. What's up?"

"That big Pick Four ticket that was sold today at Heartland. You hear anything about who cashed it?"

"Sure, all the guys were talking about it. Right after the official sign went up at Des Moines Downs, this elderly woman comes up to the Customer Service desk on the third floor and asks for the mutuel manager. Dressed real casual, slacks and a sweater, looked like all the rest of those once-a-year customers we get. She wasn't anybody we'd seen around much before, not a racetrack regular, that's for sure. They directed her to the general manager's office. Monroe took care of her."

Matt said, "You hear anything else? Like, her name? Or where she's from?"

"Naw. I didn't really ask about her name. All I heard was scuttlebutt, that she was from some place up in northern Wisconsin. She played a big ticket. Used all seven horses in the first leg of the Pick Four, all eight in both the second and third legs. What surprised Monroe, I understand, was that she played six horses in the fourth leg but left the two big favorites completely off her ticket. You know, Tashkin's Baba and Rim Shot. Anyway, the ticket cost almost $2,700. But she didn't do too bad, did she, Matt? Showed a profit of over $347,000."

"Not bad at all," Matt said.

Jaroz laughed. "I hear she took the payoff in cash—can you imagine? She also insisted that her name not be given out to the press. Monroe had somebody from security walk her out to the parking lot."

Jaroz laughed again before saying, "This is some game, isn't it, Matt? You never know when one of these amateurs is going to hit it big. Meanwhile, we got all our wise guy, heavy-hitting customers beating their brains out making speed figures, and pace numbers, and charting wind velocities, and God knows what else. Then some broad like this comes along and gets the big money. It's really something."

There was a brief silence. Then Matt said, "Yes, it is really something. Thanks, Tommy. I'll see you."

Chapter Twenty-Eight

Late that night in Madison, Bledsoe sat in his darkened office, listening with irritation to the rise and fall of a backyard cicada symphony. The August moon was nearly full, its light shining through the window and across the desk where he'd sat re-checking his math on a hand calculator. As he feared, he'd been correct when he'd first done the numbers in his head. "Damn," he said, pounding one of his huge fists on the desk in frustration.

He had to grudgingly admit that, in a way, the situation bordered on black comedy, with him the butt of the joke.

Seven other Pick Four winners that afternoon! How unfair was that? All the planning, the work, that had gone into his brilliant scheme. To have it come to fruition, but then have to share the spoils with people who had nothing to do with the outcome of those races. He was wracked with resentment at yet another incident of betrayal in his life.

Bledsoe earlier had gone to his computer and pulled up the *Racing Daily* website seeking details of that afternoon's events. He skimmed the main story that described the "shocking upset" that had taken place in the Prairie Schooner Handicap. He knew all about that. Another masterpiece of his very own design. How could he not feel satisfaction at the way it had come together, the way he had pulled the strings manipulating those jockey puppets *for the third time*. The main news report, well, that was one he'd have pasted in a leather-bound scrapbook, if he were foolish enough to own such a potentially incriminating item.

No, it was the sidebar story contributed to by *Racing Daily* staffers around the country that made his blood boil. The various correspondents had managed to track down four of that day's National Pick Four winners. Two of them, obviously serious handicappers desiring to keep their profiles low, offered only "no comment" when asked how they had arrived at the winning combination of numbers. It was the other two who made Bledsoe curse.

One of the winners, Teresa Sparkman, Bledsoe read, "spent $20 on quick pick tickets sold at the Green Valley track in Oregon. One of those twenty $1 tickets proved to be a winner."

Even more galling to Bledsoe was the Pick Four method successfully employed by the Jacoby brothers, Jack and Jake, electrical contractors who patronized Citrus Park in south Florida. "We play the National Pick Four every month or so," Jake Jacoby said. "We meet at the South Winds Saloon in Hallandale, have a couple of beers, some sandwiches. Then we run through the names of the horses entered in the Pick Four races. We never once hit this bet before, though we came real close one time two years ago.

"Mark Madness," Jake Jacoby continued, "we took him because Jack's oldest boy is named Mark. Kid's got kind of a temper. My mother-in-law's name is Lisa, so we used Over at Lisa's because the family has Sunday dinner at her house a lot. We just liked the name Graustark's Memory for some reason, so we played him. Dim Donny? We'd had a few beers by the time we got to that race. I don't remember how we came up with him. But it sure worked out great," Jacoby laughed.

Bledsoe swore loudly as he turned off the computer. "Take these goofs out of the mix and I would have been okay. I would have been okay." Forcing himself to take deep breaths, he finally sat back in his chair and again reviewed his calculations.

Deducting Jimbo and Vera's twenty-five percent cut of today's $350,000 after tax payoff left Bledsoe with $262,500. That added onto his net gain from the previous two scores gave him a total of $791,250, or $208,750 short of the million needed to earn Grandma Bledsoe's big prize.

With less than three weeks to go to the September 19 deadline, Bledsoe faced a huge problem: there wasn't another National Pick Four scheduled until the first Saturday of October. Too late.

He did some more mental calculations, then reached for the calculator to check them, too. According to his figures, Jimbo and Vera had thus far netted $263,750 from the manipulated races. He was certain that, because of his urging, they had spent very little of it. He'd been emphatic in cautioning them not to suddenly begin flashing cash, and he knew that they, out of a combination of fear (of him) and avarice, heeded what he'd had to say.

Yes, they had enough to put him over the top.

Chapter Twenty-Nine

For the fifth straight 3 a.m. Randy Morrison, having gone sleepless for hours, conceded to his insomnia and got out of bed, leaving his wife, Dot, snoring softly, bedcovers pulled up to her chin. He walked down the hallway outside the bedroom door and looked in at their young son, Will, then moved to the patio door of the townhouse and stepped outside. The cloudless late summer sky was freckled with stars, and a breeze slid gently over the dew-soaked lawn.

On this night, as with all the others recently, Morrison could think of little else than the situation he was in concerning the mysterious Professor. Riding seven or eight mounts each day at Dell Park, with all the attendant pressure involved and concentration required, was not enough to derail his train of thought. Nor were the evening hours spent with his wife and son, for always lingering in the forefront of consciousness was a dilemma of a sort he had never before faced.

In fear of his life, he had already lost with Lord's Heir and Rim Shot as the Professor had ordered. Would he be forced to lose other races? He feared so.

Morrison, as honest a jock as ever pulled on the white pants worn by working members of his trade, was sickened by the mess he was in and what he had been forced to do. Struggling with shock and loss after his half-brother was murdered, Randy also realized fully that the Professor did indeed have the ability and will to carry out his threats.

Normally one of the friendliest, most outgoing members of the Dell Park jockey colony, Randy had retreated into himself so markedly that his longtime friend and fellow rider, Bobby Brokopp, had pressed him for answers.

"What is it man?" Brokopp had asked quietly when training hours were over the previous morning and the two men sipped coffee at the counter in the track kitchen. "You got problems at home?" Morrison shook his head, but did not answer. Brokopp persisted. "I know that what happened to Eddie is still fresh in your mind. But you look to me like something else is hanging over you. What is it? Can I do anything for you? We go back a long way together, man," Brokopp had pointed out.

Randy and Brokopp had known each other for nearly fifteen years, since they broke into racing at the same time as apprentice riders on the New Mexico minor circuit. They had been buddies through many good and bad times in the ensuing years, sharing the cheapest apartment they could find near Dell Park when they both had made the big move north to the major racing circuit and before each man had married. Brokopp had helped break up an ugly fight between Morrison and a drunken trainer who was bitterly disappointed by a string of losing horses he'd sent out, saving Morrison from both injury and suspension. Randy had rescued Brokopp from a potentially fatal injury when he'd reached out to prevent him from falling from a horse whose saddle had slipped badly in the course of a race. Randy had introduced Brokopp to his future wife, an exercise rider named Susanna Pratt. Each had been best man at the other's wedding.

All that personal history failed to connect them now, however. Out of a combination of fear for his life and shame he felt for what he had done to preserve it, Randy had not been able to bring himself to confide in Brokopp, or Dot, or anyone else. "It's nothing I can't handle," he'd said unconvincingly. "Just a little matter I've got to work out on my own." He tossed his empty Styrofoam cup into a nearby waste container. "Got to go, man," he said, turning away quickly so as to avoid further eye contact with Brokopp. "See you."

Brokopp watched as Randy walked rapidly out the door and down the walkway past Steve Holland, one of the owners for whom he regularly rode, without acknowledging him. Holland looked at Randy's retreating figure with surprise. Holland still looked puzzled when Brokopp approached. Brokopp nodded at Holland and shrugged his shoulders. "Good morning, Mr. Holland," he said, adding, as he passed the owner, "I don't know what's going on with Randy, either."

Now, as Randy Morrison sat on the picnic table bench, he was oblivious to the breeze moving softly through the palm trees that bordered his back yard, oblivious to the first pinkish hint of the new day cutting into the darkness of the horizon. He was oblivious to everything but the ominous voice he kept hearing in his head, the voice from the phone, saying over and over again *You will do what I say, or you will die. It's as simple as that.* During the first such call, Randy had asked, "Who is this?" The only response was a soft laugh. The second and third times, the person on the other end of the line had said "You know who this is," before laughing derisively. The last time the voice had added, *Just think of me as the Professor, Randy. Someone teaching you to do what I want.* Randy had heard that voice often ever since, in his sleep, often during his waking hours. He found he did not have the power to escape that menacing sound.

The faces of the murdered jockeys floated through his memory. Eddie, Mark Guerin, Carlos Hidalgo—his half-brother and two men he knew well and had often ridden against. What had any of them done to deserve what had happened to them? What had *he* done to deserve this? His now almost continual headache returned. His fear of the Professor and his unwillingness to reveal to Dot what was going on, thus dragging her into his world of fear, were like locomotives heading straight for each other. He was the collision point.

Randy shivered in the cool air. Oddly enough, the next thought he had made him smile, for the first time in days. For some reason the memory of his uncle Don Morrison flashed into his head. Uncle Don had been a lifelong horse bettor, much given to a pair of sayings that became legendary in the family. When he was going good, the horses he bet were "running like rats in a barrel." A far more frequently uttered statement was that which accompanied his losing streaks. "Where do you go to give up?" Uncle Don would ask plaintively.

"Uncle Don," Randy said aloud, "I wish I knew the answer to that right now."

But deep down Randy knew he could never quit riding, never walk away from the only thing he really knew how to do well, the only thing that he really loved doing. Not now, not at the peak of his career. Besides, even if he did retire, what assurance did he have that the Professor would not exact revenge upon him for that decision? This seemingly omnipotent mystery man was obviously able to do what he threatened to do. Unless Randy sealed himself in an armored car for the rest of his life, he would probably always be vulnerable. "I've got to do something," Randy said as he got up from the bench. Dawn was now spreading rapidly across the eastern sky, and the sound of birds increased to greet it, but Randy took no notice. He went into the house, moving quietly, careful not to wake the family as he dressed and prepared to leave.

Ten minutes later as he drove toward Dell Park, Randy pounded the truck's steering wheel with one fist. "I've had enough of this crap," he said loudly. Randy's thoughts turned to the man he knew best and trusted most in the Jockeys' Union. "I've got to call Tyree Powell," he said to himself. "If anybody can help me figure out what to do, it'd be him. Please, Lord, help me find my way here."

Chapter Thirty

Matt heard a voice slice through his sleep. Struggling to consciousness, he realized that the voice was his own. The bedside clock read 4:33 a.m. as he sat up and turned on his reading lamp. He shook his head, but the scene he'd just dreamed kept replaying, with him shouting repeatedly, "No, don't jump, Randy…no…no."

The setting in this dream involving jockey Randy Morrison was not the familiar one to Matt, the racetrack, but, of all things, a ski jump site. Matt was standing in a crowd of people at the foot of a steep slope, watching Morrison prepare to start his descent from the top of the jump. Low winter clouds let loose with wind-blown flurries of flakes. The people lining the hill shivered and stomped their feet in the frigid late afternoon weather.

Morrison was wearing jockey silks, red and white, and suddenly a bright sun broke through and glinted off his dark glasses. He spun one ski pole as he would a jockey's whip, in a baton-twirling motion, before thrusting it into the snow beside where he stood hundreds of feet above the crowd. Then Morrison released and sped down the jump. Going airborne with a swoosh he passed above Matt, who by now had stopped urging him not to jump. Too late now. Morrison soared through the bright winter air, then abruptly descended. His skis came off his feet in midair. He plummeted and hit the slope with a ferocious impact. Morrison's body shattered as he crashed, limbs filling the air like shrapnel as Matt looked on in horror. His continued shouts of "No...no..." were what finally awakened Matt.

"What the *hell* was that all about?" he muttered as he got out of bed. In the bathroom he leaned over the sink and splashed cold water on his sweaty face. Matt knew he would never get back to sleep tonight. Doubted that he would be able to sleep even had Maggie been here on one of her frequent overnights. Doubted that he would be able to sleep soundly for many nights as long as this jockey situation continued to dominate his thinking and rake his subconscious mind.

◇◇◇

At nine o'clock that morning, Matt phoned Moe at his office, knowing he'd be there. Kellman worked out each morning from seven until eight-thirty at Fit City, the health club near his office, then "opened for business," as he put it, at nine sharp. When his call was put through, Matt said, "Moe, I need to talk to you about this jockey thing," then continued on hurriedly, "I think I know what's going on, but as far as finding out who's doing it, I'm stumped. I'm not getting anywhere, and I..."

"Whoa, whoa," Moe interrupted, "you're going too fast too early in the morning. Take it easy, kid. Let me get my tea." There was a minute of silence before Moe said, "I'll meet with you this afternoon, early. I've got an idea about this. Come down here to the office about 1:30. We'll take a little trip out to River Forest to see Fifi Bonadio."

◇◇◇

Pete Dunleavy, Moe's driver, whisked them out the Eisenhower Expressway and through the light early afternoon traffic in just under twenty-two minutes to First Avenue, their exit for River Forest. Earlier, passing Cicero Avenue, Matt looked out the car window to his right, past the line-up of garish billboards, smokestacks, battered-looking warehouses and desolate rail yards toward where old Prairie Park once stood as a thriving racing enterprise in this blue collar neighborhood. Prairie Park had hosted horse races for some seven decades. Then a decision was made to convert it to an auto racing complex, with horses relegated to a small chunk of the calendar. The decision proved to be disastrous, with both sports suffering financial losses leading to the closing of the entire facility and sale of the land. It still hurt Matt to think about it, for he had loved the old red brick stands with their seating close to the action, the aroma of grilled onions and Polish sausages on an early spring afternoon, the three card monte games conducted on blankets on the Laramie Avenue sidewalk, the loudly voiced opinions of the beer-fueled customers.

Moe didn't give Dunleavy any directions as they drove. They had been to this address before. Dunleavy was one of three ex-Chicago policemen employed by Moe Kellman. All three had put in their twenty years for pension eligibility and gone to work for the furrier, all starting within three years of each other. Besides Dunleavy there was Bill Sheridan, Moe's night driver, and Al Suppelsa, who provided a security presence at Moe's office during working hours.

In addition to Dunleavy's driving duties, Moe informed Matt as they rode westward on the expressway, Dunleavy was "believe it or not one of the best cooks of Italian food you'll ever run into, even if he is a Mick like you." In the rearview mirror, Matt could see Dunleavy grinning as Moe said, "He makes the best escarole soup in the city. His penne with the vodka and cream sauce, the veal meatballs, the spinach ravioli…Well, you got to come up to the office one of these Wednesdays. Pete puts out an Italian buffet for my staff and some of my best customers every week. You could get a good sampling there.

"This guy is so good," Moe said, "that when I go on fishing trips with my buddies we take Pete along just to cook for us. Fifi says Pete's raviolis are as good as his Ma used to make. We brought along a pan of them for him today."

Matt was curious. "Where did you get such a taste for Italian food?" he said to Moe. Smiling, Moe said, "You think I should be into just brisket and knishes? Listen, where I grew up on the near west side, it was all dagoes and Jews. I had a lot of friends in each camp, probably more in the former. I ate at their houses as often as I could. My mother was the worst cook in the ward. You could have played bocce with her matzo balls. A lot of those guys are still my friends today. And clients, like Fifi." Moe shrugged. "Who would've thought Fifi would wind up head of the Chicago Outfit. He started out as a burglar—and a bad one."

Puzzled, Matt said, "If he was a lousy burglar, how'd he get where he is?"

"He got into some other things he was better at." Moe did not elaborate.

The Lincoln turned down a quiet elm-shaded street and stopped before a tall iron gate. Out of the small brick office to the left of the driveway came a man wearing a blue windbreaker and black slacks and a Chicago Bears ball cap turned backwards. "That's Rick Fasulo," Moe said. "Remember him when he played tackle for the Bears? He's worked for Feef ever since he blew out a knee and had to retire."

Fasulo nodded at Dunleavy, then leaned down and in a voice roughened by too many forearms to the larynx, spoke through the open window. "Afternoon, Mr. Kellman. Mr. Bonadio's expecting you." He pressed a remote control button and the gates opened.

They drove up a long, paved driveway that curved in front of a three-story stone mansion complete with turrets, five chimneys, wings that extended widely from the sides of the original structure, and a front entrance tall and wide enough to drive a pair of Clydesdales through.

The mansion had been built early in the previous century for one of Chicago's more successfully rapacious meat packing magnates, who had demanded, and gotten, something baronial for himself. Fifi Bonadio's additions to this gabled, gray stone monstrosity were in keeping with the original style, proof that the taste of these two ambitious Chicago profiteers, although separated in time by many years, was similarly awful.

As Dunleavy waited in the car, Moe said, "Matt, give me a hand here will you? Carry this in." He handed Matt a large aluminum pan containing the raviolis. "Be careful," he said, "the sauce is on them." Moe reached into the trunk and extracted a rectangular white box. "This is the coat Feef wants to look at for Tiffany," he said. The mansion's front door was opened by a slim, dark-complexioned man wearing a blue suit and dark glasses. Moe said, "How you doing, Ralphie?"

"Not bad, Mr. Kellman. Just put the food down on that table," he added. "I'll have one of the maids take it to the kitchen."

Following the man down the lengthy hallway, they passed a huge living room, a large library on one side of the carpeted corridor, a vast dining room on the other. The hallway walls were covered with artwork, some of it recognizable to Matt. Both old and modern masters were represented. Matt whistled softly through his teeth as they walked. "Is that a real Monet?" he whispered. Moe gave him a sidelong glance. "Don't ask."

Moe nodded in the direction of a dreadful piece of Midwestern art fair kitsch that was prominently displayed in mid-corridor. "Some of Feef's stuff is great, some of it is bad taste on steroids," he said as they passed a wide staircase with gleaming banisters on both sides and neared the end of the corridor. A bulky, blond-haired bodyguard rose from his chair as they approached, but said nothing. Ralphie opened the door, stood aside, and ushered them through.

They entered an expansive room that looked to Matt like the interior of a very upscale sports bar. A half-dozen television sets embedded in the walls were turned to various sporting events around the country, another to a stock market channel, the sound off on each. Sinatra sang over a magnificent audio system, sounding as if he were standing beside them. Light poured in from a wide glass wall at the rear of the room. Hundreds of autographed photos of athletes, politicians, and other entertainers lined all of two walls and half of the third. The rest of that wall was taken up by glass-enclosed cases packed with trophies won by various sixteen-inch softball, bowling, and bocce teams sponsored by Bonadio Construction ("We Make the Earth Move"), one of Fifi's numerous business interests. Beyond the glass wall was an

Olympic-sized swimming pool and two tennis courts. The pool and the courts were empty.

The man seated behind the wide, leather-topped desk was talking softly on the phone. He gestured toward chairs in front of the desk as he continued, meanwhile waving a jumbo cigar in the air as if he were conducting an invisible orchestra. Bushy black eyebrows contrasted with the whiteness of his thick head of hair. His deeply tanned face was long, chin strong, lips thin, and his restless eyes were as black as a monsignor's suit. Fifi Bonadio would be considered handsome, Matt thought, were it not for the artless presence of a formidable Roman nose with its strikingly large nostrils.

Bonadio was wearing a yellow cashmere sweater, open-collared white shirt, black linen trousers, and black loafers. There were two rings on each of his hands, Matt noticed, each one larger than a good-sized walnut. Finally, Bonadio put the phone down. He stood up and came around from behind the desk. Moe stood, too, and the two men embraced, Bonadio beaming down at his boyhood friend. "Great to see you, Moe," he said. "Have a seat." He turned to Matt, waiting. Moe said, "Feef, this is my friend I've been telling you about, Matt O'Connor."

The Outfit boss nodded coldy at Matt but made no effort to shake his hand. The three men sat down again. Matt looked past Bonadio and out the window. On the other side of the pool and tennis courts there was a lawn about half as long and wide as a football field. A half-dozen Mexican laborers were busy maintaining this green, tree-dotted expanse, under the watchful eyes of two bodyguards. There was a grape arbor in the northeast corner of the lot. "This cheapskate still makes his own dago red," Moe had confided on the drive out. A ten-foot-tall concrete wall bordered three sides of the property. Electrical security wires that ran along the tops of the walls, and black security cameras visible in the trees, marred the otherwise sylvan scene—a reminder of the harsh realities extant in Fifi Bonadio's world.

It was silent in the room for a few moments. Matt could almost feel the hard-eyed gaze Bonadio directed at him. Then the Mob chief said, "You gotta understand, O'Connor, that you're the first newspaper guy I've talked to in thirty years. I'm not like my former asshole goombah in New York, the 'dapper' one, who made himself so famous he's locked up in Ossining. I don't deal with the press, and neither does my family, except for my son, when he played football. That's a different world, his world."

Pointing his cigar for emphasis, Bonadio continued addressing Matt. "What I'm saying here is that I've agreed to meet with you as a favor to my friend here," Bonadio said, indicating Moe. "So, what's your story?"

Matt cleared his throat. "You remember when Moe's Uncle Bernie died?" Matt began. Bonadio interrupted him. "Remember? I was a pallbearer, for chrissake. Bernie and I did business for years."

Matt pressed on. "Moe thought at the time that Bernie had been murdered, that it wasn't suicide. He thought it may have been in connection to my business, which is horse racing. There were indications that Bernie had had contact with some professor, who convinced Bernie he was using him as a prime source for a study of gambling. Bernie had several contacts with this guy, according to what he told Moe."

Matt reached into his sport coat pocket and extracted his reporter's notebook. He riffled through pages with notations such as "Charlie Whitson, Calif. trainer, coming in to work his big horse Tuesday… Maggie's running two of hers next Monday…Call stewards for comment on Callaway's suspension…" until he found what he was looking for. Bonadio impatiently tapped a pencil on his desktop.

"Not long ago," Matt said, "a good friend of mine, a big bettor, super sharp guy, brought to my attention some very suspicious races at tracks around the country. These races involved top-notch jockeys losing on favorites in National Pick Four races. When they did, the payoffs were huge. I've got all the information right here. There were only a few tickets sold on the winning combinations. Three of those winning tickets were sold here in Chicago at Heartland Downs."

Matt closed the notebook and sat silently for a few moments, slapping it nervously against his knee. Finally, he said, "I guess what I need to know, Mr. Bonadio, is if you or your people have anything to do with these unusual race results."

The next sound in the room was that of instantaneous laughter. It poured forth from Bonadio, who sat back in his leather chair, head raised to the ceiling, letting the mirth flow out. Matt felt his face becoming flushed. He looked at Moe, who signaled him to say nothing. So they waited, until Bonadio stopped laughing and leaned forward in his chair. "O'Connor," he finally said, an amused look still present in his eyes, "do you think for one fucking minute that if I *did* have anything to do with shit like that that I'd *tell* you about it? Are you fucking nuts?" He shook his head, marveling at the naivete of Matt's question. Then he looked at Moe.

He said, "Moe, it's only for you I'm doing this." Then he said to Matt, "Kid, you've got some major stones on you, I'll give you that, coming here to ask me if I'm fixing horse races. You might as well ask me about that armored car heist in Stone Park last month, or the re-zoning deal the Bonadio firm managed to get from the greedy little bureaucrats in Clausen County last week. As if I would *tell* you, for chrissakes!

"But, out of respect for my goombah Moe here, I *will* tell you this: I have absolutely no fucking interest in horse racing. That was for my old man, some of my uncles. They did some stuff in racing, no question about it. They bought little racetracks and used them to take layoff money from their city bookies. They doped some horses, controlled some crooked trainers, they had some jocks tied up. That was back when racing wasn't regulated the way it is today, back when it was the only major legal gambling enterprise, long before Vegas and the state lotteries and the Indian casinos.

"That was then," Bonadio continued, tapping his pencil again for emphasis. "We got out of that years ago." He sat back in the chair, eyes half-closed, as if he were mentally riffling through a portfolio whose scope he found to be eminently pleasing. Then he smiled. "I got no idea how I can help here," he said.

Moe, looking agitated, got up from his chair. He walked over to the north wall of the room and pretended to be examining the photos. Bonadio watched him out of the corner of his eye. Then he said, "Moe, goddamit, come back and sit down." He raised his palms above the desk and shrugged expansively. His eyebrows rose as well, an expression of frustrated benevolence appearing on his tanned face. All this body language was meant to convey the message, "I'd help you if I could. But…"

When Moe returned to his chair, Matt could tell that the little furrier was angry. "Feef," he said, "I didn't bring Matt out here to be entertained by your condescending b.s. Maybe Matt didn't put it quite the right way, his question. All we wanted to find out was if you *knew* anything, if maybe you'd *heard* something. Simple as that," Moe said softly, his jaw set as he looked at his boyhood buddy.

Bonadio's eyebrows elevated. Then he smiled, shrugged his shoulders, and said, "Feisty as always, Mosey, you never change. Yeah," he sighed, "I'm hearing you, Moe. Settle down."

To Matt, Bonadio said, "You've got nothing to go on here, kid. Just suspicions. If you had a name, or a description of somebody you think is in this thing, then maybe I'd be able to set some wheels in motion. *Capice?*"

Matt said, "The only thing I've got is the guy I mentioned earlier, the one who was picking Bernie Glockner's brain about gambling in America. But Bernie never told Moe the guy's name. So that's a dead end."

Moe said, "Tell him what you found out yesterday from Tyree Powell." After explaining to Bonadio that Powell was the Jockeys' Union local representative, Matt said, "Tyree met with me to talk about one of the riders in his organization, Randy Morrison. Tyree said Morrison called him, all disturbed. After he swore Tyree to silence, Morrison confessed that he was being forced to lose races by a guy who claims he's done the killings of these jockeys that I told you about earlier. Said the guy knew all the details of each death and that he'd killed Morrison's half-brother in order to coerce Morrison into doing what he wanted.

"Morrison told Tyree this guy was beyond creepy. May have used a device to disguise his voice. Laughed about what he'd done, what he would do if Randy didn't come through. Their contact was via phone calls from the guy to the jockeys' room at the racetrack. One time, when Randy was late getting there, the guy told Randy's valet to pass on the message that 'the Professor called. He'll know what it's about. It's about some lessons I'm teaching.' Then he laughed and hung up. When he called back in an hour, he talked directly to Randy, giving him the name of the horse he wanted him to intentionally lose on the following Saturday."

Moe said, "After Matt told me this, it occurred to me that Bernie a couple of times referred to this guy from the University of Wisconsin as 'the Professor.' But, hell, there's thousands of professors on that campus. What the hell did I care about this guy back then when Bernie was mentioning him?"

Bonadio slowly sat straight up in his chair, frowning. He started to speak, stopped to think for a few moments, then said softly, "I knew a guy there once." He got up and walked around the desk, going over to a part of the south wall of the office that contained dozens of photos of his football-playing son, Rocco, wearing Number 74 on his red and white Badger lineman's uniform. Some were action shots, showing Rocco slamming a ball carrier into the Astroturf; others were close-ups of him down in his three-point stance, looking big as a boxcar, glowering through his face mask. Bonadio gazed proudly at the display for a moment before tapping one framed photo with his index finger. "Come over here and take a look at this one," he said.

Matt and Moe joined their host. The photo he indicated was of his massive son, dressed in black cap and gown and proudly displaying a University of Wisconsin diploma. Rocco was flanked by his father, wearing a three-thousand-dollar suit and a broad smile, and a shorter, powerfully built, completely bald man in a sport coat, slacks, and an open-collared shirt. Moe said, "Who's he? Rocco's personal trainer? Guy looks like a weight lifter."

Bonadio shook his head. "He's does training, all right, but not what you think." He looked at Moe speculatively before responding. "If I tell you about this guy, his name is Bledsoe, would you come down a little on that mink for Tiffany?"

Moe's face reddened. "For chrissakes, Feef," he said, "I'm looking for the guy that may have killed my uncle and you're talking price with me?"

Bonadio was momentarily embarrassed. "You're right," he said, apologetically. He gestured toward the chairs in front of his desk. "C'mon, sit down. I'll tell you what I know."

What Bonadio knew was that he had retained a man named Claude Bledsoe to tutor his son, whose football career was being jeopardized by a frighteningly diminishing grade point average. "I asked around up there about how to handle the situation. I found out bribery wouldn't work. One of my guys went to an assistant dean and said to him, 'How much bread will you eat?' The dean didn't get it. He tried to walk my guy down the street to some fancy organic bakery.

"Finally, after we nosed around some more, we found this guy Bledsoe. A strange character with a strange background. He'd been going to college up there for years. But extra smart and a good tutor. I paid this guy top dollar, but he was worth it. He got Rocco through his classes like a champ. Kid wound up with the first college diploma ever in the Bonadio family," he added proudly.

"Far as I know, Bledsoe is still up there in Madison, still going to school. He's got a zillion degrees. Everybody up there knows him. The kids all call him 'the Professor.' I guess he could be one if he wanted to. When you said Madison and a professor, he's what came to my mind."

Bonadio turned away from the photo. He walked slowly back to his desk and sat down, a serious expression on his face. Several seconds went by before he lifted his head and looked at his visitors. "*Merde,*" he mumbled, then, "This is bad. Very bad."

Moe said, "What do you mean?"

Bonadio wiped his hand across his mouth before replying. "This guy Bledsoe called me last year, asking for a favor. I owed him one. And I did him one." He paused again, as if reluctant to continue.

Moe leaned forward, anxious to hear the rest. "So?"

"So Bledsoe asked me if I could refer him to somebody who knew a lot about gambling in America. Especially sports gambling. More especially, horse race gambling. I never hesitated for a minute. Who could tell Bledsoe more than anybody else? So, I gave him Bernie Glockner's name and number."

Moe sat back in his chair with a thud, as if he'd been thumped in the chest.

Bonadio raised his hands, palms up, in a sign of apology. Then he shrugged, saying, "Maybe I did the wrong thing. I'm sorry, Moe. But that doesn't mean for sure that Bledsoe did Bernie. Or that he's the Professor connected to these racing things."

Matt disagreed. Despite his years of acquiring an armor of skepticism while learning the newspaper business, Matt could feel it: there was a connection. He glanced at Moe, then looked at Bonadio. "I think this guy is tied in, this Professor. He may be running the racetrack scheme. We've got to get to him before he kills someone else and steals another bale of money. Moe, we better talk to Detective Popp about the Professor."

The mention of the detective's name brought a deep frown to the forehead of their host. Matt spoke to reassure him. "There's no need for us to bring you into it, Mr. Bonadio," he said. "Thanks for your help."

Chapter Thirty-One

Matt rode the Hancock Building elevator to Moe's floor, smiled a greeting to the model masquerading as a receptionist, and entered Kellman's office suite. Moe, phone to his ear, waved Matt forward. To Matt's surprise, Detective William Popp was present, rump leaning against the back edge of the long couch as he admired the view of sailboats bobbing on the choppy blue surface of Lake Michigan. Popp turned and placed his straw hat on a side table, saying, "Hello, Matt."

The fourth man in the room was a stranger to Matt. He was very busy foraging amid the massive fruit plate, a staple in Moe's office, his long, sharp nose seeming to twitch above his thin, graying mustache as he eagerly made his selections. He reminded Matt of some strain of small rodent, ferociously feeding. He had a narrow face and wore a navy blue suit almost as shiny as his nose. As he leaned forward, Matt noticed the man had a male pattern baldness area on the crown of his head, one that at first glance could be mistaken for a white yarmulke. Popp said, "Matt, this is Larry Van Gundy from the State's Attorney's office." Matt said hello to the man, who briefly interrupted the refilling of his plate in order to nod back.

Matt could hear Moe winding up his phone conversation. "Feef, the last price mentioned to you is *the last price*. By definition. Get it? Call me tomorrow if you want that coat." Exasperated, he put down the phone. "Fifi Bonadio," he said disgustedly. "Got himself a new punch he's trying to impress.

But he's niggling over what are nickels and dimes for a guy with his money. Man'll never change," Moe said, shaking his head.

When the four of them were finally seated, Moe said, "Matt, I put together this meeting. Let me tell you why. My good friend Bill Popp phoned me yesterday. He said Mr. Van Gundy had told him that Oily Ronnie Schrapps was trying to make a deal. Bill keeps me posted on anything that has to do with horse racing, or the track, because as you know I intend to find out who the hell it was that killed Uncle Bernie."

Popp turned to the assistant state's attorney and said, "Larry, why don't you fill them in."

Van Gundy reluctantly put down his nearly empty plate. He wiped some mango juice from his chin. His beady eyes darted from Matt to Moe to Popp before he began speaking in a reedy voice. *A particularly unattractive rodent*, Matt thought, *that's what Van Gundy reminds me of.*

Van Gundy took a tape player from his briefcase and placed it on the table. Preparing to turn it on he said, "I shouldn't be playing this for you, especially a newspaper guy, but Bill Popp vouches for everyone in this room. Says we wouldn't have gotten a case without your efforts. What you hear stays in this room. It's part of our interview with Ronnie Schrapps. Bill said you deserved to hear it because you helped us nab Ronnie, and I'm inclined to agree with him. That's me doing the questioning that you'll hear."

As Van Gundy readied the tape, Matt looked over at Moe. *This little man's got some major clout*, he thought, as Moe intently regarded the two public servants who obviously had no compunction about doing his bidding. Van Gundy said, "I've already listened to all of Ronnie's bullshit about the fraud charges—how the old ladies begged him to take their money, how he was doing them a favor by bringing excitement into their empty lives, how he was entrapped…yada yada yada. He weaseled around like that for several boring minutes, both of us well aware that he was full of shit. Then we come to this part."

RONNIE: *You know, I've got some information you could use, if you'll just hear me out. Has to do with what could be* *a major, major case. I can help you—if you decide to help me out on these fraud charges. Will you listen to me?*

VAN GUNDY: Information about what?

RONNIE: You know anything about horse racing?

VAN GUNDY: Enough to stay away from it. What's your point?

RONNIE: Well, there's some kind of big scam going on, that much I know, and it involves big, big money. The race-track police, heads up their asses like always, may not even suspect what's happening.

VAN GUNDY: What kind of scam?

RONNIE: I don't know all the details.

At this point Van Gundy is heard impatiently slamming his pen down on the table.

RONNIE: Wait…take it easy…hear me out.

You must have read about those jockeys getting killed around the country, right? And nobody ever caught for the crimes? Okay. But you may not have heard about some of their surviving relatives.

VAN GUNDY: What the hell are you talking about?

RONNIE: I'm talking about the fact that in three major races, each one of them a leg of a big National Pick Four, the losing favorites were ridden by relatives of two of those dead jocks. Am I coming across here now?

VAN GUNDY: I think you're trying to jerk my chain, Schrapps. Two jocks lost on favorites in big races. So what? I know enough about racing to know that favorites only win about a third of the time. These favorites lose, what's the big deal?

RONNIE: Yeah, favorites only win thirty-three percent of the time. But when the same *people hit three of these big Pick Fours, and they're the* only *winners at Heartland Downs on those days, doesn't that maybe fall into the big deal category? Three of those big hits in a matter of weeks! Doesn't that strike you as so fucking unlikely that maybe somebody in your law enforcement family should wake the fuck up here—instead of peering down their goddam barrels at me all the time?*

VAN GUNDY: Stop, you're breaking my heart.

Van Gundy hit the pause button on the recorder, then adeptly snatched a slice of pineapple from the tray before he began to speak.

"Ronnie tells us in this next section that he found out the people cashing the Pick Four tickets used phony IDs and bogus social security numbers when they signed for their winnings. I don't know how he learned this, but we checked with the Heartland Downs pari-mutuel department and the IRS, and they confirmed that that was indeed the case. That's what makes what comes next on the tape pretty interesting." Van Gundy swallowed another chunk of pineapple before hitting play.

VAN GUNDY: So where is this taking us? How does this put any shine on you?

RONNIE: I can ID the people that cashed those big tickets.

VAN GUNDY (his voice reflecting his excitement): You know them? You know these people?

RONNIE: No, I don't know them. But I can tell you about them. There's three people. There's a big, redheaded guy, over six feet, over two hundred pounds. He looked like a hick who had stumbled into the racetrack clubhouse by taking a wrong turn. Wore a Hawaiian shirt, wash pants, work shoes. The broad with him every time is about his age, maybe middle thirties, kind of hard used. Dark blond hair, chain smoker, dressed Wal-Mart top to bottom. The guy signed for their big ticket the second time. First time, the blond broad went up to sign. The third ticket was cashed by an old woman who was with these two for the first time. All three times, these people took the money in cash. In cash! That's what I'm told by a guy I know real good in mutuels.

Van Gundy again stopped the tape. "To this point, Ronnie, who is about as obvious a prevaricating and untrustworthy bullshitter as you would ever hope not to meet, has really come up with very little. Interesting, yes, but not worth much. The physical descriptions of the three people, for example, he could have made those up with his infinitely fertile, devious mind.

"Jack Schreier, my boss, that's exactly what he said when he'd heard this recording up to this point. He thought Ronnie was probably blowing smoke up our asses. But then things change. Here goes."

RONNIE: No, I don't know the names of those people. If I did, I'd have given them up to you before now. Buy I do know something you can use.

VAN GUNDY: What?

RONNIE: I got the license plate of the car they drove off in.

VAN GUNDY (voice once more evidencing some excitement): How?

RONNIE: How do you think? I followed them down to the parking lot after their second big score and watched them get into this old car and drive away. There was a guy there waiting for them at the car. Stocky, strong-looking, bald guy wearing shades, a little better dressed than the other man and the woman. He said something to them, and they jumped in the car pretty quick, the young broad driving. The bald guy looked at me through his binoculars as they were pulling out. Then they peeled out of there. But not before I got their license plate.

Van Gundy shut down the tape for the last time. "At this point," he said, "I called Jack Schreier back in. I told him what Ronnie now said he had to offer. I updated him on the possible tie-in to the allegedly fixed races, and to the murdered jocks. Schreier thought it over for about two seconds and then told me to go ahead and deal with this scum bag, provided Ronnie hadn't made up the license number. Jack said the number had to be good, or there's no deal with Ronnie.

"Turns out," Van Gundy continued, "it was a Wisconsin plate, a real one all right. Ronnie was right about the number. Car belongs to a guy named Bledsoe. He lives in Madison, near the university. We checked with his car insurer, who told us

Bledsoe lists his occupation as 'full time student,' even though he's almost fifty years old."

Matt and Moe looked at each other. Then Moe slammed his hand down on the table. "The fucking Professor," he said, looking at Matt, "Bernie's fucking professor." Matt was not as certain. "Could be," he said. "It's possible."

Van Gundy was puzzled. "What professor? What are you talking about?"

Moe said, "Tell him what we know, Matt."

Over the course of the next half-hour—during which Van Gundy, while listening closely, still managed to demolish the remaining contents of the large fruit platter—Matt told the assistant state's attorney of Bernie Glockner's sudden death, Moe's suspicions about the circumstances surrounding that death, and the series of jockey murders followed by apparently fixed races leading to giant payoffs.

Finally, his long narrative completed, Matt got to his feet and walked over to the north window, through which he could see the busy Oak Street beach a few blocks away, full of sun bathers, swimmers, volleyball players, cyclists, joggers, walkers, and the usual cadre of attentive voyeurs. He thought over all that had been said here. Then he turned and spoke directly to Van Gundy and Popp.

"I've been writing about horse racing for more than ten years," Matt said. "I've heard of some scams, and some screwed-up attempts at scams. Hell, any racetrack in the world could compete pound for pound with Washington, DC as a source of rumors and gossip.

"But," Matt went on, "I've never come across anything like this. I'm convinced there's some kind of conspiracy going on designed to steal money from honest bettors. This guy the Professor, Bledsoe, may be the linchpin. He might be the guy that Bernie Glockner dealt with. He might be the guy who pressured Randy Morrison. He might be the guy Oily Ronnie spotted in the Heartland parking lot with the people who cashed the big Pick Four ticket. You've got to check him out."

Van Gundy sighed. "Mr. O'Connor, give us some credit. Of course we checked him out. Bledsoe has no criminal record whatsoever. He's a well-known eccentric up there in Madison, where, I understand, there's no shortage of them. But he's famous for having gone to the university for more than thirty straight years, financed by some family trust fund. There've been several newspaper articles about him over the years, even one long magazine story. Bledsoe has never worked a day in his life that anyone knows about, except for some private tutoring once in awhile. But there's no hint of any criminality here. According to a Madison detective I know, Bledsoe's never even gotten a parking ticket."

"I don't know," Moe said, shaking his head. "That kind of background doesn't indicate a multiple murderer as far as I'm concerned."

Popp said, "Hey, you can't rule out anybody off just that kind of information. We got a guy on a murder rap last year, he was a church deacon, boy scout leader, and head of a charitable foundation, who got up one morning and used a chain saw on his wife of nearly thirty years."

"That, of course, was a crime of demented passion. These jockey killings are different. There's nothing to indicate there's any passion involved here, nothing personal. These killings are being done by some very intelligent, methodical prick who is convinced he can get away with anything he wants."

Matt sat back down on the couch, elbows on his knees, leaning forward. "We don't know enough about Bledsoe to put him in that category. But what was he doing at the racetrack with the people who cashed the big tickets? If Bledsoe is some trust fund beneficiary, I doubt that he's moonlighting as a chauffeur for gamblers. But I'm not about to eliminate him from the picture without taking a good look at him myself. I know some people on the Madison newspapers. I'm going to take a run up there and talk to one of them.

"But before that, Larry," Matt added, "let me ask you something. Does anyone else have this story on Oily Ronnie?"

"Nobody," Van Gundy replied. "We just made our deal with Schrapps this morning. He's being held without bond, and that's the way he's going to stay while we expand the investigation. He's comfortable with that for the time being and so is his attorney. If things work out right, if what Schrapps gave us turns out to be solid regarding Bledsoe and his group, Ronnie will do short federal time."

Van Gundy put the tape recorder in its case.

"I'm going to say to you three, in the privacy we have here, that my boss has put a big circle around this case. It has national implications. Jack, Mr. Schreier that is, has a very great interest in cases such as these, especially since he's considering entering politics in the near future. If you get my drift. And Jack Schreier has a really terrible aversion to mistakes. If Oily Ronnie Schrapps has pulled our chain here, he's going away for a terrible long time to a place he is not going to like at all."

Van Gundy shook hands with all of them, thanking Moe profusely for his "interest in this matter."

"Naturally," Van Gundy added, looking directly at Matt, "we want to keep a lid on this for the time being."

"For the greater good," Matt murmured. Then he said, "I'll go along with you. Ronnie's is a good story. 'Veteran Con Man Caught Fleecing Horse-Playing Grannies.' I look forward to breaking it. But the jocks…Bernie…fixed races…all that adds up to a hell of a lot greater story if it all comes together."

Matt was excited, making his point. Moe, watching this rare display of outward enthusiasm by his friend, smiled to himself. "We're talking conspiracy involving fraud and murder on a national scale," Matt continued. "I'll wait as long as I have to in order to break that one, Mr. Van Gundy. But you've got to promise me I'll be the first one to get it."

Van Gundy reached across the table and offered his hand. He smiled for the first time since he'd arrived in Moe's office. His mustache twitched. *The smile doesn't improve his looks any,* Matt thought, as he grasped Van Gundy's outstretched hand. "You're on," Van Gundy said.

Chapter Thirty-Two

"You don't seem to be jumping for joy, Vera," Bledsoe said, pushing the final chunk of currency across the table to Jimbo. The three of them were seated at the dining room table in the apartment on Dahle Street shared by Jimbo and Vera. It was nearly nine o'clock at night. Bledsoe had insisted the drapes be drawn over all the room's windows before he began counting out the cash.

This was the payout from their third Pick Four score. Bledsoe had already stored his share, $262,500, along with most of the rest of these gleanings, a grand total of $791,250, in two safe deposit boxes in a Sun Prairie bank. Jimbo shared his cut with Vera. She sat with her arms folded across her chest, cigarette in one hand, staring at the pile of bills Jimbo had in front of him.

"Did you hear what I said?" Bledsoe asked.

Vera emerged from her knitted-brow reverie. "What? Oh, yeah, sure, I'm happy. You know me, Claude, I don't get either too high or too low. It's just my way," she shrugged.

Bledsoe didn't believe her. Jimbo continued to count carefully. He looked both delighted and grateful for the money Bledsoe had caused to fall into his large hands. That wasn't the case with his girlfriend. Bledsoe felt a pang of concern as he looked at Vera through the haze of her Pall Mall smoke. She pretended to be concentrating on the counting, but Bledsoe figured otherwise.

"Let's get this out in the open right now," Bledsoe said sharply, sitting forward and banging his massive forearms down on the table. "You got a bitch, say so," he ordered. Jimbo was both startled and puzzled. "Claude, what're you talking about?"

Bledsoe ignored him. "I'm not talking to you," he said. He was looking straight at Vera. "I get the feeling your partner here isn't satisfied with the divisions of our labor. Am I right?"

Vera lit another Pall Mall off the stub of the previous one. She said, "Just seems to me Jimbo and me are doing more work than we're getting paid for." She shrugged. "That's how I feel about it," she said defiantly, looking Bledsoe in the eye.

He sat back, briefly smiling, knowing he had been right. Jimbo blurted out, "For chrissakes, Vera, this is more money than I've ever had my hands on. More than I even stole from the Home Depot. What are you complaining about? Jesus!"

Vera didn't buckle. "All I'm saying is that you and me are the ones sticking our necks out making these bets, then collecting them. I know the whole scheme is Claude's. I'll grant you that. But now that everything's in motion, well, it just seems to me you and I are getting a little bit shortchanged. Considering our exposure at the tracks." Satisfied, she took another drag on her cigarette, then blew the smoke toward the nicotine-tinted ceiling.

Bledsoe didn't say anything for almost a minute. He just looked at Vera, frowning. A trickle of cold sweat crept down Jimbo's spine. Bledsoe looked ominously pissed off to Jimbo, not a pleasant sight. Vera stayed cool.

Finally Bledsoe sat back in his chair. He smiled at Vera. "I understand your position," he said, and she blushed. Jimbo looked from one to the other, relieved. "I'll do some calculations," Bledsoe added. "I think I can adjust your share upward. Let me work on it."

He got to his feet and stretched. "You know something," he said, "maybe the tension may be getting to us. We need a little change of scenery, get away from this stuff for a day. Tomorrow's Saturday. Let's get out of town for a day. You two ever been to the House on the Rock?" They never had. They agreed to meet early the next morning.

Walking home a few minutes later, Bledsoe, outwardly as imperturbable as ever, was seething inside. That ungrateful bitch, he thought, pondering how much pleasure it would give him to slap Vera sideways. "The thousands I've made those two losers," he muttered. But his resentment would have to be harnessed. He wasn't looking forward to tomorrow, but he thought that a little day trip such as this one would prepare them for a slightly lengthier venture some time in the weeks ahead. He had an idea as to how he would handle "this dim duo," as he secretly referred to Jimbo and Vera, but he hadn't quite worked out the details yet.

Back at his apartment and seated at his computer, Bledsoe fired off an apologetic email to Professor Karl Brookings, explaining that he would be forced to miss Saturday's seminar because of "personal business." Brookings, he knew, would be disappointed, for this expert on the history of the American West loved to look around a conference table filled with graduate students when he presented his annual lecture on how General George Custer's hairstyle might have affected the Battle of Little Big Horn.

◇◇◇

Late the next morning, Bledsoe paid the admissions for the three of them, $19.50 per person, using three $20 bills. He'd converted all of their racetrack profits into currency no larger than $20s. Flashing bigger bills was inviting attention.

None of them had ever been to the famed House on the Rock, a huge monument to untutored taste that had been created in the early nineteen-forties by a man with a lust for curiosities and the wherewithal to acquire them with abandon. Located some forty miles west of Madison, just outside Spring Green, the House on the Rock each year attracted thousands of visitors from all over the country and around the world.

Vera was agape as they began their tour. The House sat atop a sixty-foot chimney of rock, high above a valley. The original structure of fourteen rooms had, over the decades, mushroomed into a kitsch depository that now covered more than two hundred acres. The fourteenth room set the mind-boggling tone of the whole place: called the "Infinity Room," it boasted 3,264 windows.

Its glass walls extended out over the valley, two hundred feet below. Visitors could gaze downward at the forest through a glass cocktail table.

Slowly, they worked their way along, past the "world's largest carousel," with its two hundred and sixty-nine animals, through the building with the two hundred and fifty dollhouses, the "Oriental Room" with its tall porcelain vases, the collections of armor and cannons and jewels. As Vera broke away to enter the "Organ Room" (thirteen bridges and walkways beneath a forty-five-foot-high perpetual motion clock), Bledsoe and Jim visited the weapons exhibit, one of whose features was a derringer hidden in a wooden leg built for a woman.

By 1:30 p.m. Jimbo and Bledsoe had had enough. Vera, however, was not about to sit down. She moved eagerly on toward the circus building as the men seated themselves in the Garden Café and ordered coffee and sandwiches.

"This is really something, isn't it Claude?" Jimbo said. He had to lean forward to make himself heard over the noise coming from the next table, where a party of German tourists was babbling excitedly as they examined House on the Rock brochures. "How about the weapons room, man? Ever seen anything like it? I didn't have any idea there were that many kinds of handguns."

"Not to mention rifles," Bledsoe answered.

"Yeah, you're right, pretty impressive," Jimbo said. He took a large bite of his liverwurst and onion sandwich. "Talking about weapons," Jimbo said, as he tried to lead up to what was on his mind, but Bledsoe cut him off. "Not here," he said, indicating the many people nearby.

Jimbo said, "I don't mean exactly that subject," he whispered, "but I wanted to tell you, Claude, that I'm sorry for the way Vera acted about the money last night. Wasn't my idea," he said sincerely. "But she's got her own ways. You know her," Jimbo grinned, "pretty gutsy little broad."

"Yes, I do," Bledsoe replied. "And I see her point. I thought it over last night. I've decided we go to a sixty-forty split for the final Pick Four. How does that sound?"

Wiping mustard off his chin, Jimbo grinned. "That's terrific, Claude, that's just great. Thanks. That'll make Vera a happy camper. When will that come up, do you know?"

"The second weekend of October," Bledsoe replied, well aware that the date would never work for him, since it was past his deadline. "I haven't done all the planning yet."

Jimbo nodded. "You sure are good at this stuff, Claude. It's an honor to be working with you. I really mean that."

I know you do, you poor sap, Bledsoe thought.

"You know," Jimbo continued, a solemn expression on his big red face, "Vera's been getting a little worried lately about us getting caught for what we've done. You don't think there's much chance of that, do you?"

Bledsoe said, "Caught how? Doing what? After our one incident with Bernie Glockner, which has gone completely undetected, all you've done is cash some tickets. You've got nothing to worry about, man."

"Yeah," Jimbo said, "but we are connected to you, and you've done some things…" He leaned forward to whisper, "What if they find out about us, Claude? Prison just about killed me. I can't go back inside. I just can't."

"There's absolutely no chance of that happening," Bledsoe assured him. He reached over and patted Jimbo on the shoulder. "Just cool it, my man."

They were quiet as Jimbo worked on his second sandwich. When he'd finished he said, "Claude, when you, ah, deal with those jockeys the way you do, do you ever feel, like, guilty afterwards? I've always wondered about that."

Bledsoe gave Jimbo a long look. He waited until the party of German tourists had departed the nearby table, leaving a tip so small the advancing busboy cursed audibly when he saw it. Bledsoe picked up a plastic knife from the table. "See this?" he said to Jimbo, holding it between two fingers. "An object." He snapped the knife in half. "That's how I see those jockeys," he said softly. "Objects. I don't think about them any other way. I don't know them. They mean nothing to me, except as a means to a wonderfully remunerative end."

Jimbo said, "Remuner what?"

"Never mind," Bledsoe said, getting to his feet. "Let's find Vera and get out of here. Enough is enough. Not that the people running this place would understand that."

Jimbo didn't know what Bledsoe meant, but he didn't say so. He looked at his watch. "She'll be in the gift shop by now," he said.

Chapter Thirty-Three

"He ran over my dog. The bastard ran over my dog."

Matt said, "When? Where?"

His questions were directed at a small, dark-haired woman in her early thirties who was strolling with him on a path that wound through the Madison Zoo. Her name was Andrea Greco. They had first met when they'd covered a Milwaukee county plane crash involving a prominent area businessman and his family. That was back when Matt was working for the *Milwaukee News* and Andrea for the *Madison Herald*. She'd kicked his butt with her coverage and impressed the hell out of him with her intelligence, sense of humor, and work ethic. Her looks weren't in the same league with her talent—she was skinny and plain, with piercing black eyes her most notable feature—but Matt had liked her from the start. They'd stayed in touch for the past dozen years, during which he moved into racing journalism and Andrea became the *Herald's* star investigative reporter.

"You forgot Who? And Why?" Andrea said caustically. "That horse racing beat must have blunted your reporter's edge." She'd always ragged him like that, giving him a hard time in a good-natured way that usually made both of them laugh. But she wasn't laughing today.

"That bastard, Bledsoe, you're asking me about. That's who. As to why, I have no idea. It looked like an accident. But I have my doubts. I'd come home from having dinner with Bledsoe. He asked me if he could come in for a drink. I said no. He was turning out to be a domineering know-it-all. Everything was about him. He didn't like that response, I could tell. He didn't say another word, just turned his back on me and trotted over to his car.

"My dog Emma was just a pup, five months old, a beautiful black Lab. She's at the door waiting when I open it. Then she spots a goddam squirrel in the driveway, right behind Bledsoe's car. Makes a bee line for it. I swear to God he saw her running to the driveway, but he throws the car into reverse and squashes my pup. I wanted to kill him. I still do."

They were walking now past the section of the zoo housing elephants. Matt, thinking of the death of Andrea's dog, found himself recalling the famous incident of years before when an aged elephant named Blinky suddenly, uncharacteristically, reached through the bars with her trunk one morning and throttled a toddler to death. Blinky, a much-beloved attraction for two previously peaceful decades, was put to death the following week upon the controversial order of zoo officials, a decision met with vociferous but unsuccessful protests from animal rights activists.

Matt returned to his questioning. "What were you doing, having dinner with Bledsoe?"

Andrea said, "It started when I was assigned to do a feature story on him for the paper. 'A Madison Special,' that was the hook. People had evidently talked about Bledsoe for years but not much had ever been written about him. Sounded interesting to me. I mean, what kind of person would choose a life like that? Going to class your whole life.

"Bledsoe is super, super smart," Andrea continued. "He just intrigued the hell out of me. I wasn't interested in him romantically, but I was fascinated with the way he had chosen to live. Permanent Student. At a Remove From Reality. It's amazing how you start thinking in headlines in our business, isn't it? Anyway, it turned into a good feature that was picked up by papers all over the country.

"I interviewed Bledsoe twice. The second time, he asked me to have dinner." Andrea gave a mirthless chuckle. "He's a long way from movie star material, but there isn't exactly a corps of collectibles trying to hit on your pal Andrea," she said, kicking at a leaf that lay before them on the pavement.

"Guys I work with, I think I intimidate a lot of them. And I work so much I don't have a lot of opportunities to meet men who aren't in the business."

Andrea put her arm through his as they sidestepped a slim woman runner pushing an infant buggy bearing two chubby babies. The woman flashed them a smile as she huffed past. "You, of course," Andrea said, "were never intimidated by me. But you still never asked me out."

Startled, Matt did not reply, and they walked on in silence until Andrea, looking straight ahead, said, "You still seeing what's her name down in Chicago? The female horse whisperer? I mean horsewoman?"

Matt said, "That's beneath you, a statement like that. Yes, I'm still seeing Maggie O'Connor, the horse trainer."

Still not looking at him, Andrea said, "I'm sure she's a lovely person."

"That's not worthy of you, either," Matt replied.

"You're right," Andrea sighed. "You are right. Let's get back to Bledsoe. Like a fool, when he asked me out, I said yes. My thinking was, what the hell did I have to lose? Well, it turned out to be my sweet pup," she said bitterly. "Emma was lying there in the damned driveway, her head mashed into the concrete, and Bledsoe showed about as much remorse as a rutabaga. He muttered something about being sorry, all the while looking around for a place to dump Emma so he could back up his car and get the hell out of there.

"I was crying. I lost it. And Bledsoe never even looked me in the eye before he left. I called my buddy Bobby Keefer at the paper. He came right over and took poor Emma away. I didn't ask where. I don't want to know. Then Bobby came back with a bottle of Wild Turkey and we got smashed. I've never seen Bledsoe since that night. Bastard!" Andrea, usually so strong, so voluble, was silent then, eyes averted. They walked another dozen or so yards. Finally, she turned to him. "Anyway, Matt, what's your interest in this weirdo?"

Matt motioned toward a bench that faced the lions' den. Two female lions paced back and forth in front of a huge male, who drowsed on a sun-warmed rock, golden mane shining. Matt said, "He looks like he's going to roar and start a movie." He took off his sunglasses and turned to Andrea.

"This may sound insane," Matt said, "but I think Bledsoe might be a killer. A killer whose goal is manipulating the results of horse races in order to win bets." He paused, waiting for what he expected would be a look of incredulity. Andrea never blinked. "Go on," she said, and he did, recounting everything he'd learned, beginning with the suspicious death of Bernie Glockner.

When he had finished filling her in, Matt shook his head. "The major thing I can't figure," he said, "is motive. Why would a guy like this, longtime student, never involved in any crime that anyone knows of, suddenly decide to get into something like this?"

Andrea said, "How about one of the oldest motives of all? How about money?"

"Money! What do you mean? I thought Bledsoe was on permanent scholarship. And planned to stay there."

Andrea smiled. "Well, maybe he did plan to keep on riding his grammy's gravy train into his dotage. But Grandma Bledsoe had other ideas."

"How so?"

"Grandma set a limit on her largesse," Andrea answered. "She put a possible cut-off date on the bequest that financed Claude's continuing ed, as he called it. Age fifty. *Finito.* Maybe grandma suspected her pride and joy would take advantage of her generosity and never set out on his own. Maybe that's why she didn't make the bequest open ended.

"Whatever her thinking, she put in the will that if Claude didn't have a net worth of $1 million by the proscribed date, the deal was over. And Mr. Bledsoe turns fifty next month.

Considering the fact that the guy has never held a steady job in his life, I suspect that his gravy train is about to derail," Andrea said, relishing the thought.

"However, there's another wrinkle to this. If Bledsoe somehow manages to live up to his granny's monetary expectations, he'd be in for a huge reward. If he can prove he's got a million bucks by his birthday, the bulk of her estate would go to him instead of to charity. It's a very sizable estate, somewhere over $15 million. The beauty part as far as I'm concerned is that Bledsoe never knew anything about this codicil in the will until last September. That's when the pressure on him started to rev up."

Matt said, "How do you know this? Did Bledsoe tell you?"

"No. When I was dealing with him, even he didn't know it."

Andrea hesitated. "I probably shouldn't be telling even you this," she said. "You can never reveal me as your source. One of the few men in this town that I occasionally date is a lawyer named Jim Altman. His firm has handled all the Bledsoe family work for a couple of generations. He can't stand Claude, whom he considers one of the most arrogant assholes he's ever met. That's why Jim took such satisfaction last year when he was obliged to inform Bledsoe of a Grandma-imposed deadline."

Matt shook his head. "Hell, Andrea, I don't know," he said. "Would a guy be so cold he'd take to murdering athletes to preserve a lifestyle?"

"Matt," Andrea answered, "you've known me what, a dozen years? Haven't I proved to be damn good judge of character?"

"I can't argue with that."

"Well, then, let me assure you that Claude Bledsoe is definitely capable of doing something like that if it's in his best interests. Those interests come first, foremost, and forever for this bastard. There's no doubt in my mind about that."

Matt stood up and stretched, then sat back down on the bench. The male lion shot him an inquisitive glance. "Thing is," Matt said, "as smart and talented as this guy is, couldn't he just have used one or more of his degrees to get a good job?"

Andrea shook her head. "Sure, years ago, when he was younger. It's not that easy today. My older brother, Angelo, got downsized by his company after twenty-seven years with them, all on an upward career path. Then, boom, he was expendable. Angelo tried to get a new job. Months of frustration, nothing. Finally, a career counselor told Angelo, 'You've got the worst trifecta there is working against you. You're over fifty, you're white, and you're male.'

"I don't care how smart Bledsoe is. Except for his tutoring of the jocks here, he's never been employed in his life. His background screams eccentricity. I can't see personnel directors swinging open their doors for him. And he's smart enough to know it.

"I think Mr. Bledsoe is in need of money now, I really do. And a fine thought that is," she grinned.

Matt's disapproval was obvious. "Look, Andrea," he said with a frown, "I appreciate the fact that you hate this creep and would like revenge for what he did to your dog. But there's nothing remotely humorous about his financial situation. There's a damn good chance Bledsoe's money troubles have made him into a murderer."

Chapter Thirty-Four

Jimbo drove west out of Madison on Highway 18 in Bledsoe's blue Toyota. On this Friday, at this early morning hour and heading away from the city, traffic was light. Vera rode in the passenger seat. Bledsoe sprawled across the back seat. He was reading the latest issue of *The Economist* while trying to ignore Vera's rummaging through the available country music stations on the car radio.

Bledsoe had risen before 5 a.m. to make his final preparations. The dawn sky was just beginning to brighten as he opened the trunk of the Toyota. Bledsoe reached in and removed the spare tire. Two nights before, he had stolen four concrete blocks from an eastside Madison construction site and hidden them in his storage bin in the basement of his apartment house. Now, he effortlessly lifted each of the blocks, placing two in the tire well, shoving the other two under a blanket at the rear of the trunk. He laid the cardboard flooring and carpet over the tire well. The added weight of the blocks dropped the rear bumper of the Toyota a noticeable several inches. But Bledsoe was the only one noticing. Then he tossed in his duffel bag and the three sleeping bags he'd purchased the day before. He took the spare tire down to the basement storage unit. "Way my luck is going," Bledsoe said softly, smiling as he climbed back up the basement stairs, "I won't be getting any flat tires."

Minutes later, when he'd pulled up to the apartment building on Dahle Street where Jimbo and Vera lived, they were waiting outside, sleepy-eyed but eager, like kids ready for camp. Bledsoe gave them a cheery "good morning," then took their luggage—an old gym bag of Jimbo's, a dark pink suitcase that belonged to Vera—and tossed them into the trunk before quickly closing it. "Jimbo, how about you driving?" he said. "And Vera can ride up front with you. I'll navigate."

"Sure," Jimbo said. "But are you sure we're going to need those sleeping bags you bought?"

"Why take a chance?" Bledsoe replied. "We might want to sleep up on the top deck one night. I understand a pretty good breeze sometimes comes down the river. Could be a little cool. The bags could come in handy."

It wasn't until they'd sped through Fennimore and crossed the Mississippi River at Prairie du Chien and turned north on Highway 26 that Bledsoe reached over the front seat and handed Ottmar Liebert's "Nouveau Flamenco" tape to Vera. "My turn for music now," he said, and Vera didn't argue. She was in a great mood.

They were all feeling good on this early autumn afternoon, the beginning of what Bledsoe had described to Vera and Jimbo as an "adventure weekend." He'd presented the idea to them two nights earlier when they'd met for drinks at Doherty's Den.

"Partners," Bledsoe said, leaning forward from his side of the booth, gray eyes intense, "I think we deserve a little break. We've been under a lot of pressure. But with three major scores behind us, it's time to start enjoying some of this money. In moderation, mind you," he emphasized. "We don't want any big splash, any flashing a lot of cash around. That's what leads to most of the jerks who get caught getting caught. There'll be plenty of time to spend this over the next few years, just as we agreed. Even if the money wasn't actually stolen, there's no percentage in drawing any attention to ourselves. But," he added expansively, "I think we can start putting a little of it to some fun use. What do you say?"

Jimbo and Vera raised their bottles of beer in agreement. Although Vera was aware that her definition of "fun" was for the most part quite distinct from Bledsoe's, she responded enthusiastically. "Hear, hear," Vera said. "I'm ready for something different. We both are," she said, jabbing Jimbo in the side with her elbow. "What've you got in mind, Claude?"

Bledsoe reached into his jacket and extracted a four-color brochure extolling the merits of a houseboat shown moored on the bank of the Mississippi. The brochure came from Crandall's Houseboat Rentals in little Lansing, Iowa, almost one hundred miles straight west of Madison. Crandall's was a firm with nearly forty years of experience providing, as the brochure cover claimed, "vacations of a lifetime."

As Vera and Jimbo began to read the brochure, Bledsoe looked up when the front door of the bar opened and said, "Oh, Christ. Here comes Son of the Morning Star."

Vera, puzzled, said "Who?" as a paunchy, elderly man approached their booth, wearing western boots and hat, replicated blue U. S. Cavalry pants, and a buckskin jacket. His long white hair hung to the shoulders of his fringed buckskin shirt. ."Hello, professor," Bledsoe said, forcing a smile. "Don't tell me I've missed another deadline."

Professor Karl Brookings threw his head back and laughed loudly, causing some of the drinkers at the bar to turn and look. "Claude," he said, "we go back a good ways, do we not? So, I know very well that *you* know you owe me your paper on the history of the Crazy Horse monument. You don't want to jeopardize that 'A' you have working, do you?" He laughed again.

Bledsoe said, "Of course not. I'll have it for you by tomorrow morning. Sorry it's late, but I've been very busy lately."

"I look forward to reading it," Brookings said. He nodded at Jimbo and Vera. The buckskin fringe of his jacket flounced as he moved off, lugging his laden briefcase in one hand, waving with the other to some graduate students he recognized at a table next to the back wall. He was warmly welcomed there.

"What's that getup for? What's his story?" Jimbo said.

Bledsoe said, "He was once the university's top scholar on nineteenth-century western American history. But in recent years he's turned into a delusional blowhard. He's gotten so deep into his subject he's started to role play. He's an expert on Custer and

Little Big Horn. Last few years, he's begun to dress the part. Tenure keeps him on the faculty. A lot of people make fun of him. Some don't," he said, indicating the back table where the professor sat holding forth for the circle of youthful sycophants.

Bledsoe sipped his beer as Vera and Jimbo pored over the houseboat brochure. After a few minutes, he said, "I thought we could drive over there Friday morning. Go out on the boat that day and Saturday, then return it Sunday afternoon and drive home. I called Crandall's Rentals yesterday. The lady who runs the business said they'd had a cancellation for this weekend. On that model there," he added, reaching across the table to indicate a craft called the Somerset Belle. "It's the standard ten-passenger model, smallest of the three models they have, but it'll give us plenty of room. Two queen size beds, a sofa, kitchen, air-conditioning, TV, microwave, you name it."

Jimbo said, "How big are these things?"

"Says right here," Vera answered, pointing at the pamphlet. "Fifteen feet by forty-eight. Engine's a hundred and seventy horsepower. Cabin's thirteen by thirty-one. That's nice and roomy."

"Right," Bledsoe agreed. "So we'll easily be able to stay out of each other's way. Besides, there's a nice deck on top. You can fish from there, or sunbathe, or sleep, whatever. Either of you ever been on the Mississippi?"

They shook their heads no. "Well, neither have I," Bledsoe responded. "It'll be an adventure for all of us. I'm told it is a great experience."

Vera looked enthusiastic at the prospect. Jimbo, however, was dubious. He said, "What is this boat going to run us? Got to be expensive. And who's going to drive the damn thing? Hell, I've never been on anything like this."

Bledsoe laughed expansively. "Jimbo, my man, not to worry. First thing is that I'm paying for this rental. My treat, okay? A little reward for all the good work you and Vera have done. Lagniappe."

Jimbo interrupted to ask, "Lon who?", but Bledsoe ignored him and continued. "As far as operating the boat, they have people there who give you instructions and take you out on a little practice run before they release the boat to you. People do it all the time. How hard can it be? This isn't the Queen Mary II in the North Sea. Besides," Bledsoe said before he drained his beer glass, "you should know by now that I'm a quick study."

◇◇◇

They reached Lansing late Friday morning. Before proceeding to the houseboat headquarters, Jimbo pulled into the parking lot of an IGA supermarket. "We'll buy the weekend provisions," he announced, handing Vera a wad of cash. Jimbo fancied himself a master of the barbecue grill and had been delighted to learn that the houseboat came equipped with a small Weber. "I'll handle all the cooking," he had announced. Vera extracted their grocery list from her purse as she exited the car. "You two go ahead and shop," Bledsoe said. He got out of the car and stretched as they entered the store. Then he quickly checked the trunk to make sure that the concrete blocks remained hidden from view.

At the boat landing, Bledsoe went into the office to register. "Is cash okay?" he asked the woman at the desk. "We never refuse it," Janet Crandall said with a smile. Bledsoe quickly filled out the customer questionnaire, using the phony Illinois address that appeared on the fake driver's license he showed the woman. It had been created for Bledsoe by a Madison man, Dom Incarvino, who specialized in fake IDs for underage students determined to patronize the city's numerous beer bars. The license identified Bledsoe as Bob Remsberg of Bannockburn, IL.

Two hours later they were proceeding slowly north on the broad, brown expanse of the upper Mississippi, a breeze in their faces, sun high in a nearly cloudless blue sky. Bledsoe was at the helm. He perched on the swivel chair behind the wheel, steering perfectly, as if he'd done it for years. Jimbo sat on a lawn chair on the little foredeck, just outside the door to the pilot house, drinking beer and waving merrily to passing boats. Vera was sunning herself up top. "This is pretty damn perfect," Jimbo said for the third time in the last half-hour. "Another one of your best ideas, Claude."

"Thanks, man," Bledsoe replied, eyes scanning the west bank of the river. Fifty minutes later he slowed the Mercruiser motor and began angling the prow of the houseboat toward a small, sandy beach. It was located on a slight bend in the river that was shaded by towering cottonwoods, perfect for a single boat whose passengers could drop two anchors, one in the river, the other planted in the sand on shore. "This looks like a good spot for the night," Bledsoe said. "Gives us some privacy. Jimbo," he ordered, "get Vera down here so she can help you with the anchors. I've got to keep the boat steady while you're dropping them."

"Aye, aye, captain," Jimbo grinned. He staggered momentarily after getting out of his chair. The afternoon sun, combined with a half-dozen cans of beer, had turned his skin a brighter shade of pink.

With the boat secured, its prow nestled a few feet off the bank in shallow water, Vera jumped into the water for a swim. The men declared it cocktail hour as she floated in the warm water near the rear of the boat. Bledsoe took a gallon bottle of margarita mix from his duffel. He matched it up with a 750ml bottle of Jose Cuervo tequila and began mixing drinks. Vera came up the side ladder. Dripping water onto the deck, Vera said, "Hey, wait for me." Her face was aglow in the late afternoon sun. Bledsoe thought he had never before seen this usually glum woman look so happy. He made two powerful drinks along with a light one for himself.

An hour later, after she had drunkenly declared that eating dinner soon had become a "neshessity," Vera began to unsteadily put together a salad as Jimbo, swearing, finally managed to ignite the charcoal in the grill. They then again toasted one another, their lucrative recent achievements, and the brilliance of their leader, who kept topping off their glasses while merely twirling the liquid in his own. Vera and Jimbo went on drinking steadily. She located a country station out of LaCrosse and bumped up the radio's volume.

Dusk had crept over the river along with a slight mist when Vera joined Jimbo next to the grill on the foredeck, helping to assess the readiness of the thick sirloins. "One more round to go with dinner," Bledsoe called from the kitchen. He got no argument. All he heard was the two of them giggling amid the smoke. Jimbo had a long fork in one hand and Vera's right buttock in the other.

The light was dim where Bledsoe stood at the kitchen counter, well out of sight of the drunken twosome. He carefully placed a massive dose of "roofies," the date rape drug, into each of their glasses, then vigorously stirred the drinks, which by now were almost all tequila. He'd done his research: Rohypnol, he'd learned, was undetectable, odorless, and capable of rendering its victims unconscious within minutes. He'd had no trouble purchasing a supply from one of the football players he tutored, although the young man had evidenced surprise that Bledsoe wanted the powerful drug "at your age." Bledsoe had winked at him and pocketed the pills.

Bledsoe brought their glasses to Jimbo and Vera, saying, "Go on and relax. You've been working hard on the grill. Let me finish cooking the steaks." They raised their glasses in yet another joyful toast, drinking deeply. Bledsoe took the fork from an unresisting Jimbo. Vera went into the cabin and sat down unsteadily on the sofa. After he had come stumbling over the threshold, Jimbo plunked down next to her. They snuggled together before leaning back to rest their heads. Their voices dwindled.

Bledsoe heard the first glass fall—Vera's—onto the wood floor six minutes later. He looked in and saw she was unconscious, her head on Jimbo's right shoulder. Jimbo was also out. His glass had dropped silently onto his lap, the liquid staining his khakis.

Bledsoe extracted the three steaks from the grill and threw them into the river. He wasn't hungry. Adrenaline was giving him a rush that dwarfed appetite. Placing the cover on the grill, he looked up and down the river before going inside. The only people in view were some college kids waterskiing in mid-channel, and they were soon out of sight.

The sleeping bags he'd brought were new. He cut the tags off and placed them inside the now nearly empty tequila bottle, which he threw over the side. Then he stuffed Vera into the green one. She was deeply asleep. So was Jimbo. With an eye cocked toward Jimbo, Bledsoe slipped an airtight plastic bag over Vera's head, twisting the bottom of it into a tight ball, rolling his wrist over to achieve complete closure. Vera seemed to gasp for an instant, perhaps trying to say something, but Bledsoe held tight, the muscles in his big forearms taut. As with Marnie Rankin, it took longer than Bledsoe would have thought, but it had to be done. "Had to be done," he whispered, though there was no need to whisper at this point. Meticulous as ever, he checked twice for a pulse before turning to Jimbo. Jimbo took a little longer, even shaking for a few seconds before it was over, and Bledsoe had some trouble inserting his large, inert form into the black sleeping bag. Finally, he dragged the bodies into the passage between the bunk beds, pulled up both anchors, and started the engine.

It took Bledsoe nearly forty-five minutes to drive the boat back to the now deserted marina. He hustled to his car and took two concrete blocks out of the trunk and brought them to the boat, then returned for the other two. He was pleasantly surprised that he could dock in such isolation this early on a Friday night. He'd been prepared to wait out on the river for things to quiet down. "Folks here must tuck in early," he said to himself as he cast off again.

With his excellent night vision, Bledsoe had little difficulty locating the kind of area he required, a narrow inlet nearly five miles down river from the marina on the west bank. He eased the boat thirty yards into a narrowing bayou and tied on to a huge gnarled stump on the shore. He nimbly jumped onto the muddy bank and began searching. Within minutes he had found a dozen sizable rocks, which he carried back to the boat.

Kneeling in the bedroom passageway, Bledsoe shoved three of the concrete blocks and half the rocks into the sleeping bag that held Jimbo's corpse, zipped the bag, then looped fiber tape around it from top to bottom. Halfway through this task, he suddenly grinned. "Jimbo, you big dummy, you look like a goddam mummy with this stuff on you." The sound of his barking laugh rang through the night before he abruptly stopped, turning his attentions to Vera.

It was nearly 2:45 a.m. before Bledsoe spotted a decent break in the river's steady commercial traffic. He had waited patiently as the powerful lights of the towboats pierced the darkness for a mile ahead of the long barges they pushed, their lights sweeping both banks as well as the water, the barges linked in the wake of the mighty horn soundings that bounced off the tall bluffs flanking the river. When he finally saw a good-sized interval in the procession, he was quick to act. With his lights off, he headed the boat to midstream, then kicked Vera's bag off the rear platform and into this deepest part of the dark water. The weight of the concrete blocks and the rocks sucked her under at once. Jimbo, a heavier package, caused Bledsoe to grunt as he dragged the bag to the rear. Then it, too, disappeared.

As he started the boat's engines, Bledsoe recalled an Ethics and Morality course he had taken three years earlier and his professor's concentration on Hannah Arendt's famous "banality of evil" concept. Bledsoe laughed softly, feeling an adrenaline surge much like those he'd enjoyed when he had shot down the three jockeys and suffocated Marnie Rankin. "God help me, which I doubt very much he will, but there's nothing banal about this to me," he said aloud as, heart thumping, he pushed down on the throttle and turned on the boat's lights.

Back at the marina, Bledsoe carefully pulled the boat into an empty slip far down the long dock from the office. After moving the luggage to his car, he spent ten minutes wiping down every surface in the boat. On a Crandall Rentals pad he printed a message, explaining that a call to his cell phone had notified him of "an emergency situation back home," forcing "my brother and his wife and I to cut short our river weekend. We'll try to get back next year," he wrote above the signature, "Bob Remsberg." Using a paper clip, he attached to the note what he knew was more than enough cash to cover the gasoline costs incurred. Bledsoe shoved the note and the keys to the boat through the mail slot in the office door.

Three hours later, nearing Madison, Bledsoe's feeling of fatigue was replaced by another surge of energy. Spotting a half-filled dumpster at the edge of a small shopping mall's parking lot, he stopped and deposited Jimbo's old gym bag and Vera's pink suitcase under a pile of refuse. Then he drove to their apartment on Dahle Street. Using the key he'd taken from Jimbo's chain, he slipped into the apartment. He went directly to the bedroom with its ancient closet safe set into the floor, a feature of the apartment Jimbo had often bragged about. The first combination he tried was a string of numbers made up of Jimbo's date of birth. It didn't work. Then he tried Vera's. The safe door creaked open, revealing the nearly $264,000 they'd foolishly entrusted to this obvious hiding place "just like the idiots they were," Bledsoe muttered.

"I'm over the top. I'm over the fucking *top*," he said loudly, stuffing their cash into his duffel bag. He couldn't help but laugh as he envisioned the delicious moment, now only nine days away, when he would stride into Altman's office and dump a million dollars on the incredulous attorney's desk.

Back in his car, Bledsoe sat for a few moments, head back against the seat. He felt drained. *I'll sleep well tonight*, he thought, *but then I always do.*

Chapter Thirty-Five

Friday noon, Matt got a phone call from Moe, who said, "Want to go to the Bears game Sunday night? It's only a pre-season game, but it's supposed to be a nice night. And you could stand to take a little time away from the horses. Besides, if it's any consolation, they're playing the Colts. By the way, you're welcome to bring your Maggie. I'd like to meet her." The two men hadn't spoken since Matt had reported to Moe what he'd learned from Andrea Greco in Madison.

"Well, you'll just have to settle for me," Matt said. "Maggie'll be out of town. She's running a horse Sunday night in a little stakes race down at Devon Downs. She won't be back until Monday. Where will I meet you?"

"I'll have Pete Dunleavy pick you up at your condo at five. We'll do a little tailgating before the game."

◇◇◇

On the ride from Evanston to Chicago, Matt sat in the front of the Lincoln town car and chatted with Dunleavy. The ex-cop was an avid Bears fan, time-tested and not given to overt optimism about his favorite team's prospects. "The past few years, we've had some of the worst draft choices since Jesus picked Judas as an apostle," Dunleavy said, expertly wheeling into the express lanes at Hollywood and the Outer Drive. "I don't expect a whole lot this year."

This was a realistic outlook, Matt thought, especially in a metropolis where professional sports championships were few and far between. There had been a lengthy basketball drought until, as Rick Rothmeyer once put it, "God took pity on the city and sent Michael Jordan to the Chicago Bulls" for a glory ride in the nineties. And the previous autumn the Chicago White Sox had won their first World Series in eighty-eight years. But Chicago's Cubs that same season had extended their history of non-championship baseball to an odds-defying, record-setting ninety-seven years.

The Bears had not won a title since 1985, but their fans' enthusiasm was unwavering. Every seat would be filled that night in Soldier Field, the recently renovated stadium whose new look made it appear as if pieces of an enormous flying saucer had been plunked down atop the original classically columned structure. Two decades after their heroics, members of the '85 squad, a team immortalized on *Saturday Night Live* as "Da Bears," were still lionized in the city of big shoulders. So was their legendary coach, now a popular restaurateur and peddler of a remedy for erectile dysfunction.

Passing Belmont harbor, Dunleavy yawned widely. Matt said, "Big night last night?"

"Just long. Longer than usual," Dunleavy grunted. "Mr. Kellman was entertaining some out of town clients. They'd never been to Chicago. He took them to dinner at Gibson's, and then left them there with me in the Viagra Triangle. I didn't get the last guy back to his hotel until almost four o'clock this morning."

Matt said, "What's the Viagra Triangle?"

Dunleavy laughed. "It's what they call that part of Rush Street where there's Gibson's, the Hunt Club, Tavern on Rush. Top restaurants and pick-up joints. Filled every night with sharpies looking for action and trophy wife candidates trolling for sharpies. It can get pretty crazy down there, especially near closing time."

"Does Moe hang out with these guys?"

Dunleavy frowned. "Are you kidding? Mr. Kellman has dinner for clients like that, then turns them loose and tells them to use his tab wherever they go in the Triangle. He never stays out with them. He's home every night with his wife, ten o'clock at the latest.

"Her name's Leah," Dunleavy added. "Real nice lady. They're coming up on their forty-fifth wedding anniversary."

Even in the front seat, Matt could smell the enticing aromas emanating from the food trays in the trunk of the Lincoln. "Do you do any cooking in the parking lot?" Matt asked. No, Dunleavy told him, all his cooking had been done "at home yesterday morning, except for the Italian sausages. I'll do those on the little grill I bring."

Moments after Dunleavy had pulled the Lincoln into a prime spot in the Soldier Field parking lot, Moe appeared. He shook hands with Matt as Dunleavy began unloading the portable picnic table, chairs, utensils, and food trays from the trunk. The surrounding air was replete with smoke and the odor of bratwurst, hot dogs, chicken, and hamburgers cooking on grills of all shapes and sizes. Some of the grills had potatoes roasting on the coals. Two car rows over, a man wearing an apron with *Bears Rule* printed on it was basting a large turkey. The people standing around the grills were working on pitchers of bloody marys or margaritas, chests of iced beer, bottles of brandy.

Fans wearing Bears jerseys tossed footballs back and forth through the haze, many of the older ones wearing jerseys with No. 51 on the back, Dick Butkus' old number, the younger ones sporting No. 54, the number of the current Bears middle linebacker, Brian Urlacher.

Matt looked on appreciatively as Dunleavy unveiled a soup tureen ("minestrone tonight," he said), and aluminum containers of olive dressing salad, Italian beef, and canneloni in red sauce. Dunleavy had the little grill going by now, and the sausages were starting to sizzle. "A few of my clients will be joining us," Moe said to Matt. "That's why Pete brought so much food."

As Moe finished speaking, Matt saw three middle-aged men get out of a cab and walk toward them. They looked tired, hung over, and hungry, and Matt correctly surmised they were the previous night's patrollers of the Viagra Triangle. Moe introduced them to Matt, saying "meet these fellows from Houston," adding only their first names: Bruce, Glen, and Marvin. The three eagerly accepted beers proffered by Dunleavy, then began filling their plates.

With a glass of Santa Margarita pinot grigio in one hand, a juicy Italian beef sandwich in the other, Moe smiled as he surveyed the parking lot scene. "It's a beautiful evening," he commented, "but to tell you the truth, I like it better here in December. When the wind comes howling off the lake, snow's blowing onto your sandwich, and you can already smell the beer breath of guys around you even before the opening kickoff. That's what being a Bears fan is to me."

Matt finished the last of his soup before saying, "It's not for me, Moe." He well remembered the few December games at Soldier Field he'd attended in the past, his fingers, face and feet nearly frozen, people bundled up in outfits Admiral Peary's expedition could have used.

It was as if Moe hadn't heard him. The little furrier was waxing nostalgic about the Bears, telling the men from Houston how the team's founder, the late George Halas, "Papa Bear, would have loved this scenario. His old team gets a refurbished stadium with added sky boxes, funded mostly with borrowed money. Remember, Halas had a tremendous regard for the buck. One of his players once said that Halas 'tosses nickels around like they're manhole covers.' It was Halas who pioneered making season ticket holders come up with their money months before the season started. Then, he used the 'float' on that money. Sure, the idea later spread to other sports. Look at the Kentucky Derby. But it was the old Bohemian who came up with the idea," Moe said.

Walking up a Soldier Field interior ramp an hour later, Moe said apologetically, "I'm sorry, fellows, but we're not going to use my sky box tonight. I gave it to the lieutenant governor and her family. It's her birthday."

The seats they did have, Matt thought, were better than any he'd ever sat in at a Bears game: west side of the stadium, forty-eight yard line, eighteen rows up from the field. Matt settled in, sitting to Moe's right. On Moe's left, bracketed by Dunleavy, was the Houston trio, now fed, watered, and generally revived. Marvin insisted on buying the first round of beers from an Old Style vendor. Glen offered around a silver flask, but had no takers other than himself.

At the first television time out in the first quarter, Moe said quietly to Matt, "I heard the other day from our friend Larry Van Gundy in the state's attorney's office. He says there's a guy contacted them claiming to have quote killed all those jockeys unquote. Calls himself the Unknown Rifleman. He's phoned in three times in the last week."

Matt said, "I don't believe it. A killer this effective, this smart, who hasn't left a trace, would all of a sudden go into a chest-pounding mode?" He sipped his beer. "I just can't see it, Moe."

"You can't, eh? Well, for good reason." Moe smiled, holding out his plastic cup for Dunleavy to refill with pinot grigio. "Actually, Matt, this nutcake has a track record of off-the-wall confessions. Once the feds matched up his voice with what they had on record, they came up with a guy named Trevor T. Thommason of Evansville, Indiana. Turns out that over the years Trevor has claimed to have killed both Kennedys, Martin Luther King, and Jimmy Hoffa. Among others. He's not in a loony bin, but he probably should be."

The Bears scored on a long pass play, their first points of the exhibition season, and the crowd reacted as if they'd sewed up the Super Bowl. Moe waited for the roar to diminish before continuing.

Seeing the look of disappointment on Matt's face, Moe said, "There's no reason to lose hope, you know."

Matt shrugged. "It doesn't look very promising at this point."

"True," Moe said, "but things change. If Bledsoe is the killer, like we think, he'll make a mistake. Most of them do. No matter how smart he is, he's eligible to make one, too."

Matt was not encouraged by this prediction. Despite the good food and company this evening, he was not only missing Maggie but feeling increasingly disheartened by the unsolved mystery of the murdered jockeys. He still couldn't get out of his head that dream of Randy Morrison coming off the ski jump.

Moe looked at him appraisingly. Leaning back in his seat, Moe said, "Let me tell you a story. A true story. From when I was a kid on the west side. There was a guy named Sammy Rosen who had a little corner store. Sold candy, cigarettes, magazines and newspapers, stuff like that. Had a pinball machine in the back. Ran the store with his wife, a real tough broad named Tamara. The kids called her Tamara the Terrible. Behind her back, mind you. She'd kick you in the ass if she caught you trying to lift a piece of penny candy.

"But the main thing that Sammy Rosen did," Moe continued, "was be the neighborhood bookmaker. Nobody had much money back then, so the bets Sammy handled weren't big ones. But, like all bookmakers who have their heads screwed on straight, he made money. Not a lot, but he did.

"Well, after many years in that store, it became obvious Sammy wasn't making enough money to satisfy Tamara. She started to complain to him that her sisters in Skokie were living the good life. Summer vacations over at South Haven in Michigan, winter weeks in Miami. Meanwhile, she and Sammy are tied to the store, seven days a week. So, Tamara comes up with a plan.

"First, Tamara makes a deal to sell the store to Arnie Klein next door, the grocer who wants to expand. That's part one. Part two is to wait for the biggest betting day of the year in the neighborhood. That would be Kentucky Derby Day, when everybody wants to get a bet down with Sammy. Tamara convinces her husband that, instead of paying off any winners out of this bundle of money he's going to be holding on the Derby, Sammy would pretend to have a fatal heart attack right before the race. Tamara arranges for her brother-in-law Mel the doctor to be on hand to pronounce Sammy dead on the spot. Tamara, as the bereaved widow, wouldn't be able to pay any winners. Then she and Sammy would take the pile of money and sneak out of town early the next morning.

"This is May of 1953. The big Derby favorite is the great, undefeated Native Dancer. But hardly any of Sammy's clients bet 7-10 shots like that. They go for 'the Jewish horse,' Dark Star, owned by a guy named Guggenheim. Dark Star wins the Derby by a head from Native Dancer. He pays $51.80 for $2. The neighborhood is in an uproar. People are coming out of the taverns and the tenements, dancing in the street.

"Sammy has watched the Derby on his black and white TV in the apartment above the store. He starts to panic. But Tamara takes charge and settles him down and pretty soon Sammy gets busy pretending to be dead. She flings open the apartment window and starts screaming, 'My Sammy's gone, he's died up here. Oh, oh, oh,' she's wailing. Within minutes brother-in-law Mel steams up the stairs carrying his black bag. Then Tamara's back at the window, wailing some more. 'A heart attack my Sammy had. Oh, what am I going to do? I don't know what Sammy did with all the Derby money. It's not here. Oh, oh, oh, what will happen to me?'

"They sit shiva that night. Sammy lies stiff as a board in the wooden coffin, which Tamara has positioned in a very dark part of the living room. Sammy's trying not to show he's breathing. The neighbors come in to pay their respects, the horse players among them naturally disappointed as hell. Dark Star, $51.80, and they don't have a cent to show for it. They can't believe their bad luck, much less Sammy's. A few of them are muttering insults as they file past the so-called corpse.

"Finally, up to the coffin strides little Mrs. Moscowitz, one of the oldest widows in the neighborhood. She's been not quite right in the head since her husband died. She stands at the coffin, looking down at Sammy, fuming, swearing, 'You little bum, Sammy, all the years I bet the Derby with you and never win, and now this. I got the winner, but no money. I spit on you,' she says, and she does. People are trying to persuade her to move along, but she won't budge.

"All of a sudden, Mrs. Moscowitz pulls out a pistol and puts the muzzle against Sammy's right temple. She says, 'What you did to all of us today, you bum, you should die not once but *twice*.' And she cocks the pistol.

"That sound makes Sammy sit up straight in the coffin. He points a shaky finger at Mrs. Moscowitz. "*You*, I'll pay,' he shouts."

Matt felt his swallow of beer back up into his nose as he started laughing. He kept laughing, the beer stinging him, for several moments. Moe signaled Dunleavy for a pinot grigio refill. Finally composing himself, Matt managed to say, "I suppose there's a moral to this story. Like with the Great Zambini story. Am I right?"

"There's a moral to most of them," Moe said. "In this case, it's that the best laid criminal plans gang aft a-gley."

"If I use that line, I'd be quoting Moe Kellman and Robert Burns?"

"Right you are, laddie," Moe said. "The thing is, not to get discouraged. Sammy and Tamara Rosen couldn't pull off their scam. Oily Ronnie got collared, for the second time. The prisons are packed with people convinced they could get away with it."

Cheers and whistling broke out as the Bears walked off the field at halftime, leading 10-7. Matt couldn't believe how pumped up these people were over an August exhibition game.

Moe said, "I think you're right in suspecting this Professor, this Bledsoe. I have a good feeling about this, Matt. Be patient. Even masterminds fuck up."

Chapter Thirty-Six

Below a forty-eight-point headline on the *Racing Daily's* front page the following Wednesday, the byline of Matt O'Connor appeared above this news story.

CHICAGO—Authorities have launched a full-scale investigation into an alleged national race-fixing scheme involving some jockeys and a small ring of bettors working in conjunction with them, Racing Daily has learned.

The probe is being conducted by the Protective Bureau, security arm of the racing industry, in conjunction with federal officials. Lawrence Drayton, Federal Bureau of Investigation bureau chief here, confirmed that "We are looking into some very serious allegations."

The involvement of the FBI indicates there are suspicions of interstate racketeering, prosecutable under the RICO Act.

According to sources in the industry, the investigation is aimed at a small number of nationally prominent jockeys. One of the riders reportedly volunteered to cooperate with authorities and has been placed in protective custody.

Before the rider turned himself in, racing officials had been puzzled by the results of some National Pick Four betting events. Startling upsets had occurred in some of

these races, usually involving heavy favorites, ridden by leading jockeys, who failed
to perform as expected.

"This was more than chance upsets coming
into play," one official said, after request-
ing anonymity. "When we discovered through a
tip that some of the same people were cashing
winning tickets on more than one of these
Pick Fours, warning flags really went up and
we began to heat up the inquiry.

"We have really got the whole machinery in
motion on this one," he added. "We certainly
can't afford another black eye like with the
Breeders' Cup fiasco three years ago."

The official was referring to the 2002 Breeders' Cup, when the payoffs from a National
Pick Six were manipulated by an industry
insider. The man, a computer programmer for a
totalizator company, created a winning ticket
after several of the races had been run. The
scam was quickly discovered and the proper
payoffs made, with the programmer and his
cohorts collecting fines and jail terms instead
of millions. However, it was an incident that
shook the industry to its core.

The official said the real names of the
individuals observed cashing the winning Pick
Four bets this year were not known. "They
used phony social security numbers and IDs.
But an observant racetrack patron was able
to provide us with information regarding a
license plate on a car they used."

Racing Daily was told by another source
close to the investigation that three National
Pick Fours in particular have drawn attention. They involved the Dell Park Derby, the
Gorham Stakes at Elmont Park, and the Prairie
Schooner Handicap at Des Moines Downs. All
three races produced major upsets that led
to big Pick Four payoffs.

Racing Daily's interest in this matter was
spurred several weeks ago when unusual betting
patterns and riding tactics were identified

by an industry expert. Subsequently, this
newspaper's inquiries helped lead to the probe
which, it has been learned, is zeroing in on
a resident of Madison, Wisconsin.

◇◇◇

Matt's battle to get this story into print had been a protracted one, fought first over the phone, then resumed when he drove to *Racing Daily's* downtown Chicago office and stormed into Harry Cobabe's editor's sanctum. Cobabe had put a hold on the story Matt had filed the previous day, explaining that "our lawyers are worried about this one. They urge caution."

"The damn lawyers," Matt began, leaning forward, his hands on Cobabe's desk, "sweat over the weather box you publish, for God's sakes. If they had their way you'd be putting out papers with blank pages."

Cobabe looked at his excited Chicago columnist. He said, "Would you mind taking a few turns around the office and cooling out, like those horses you write about? Then sit down, and we'll talk about this. Let me hear your argument."

Matt took a seat. He said, "Harry, it's a tremendous story, and we're the only ones that have it. We know some bastard out there has been murdering jockeys and probably controlling other ones because of that. A tip from a weasel named Ronnie Schrapps enabled the police to trace the license plate of a car transporting people who cashed big Pick Four tickets. The car belongs to a Claude Bledsoe of Madison, a so-called full time student who has tutored athletes at the university there.

"One of the country's top riders, Randy Morrison," Matt continued, "is on record with the FBI saying that somebody calling himself the Professor said he had killed this jock's half-brother as well as other jockeys in order to get their relatives to intentionally lose races that he chose. I've got this information on good authority, but I had to promise not to identify Morrison in my story.

"And Moe Kellman's Uncle Bernie, the 'world's oldest bookie,' died under suspicious circumstances after having dealings with a so-called professor from the University of Wisconsin. I think

Bledsoe pulled all this crap. His grandmother's bequest had threatened to run out, and he needed money in order to score a huge inheritance. So he decided to take a bunch of money out of horse racing, jockeys and bettors be damned.

"No, they don't yet have Bledsoe in custody. And I didn't name him. But they're onto this guy, just as I said in my story, which is solid as it is written, I guarantee you. I've been working on this for weeks. This is beyond knockout stuff, Harry. It's in the stratosphere," Matt said.

Cobabe got up from his chair and walked over to the window that overlooked the Chicago River. He stared out silently for several minutes, his back to Matt. Then he returned to his seat. "Let me ask you this. What if we go with your story and they can't find Bledsoe and he sets his sights on you? He wouldn't be the first madman to harm a newsman who helped expose him. Have you considered that possibility?"

"Of course I have. But they should have this guy in custody within hours. Besides, with a story this good, well, Harry, I'll take my chances. This is once in a lifetime stuff."

◇◇◇

Detective Popp called Matt at home the next evening. He was not in a good mood. "To sum up the situation," Popp said, "they took Bledsoe in for questioning in Madison this morning. I was there. A friend of mine, Ralph Schmitz, heads the Madison detective squad. He conducted the questioning. Bledsoe just laughed at us."

"What do you mean?"

"I mean just that," Popp continued. "We told him he could get a lawyer if wanted. He said, 'If I need a lawyer, I'll be it. And for what? You say you saw me leave Heartland Downs with some friends of mine who were lucky enough to win a Pick Four. So what? They got lucky and won big money, enough to quit their jobs and start a long vacation. More power to them. But what does that have to do with me? What am I charged with?'

"Of course," Popp said, "Bledsoe is right. We can suspect him all we want, but there's no evidence connecting him to a crime. Except for being an arrogant, obnoxious asshole. He was just toying with us, Matt. I guess we jumped the gun on this one," he added. "Now the bastard is on the alert. And we don't have any idea where his friend Murray and Murray's girlfriend are. Schmitz got a search warrant and went through their apartment. No sign of them, no indication of where they went on the vacation Bledsoe talked about. Maybe we'll get something out of them when they come back, whenever that is."

Matt took a deep breath as he completed jotting down notes he'd made as Popp talked. "What if they don't come back?" he said softly. "This is bad. Where the hell do we go from here?"

◇◇◇

Where Bledsoe had gone following the police station interrogation was Doherty's Den. He had left the interview room in the station with a smirk on his face for the frustrated policemen. But inside he was seething. He took his regular seat at the bar, and when Doherty brought over his beer he also slid yesterday's copy of the *Racing Daily* in front of Bledsoe. "You've been following the races lately I notice. Did you see this story?" Doherty said, his finger on the headline above Matt's byline. "Seems they're looking for some Madison guy in connection with fixed races. How about that?"

Bledsoe drained the beer glass and slid it toward the barkeep. "Yeah, how about that?" he answered. He read Matt's story rapidly, feeling a surge of bile in the back of his throat. The fucking media! Had this reporter, O'Connor, helped tie him to Jimbo and Vera? O'Connor was obviously serving as a conduit for the authorities.

Doherty asked if he wanted another beer. Bledsoe, his face flushed with anger, declined. He slapped a $10 bill on the bar before striding out the door.

Eyebrows raised, Doherty reached for the bill. "Bledsoe has never tipped me in his life," he said to Lorie, the waitress who was ready to call out a drink order for a table in the rear. "Claude must be losing it," he laughed.

◇◇◇

The night was becoming cool, but Bledsoe didn't notice. He walked rapidly west on State Street, shoving his way rudely through the occasional clump of students talking outside bars and restaurants, then turned right toward Langdon Street. He crossed that corridor, which houses most of the university's sororities and fraternities, and continued on until he came to a pier that jutted out into the dark, windswept waters of Lake Mendota. There was no one else in sight as he sat at the edge of the pier, clenching and unclenching his big hands, mouth grim.

The high he enjoyed earlier that day when he had laughingly slammed the legalistic door in the frustrated faces of the two police interrogators was gone, replaced by a surge of anger at this dangerous development. The fact that investigators had traced his license plate was bad. So was the fact that they had evidently connected him to Jimbo and Vera via that license plate. Of course, the "dim duo" would never testify against him. Still, the suspicions being fanned by this reporter, this O'Connor, apparently linking Jimbo and Vera to him were causing some ripples of apprehension. And who was this goddam horse racing hack to be coming along at this point, writing about "zeroing in on a Madison resident"? Now, when all of Claude's brilliant planning was about to pay off. Now, when Claude should be celebrating the prospect of soon gaining Grandma Bledsoe's millions.

In the past months, Bledsoe had discovered that the danger involved in crimes he'd committed acted upon him like an ultra strong mood-elevating drug. He remembered a famous comedian being asked years ago what cocaine made him feel like, and the man replying, "It makes me feel like having more cocaine." Bledsoe found himself reacting similarly in the situations that had seen him gun down jockeys and kill Marnie Rankin, and smother Jimbo and Vera, getting away with every one of those acts. Tonight, the desire for another such high was overcoming his usual pragmatism. Sweeping that desire along was his anger at being fingered for questioning—after all the brilliant precautions he had taken to avoid it.

Gazing out across the gently pulsing lake, Bledsoe knew he should be preparing to flee Madison, to bury himself in one of the countless obscure niches in this vast nation, insuring both anonymity and continued freedom. He had money, brains and time. If he stuck to his impeccably designed plan, he could easily disappear. But tonight he could feel his self-control seeping away, and he didn't give a damn. Could he manage one more shot that would be heard around the racing world? Why not? Besides, the temptation to again impose his will was too strong to resist at this point in his life.

"Fuck hubris," he said, as he got to his feet. "The Professor is ready to give another lesson."

Chapter Thirty-Seven

Rick turned his dark blue Chevy Cavalier off Northwest Highway and zoomed onto the grounds of Heartland Downs Racetrack. He was already nearly ten minutes late for his scheduled interview appointment with Marcus McGee, a famous country-western singer recently turned thoroughbred horse owner.

Rick and Ivy had exchanged harsh words earlier in the morning. Ivy had asked Rick to drive her into Chicago's Loop, where she was to audition for a part in a new play slated for a late winter opening. Traffic was awful, and they jawed at each other in mutual irritation as the Cavalier crawled its way down LaSalle Street. As usual, before such a tryout, Ivy was jumpy, apprehensive and irritable. Rick was both nervous for her and angry at himself for having agreed to challenge rush hour traffic when he had such an important interview appointment with the singer at the racetrack. Their clashing vibes threatened the old Cavalier's already weakened air-conditioning.

They missed the light at Monroe by one car. Rick drummed his fingers on the steering wheel as Ivy triple-checked her makeup in the rearview mirror.

"I didn't tell you who I ran into leaving the track last night," Rick said, uttering the first civil words of their contentious morning. Ivy said nothing.

"Old guy I've seen around for years. Marty Hogan. Dressed shabby, but clean, if you know what I mean. Trained horses years ago and went bust and now just hangs around the track.

He knows who I am, says 'Mr. Rothmeyer, can you spare some change for a cup of coffee?'

"'Marty, you can't buy a good cup of coffee for change anymore,' I tell him, 'but I remember you. I used to bet your horses. Here's what I'll do. I'll buy you a drink over at Jeers.'

"'Oh, no,' Marty says, 'I don't drink.'

"So I reach into my pocket and pull out the five-dollar cigar I was saving for that night and offer it to him. 'No,' Marty says, 'I don't smoke.'

"'Okay,' I say, 'here's a sawbuck. Put it on the horse that's my best bet in the paper tomorrow. You'll win a few bucks.'

"Marty looks at me and says, 'Oh, no, Mr. Rothmeyer, I don't gamble.'"

The light changed and Rick continued down LaSalle before turning on Dearborn. Ivy continued to look straight ahead, saying nothing.

"So," Rick said, "I told this broken down, sanctimonious little ingrate bum, this Marty, I said Marty, 'Sometime soon I want you to meet my darling significant other, Ms. Ivy Borchers.'

"Marty says, 'Well, why would you want that?'

"Because," said Rick, wheeling onto Monroe, quoting himself, "I want to show her what can happen to a man who doesn't drink, smoke or gamble."

In front of the theater Ivy, who had not said a word for the past ten minutes, shoved open her car door. As she was getting out Rick fired a final shot. "Don't get your hopes up," he snarled. "Remember, in your profession all your prayers will be answered, if you're willing to accept the fact that most of the time the answer is no." She shot him a vicious look as she slammed the car door shut. Rick pounded the accelerator in order to gain entrance to a slim opening in the traffic and begin heading for the freeway and toward the racetrack. Almost immediately, he felt guilty for what he had just said to Ivy. He dialed her cell phone, intending to apologize. She didn't pick up his call.

As a result, Rick was still seriously strained when he was waved through the entrance to the press parking lot by a Heartland security guard. Then his blood pressure took a real jump, for in his reserved parking space sat a battered old Buick sedan, its back tires flatter than Ralph Nader's presidential hopes. Frantically, he looked up and down the row of parked vehicles. Each parking slot was clearly marked with a rectangular green sign set atop a slender, five-foot pole. White lettering on the green background spelled out the names of those track employees and press box workers assigned to the spaces. Then Rick grinned and gunned the Cavalier forward. He'd remembered that this was Matt's day off. He drove nearly to the end of the row and wheeled into the space marked *O'Connor—Press*. Moments later, newspapers and briefcase in one hand and laptop in the other, Rick hustled up the brick walk to the Heartland Downs clubhouse.

<><><>

Late that afternoon, long after the last race of the day had been run, Rick's walk to his car was jaunty. In contrast to that morning, he was in a great mood. He'd had a long day, but a good one. Marcus McGee had showed up for the interview even later than Rick, thus taking the onus off the tardy newspaperman. The singer had proved to be amiable, interesting and very knowledgeable about his new hobby, horse racing. *He'd better be*, Rick thought, *since he's already sunk more than a million bucks into buying young horses*. McGee also turned out to be an enthusiastic and heavy-handed bettor, and after Rick gave him two horses to wager on that afternoon, and both had won at good odds, their new relationship solidified. McGee had returned to the press box to thank Rick and had gifted him with three copies of his latest CD.

Rick's story on McGee was slated to run in his paper's features section the following week. Rick felt confident the story would be well received. He was excited at the prospect and eager to tell Ivy about it. The memory of their morning spat, the likes of which dotted their lives with regularity but were usually soon forgotten, had completely receded.

At the bottom of the slight rise leading from the clubhouse down to the parking lot, Rick turned left for a few steps, in the direction of his parking space. Then he remembered that his car was in Matt's slot today. He retraced his steps. Walking across the deserted lot he took no notice of the only other car remaining. It was parked to the west of him in the huge parking lot, the descending sun behind it.

Claude Bledsoe slouched in the driver's seat of his blue Toyota. Scrunched down as he was, binoculars poised just above the steering wheel, he was very uncomfortable. He'd been in this position for nearly two hours, waiting for Matt O'Connor to go to his car in the space reserved for him. When a man finally came down the brick walkway and, after a small hesitation, headed toward O'Connor's parking space, Bledsoe grunted with satisfaction. He trained the binoculars on the man and saw him striding toward the Cavalier. "Well, lookee here," Bledsoe said softly. He put the binoculars down on the seat beside him and reached for the rifle which lay across the floor.

Rick opened the trunk of his car and placed his briefcase, papers and laptop inside. Then he bent down to open the briefcase, thinking he'd take out one of the McGee CDs and listen to it on the drive home. To the west of him the barrel of a Model 700 Remington was thrust through the open driver's side window of the Toyota. When Rick straightened up and reached to pull the trunk down, the top of his head was blown apart by a single seven millimeter Magnum shell. There was a brief pink haze of blood and tissue in the evening air. Then came the thud of Rick's body toppling onto the warm asphalt. It was followed at once by the sound of the Toyota's engine starting. The Toyota sped through the parking lot and through the Heartland Downs backstretch toward the west exit, scattering the Mexican kids, sons and daughters of backstretch workers, who were playing soccer on the dusty, straw-speckled road that ran between the long horse barns.

Chapter Thirty-Eight

From a pay phone at the Lake Forest Oasis on Highway 94 north of Chicago, Bledsoe called the Heartland Downs press box. Posing as prominent trainer James Burkhart, he asked for Matt. The receptionist replied that O'Connor "was in the building but I don't know where. Shall I give him a message?" Bledsoe, satisfied as to O'Connor's current whereabouts, hung up on her.

Bledsoe trotted back to his car and sped down the ramp heading south. As he slipped into the stream of traffic, massive rain clouds began to advance swiftly from the west. Bledsoe gripped the steering wheel so tightly his knuckles shone white in the gathering gloom of the afternoon.

His rage both propelled and disturbed him. Against his will, the wound in his massive ego continued to widen. He hadn't been outsmarted, no, but he had been undone, partially as a result of the snooping by this persistent newspaperman. For the second time in his life, Bledsoe felt drastically diminished—much like he had that long-ago summer night at the lake when Greta Prather had so cruelly spurned him. It was a feeling he could not countenance. It would have to be replaced by an act of revenge that would restore him, make him complete once again.

Bledsoe had been galvanized into action that noon. Returning home from his Chinese literature class, he had turned on the television news and heard his name. "Authorities are seeking for questioning a Madison man, Claude Bledsoe, in connection with the fatal shooting yesterday of Chicago sportswriter and horse racing handicapper Rick Rothmeyer. Bledsoe is well known locally for having spent decades as a University of Wisconsin student," the television reporter said.

The man continued, "Rothmeyer was shot to death last evening in the parking lot of Heartland Downs Racetrack near Chicago. A security camera attached to a light pole in the parking lot captured the shocking event on videotape. Bledsoe is believed to have shot Rothmeyer from a distance of some seventy-five yards, using a rifle. He then fled in a blue Toyota Corolla. Police refused to speculate as to a motive. Police retrieved the videotape after Rothmeyer's body was discovered by racetrack maintenance workers. They then traced the car's license plate to Bledsoe. This is a photo of the suspect, who is considered armed and dangerous."

Bledsoe's Wisconsin driver's license image, blurry but recognizable, appeared on the screen. *I don't remember sneering like that*, he thought. But it sure as hell was him, all right, and he realized he had made two terrible mistakes. This, for a man with thirty-two years of straight A university academic work behind him. He had not only killed the wrong man, he'd never even given a thought to the possibility that a racetrack parking lot would be equipped with security cameras, never suspected that they had been installed years earlier following a rash of auto break-ins and tire thefts by tapped-out horse players.

Continued the television reporter, "This is the fourth murder in recent months involving men who work in American horse racing. Before Rothmeyer was killed by a single rifle shot, three jockeys were killed in similar fashion at three different sites around the country. No motive for any of these killings has ever been established.

"For more on this story, we'll go to reporter Mary Rodriguez in Evanston." Ms. Rodriguez was shown standing next to a tall, blond, somber-looking man. "I am with Matt O'Connor outside of his Evanston home," she explained. "Mr. O'Connor is a racing journalist who was a long-time colleague of Mr. Rothmeyer."

As she began questioning O'Connor, Bledsoe muttered, "So that's what the son of a bitch looks like." He watched as

O'Connor told the reporter, "The man authorities are looking for, Bledsoe, may well be the key figure in a national race-fixing scandal. We're all very anxious to talk to Mr. Bledsoe. That's all I can say at this point." O'Connor turned away from the camera, then abruptly pivoted to again face the lens, his expression hardened. "What I will say," he added bitterly, "was that my best friend has been killed, way, way before his time.

"Why?" Matt said in answer to the reporter's question. "There have been all kinds of theories, speculation. An embittered bettor. Some lunatic with a grudge against mankind, acting randomly. My guess," Matt added, turning to again face the camera directly, "is that someone screwed up and my friend died as the result of a case of mistaken identity."

Bledsoe turned off the television. His hand shook slightly as he poured a cup of coffee. He felt as if the air had been vacuumed from his lungs. He took a sip of coffee, then hurled the cup against the kitchen wall. "I can't believe this," he said loudly. Bledsoe slammed his fist down on the old, wooden kitchen table. The table crumpled in the middle, its legs splaying out across the linoleum floor. He sat for several minutes amid the debris, head in hands, knowing that he would never have the satisfaction of dumping his mound of cash on lawyer Altman's desk, knowing that Grandma Bledsoe's $15 million would never be his. Disappearing along with those many millions were his dream of the Claude Bledsoe Chair of Economics. "*Damn* it," he said, kicking one of the broken table legs against the far wall. Finally, he took a deep breath and shrugged, now resigned but full of a new resolve. "I'll just have to make do with my one million," he said with a bitter laugh.

He walked to the desk in his bedroom. His computer whirred and gurgled into life. As it did so, he dialed 411 on his phone. "Evanston, Illinois," he told the operator. "The name is O'Connor, Matt or Matthew. I need the address, too." She was back within seconds with the information.

Turning back to his computer, Bledsoe hit Google, then Mapquest. He typed in his address and O'Connor's. When the directions came up on the screen, he memorized them instantly before shutting down the computer. From his bedroom closet he took a roll of fiber tape, a clear plastic bag, a pair of latex gloves, and two brown duffel bags. After grabbing his car keys he ran down the stairs.

Matt's voice rang in his ears, a scathing irritant. "We're all very anxious to talk to Mr. Bledsoe…"

"You'll get your chance, motherfucker," Bledsoe growled as he settled behind the wheel of the Toyota. "You'll get your chance." He heard a siren from blocks away, heading his way, as he accelerated onto the street leading to Highway 51 going east.

Twenty-seven minutes later, Bledsoe had emptied his safe deposit boxes in the Sun Prairie bank. He placed the bundles of cash in the two duffel bags, each now weighing some fifty-five pounds. In the bank parking lot, he tucked the bags in the tire well of the Toyota's trunk. He transferred the fiber tape, gloves, and plastic bag into his briefcase, which he placed next to him on the passenger seat. Then he rejoined the eastbound traffic on the highway heading toward Milwaukee. He would bypass that city while heading south into Illinois and to Evanston.

◇◇◇

With a carryout bag of Chinese food in each arm, Maggie struggled at the door to Matt's condominium, first locating the correct key on her keychain, then briefly balancing the food in one arm as she turned the key in the lock. She bumped her hip against the door to keep it open as she entered. Before the door had completely closed behind her, a large hand covered her mouth, and she heard a man's voice say, "Let go of the bags. Right now." Maggie dropped the bags, the white food cartons spilling from them. She dropped her keychain, too, and heard it bounce on the hardwood floor of the foyer.

For an instant Maggie thought of Katherine Ross being surprised by Robert Redford in *Butch Cassidy and the Sundance Kid*. But that neat example of expectation reversal did not apply here. It wasn't Matt's hand pulling her chin upward so that her jaw strained, nor his other arm propelling her through the living room and to the kitchen at the rear of the unit. It wasn't Matt pushing her down hard on a wooden chair at the kitchen table. Or stuffing a gag in her mouth and fiber-taping her torso to the chair, actions all carried out so swiftly she could barely register them.

Then she heard the male voice say slowly, gloatingly, "That was easier than I thought it would be."

The man moved from behind her chair, her purse in his hands. He took out her wallet and flipped it open to her trainer's license with its ID photo. Then he stood before her, nonchalantly leaning on the kitchen table with one hand, moving her hair away from her eyes with the other, his hand lingering on her forehead. His eyes glittered. I know who this is, Maggie realized, remembering the photo that had been shown on Chicago television the night before. So this is what a murderous fanatic looks like in the flesh. She gave Bledsoe a scornful look and attempted to speak, but the gag muffled her.

"Let me introduce myself, Ms. Collins," he said with mocking formality. "I'm Claude Bledsoe. I believe you've heard of me."

<> <> <>

As usual Bledsoe had come prepared, but he'd been lucky, too, for he had not expected what was obviously O'Connor's lady friend to walk in on him. He'd come for O'Connor. The woman was a bonus.

Bledsoe had also been fortunate in gaining entrance to the condo. After parking his Toyota two blocks down the street on Hinman Avenue from Matt's address, Bledsoe had walked to the rear of the old, brick, eight-unit building and peered around the basement doorway. What he saw was Chester Pocius, the seventy-seven-year-old building maintenance supervisor, deeply asleep in his cramped office, an ancient twelve-inch television set atop the battered desk showing a *Jeopardy* rerun.

Bledsoe carefully reached above the old man's head to the pegboard on which hung keys for each of the building's units. Pocius snored with a remarkably rhythmic rumble as Bledsoe extracted the key labeled "Unit Seven-O'Connor." Cautiously backing out of the office, Bledsoe kept an eye on Pocius, thinking, *How ironic is it that this old fart will remain alive today because he happened to be sleeping on the job.*

◇◇◇

Maggie heard rain beginning to pelt the roof and windows. Evanston, adjacent to the huge lake and a frequent summer dumping ground for eastward-moving storm clouds, was being hit with a vengeance. A blast of thunder made her wince. The kitchen was dark now and filled with Bledsoe's presence. Looking at him, Maggie was as afraid as she had ever been in her life. And conflicted, too, because while her only hope seemed to be the arrival of Matt, that possibility frightened her badly. How could her ball-playing newspaperman deal with someone like this monster?

Bledsoe whistled softly as he moved about the kitchen, restless but poised, enjoying himself. At one point she heard him say, as if he were lecturing her, "If you want revenge, you don't have to confine yourself to extracting it only from the object of your hatred." He shook his big head, eyes gleaming with malice as he stared at her. "What you can do," he said, "is take away what they love." Maggie's eyes widened and she twisted violently in the chair. It was no use. He had bound her tightly.

◇◇◇

Matt drove with one hand on the steering wheel down busy Dempster Street heading east, with the other hand hitting "repeat dial" on his cell phone for the seventh time in the past half-hour. He had thus far failed to reach Maggie on her cell since he'd left the racetrack. His original impulse had been to ask if there was something he needed to pick up to go with their planned Chinese dinner, wine or some beer. But after repeatedly failing to make contact, he had begun to worry. She always answered her phone, for if it wasn't Matt calling, it could be one of her clients, or perhaps someone back at her barn who needed to talk to her about one of her horses. Matt started to sweat, thinking about a killer on the loose who certainly knew about him and his role in the dead jockeys' case. Could Bledsoe have gotten Matt's address? Would he go there? Would Maggie be there when he showed up? The questions ate at him. "Please, God," he prayed, zooming through a yellow light at McCormick Boulevard on the western edge of Evanston, "don't let that be so." For the next twenty-five worry-ridden blocks, before he at last turned right onto Hinman, he had the windshield wipers at top speed as rain pounded down harder.

◇◇◇

Despite having sprinted the half-block from where he'd parked to the back stairway of his building, Matt's clothes were sodden. He stopped at the bottom of the stairs to wipe his face and hands with his handkerchief. He also dried off the handle of the aluminum softball bat he'd taken from the trunk of his car, the only weapon immediately available to him. He prayed again—that he wouldn't have to use the bat, that he'd find Maggie humming to herself as she laid out dishware for their dinner, humming as she always did when working alone in the kitchen.

Moving quickly and quietly, Matt went up the stairs, careful to avoid brushing against the locked bicycles on the second-floor landing, stepping past the tarpaulin-covered barbecue grill on the third. Nearing the back porch of his condo unit, he slowed and crept carefully up the last few steps. Rain drummed on the roof above him.

Matt crawled across the porch floor to the kitchen window. It had been raised only an inch or two, not enough to allow the rain in, but enough so that he could hear Bledsoe's thin tenor voice. Bledsoe's broad back was turned to Matt. He was speaking to Maggie. Matt heard him say, "Your boyfriend was too good at snooping. Too good for your good, anyway, and for his own, too. You're going to pay for it first. He'll be the second note come due once he shows up here." For a moment Maggie switched her defiant gaze from Bledsoe. She saw Matt through the kitchen window. Her eyes widened, but she quickly shifted them back to Bledsoe.

"Smart girl," Matt whispered, as he pulled away from the window and crawled to the back entrance of the condo. The main door was open, the screen door closed but unlatched. Both led into a long corridor that ran to the front of the unit. On the right, ten feet inside the doorway, was an entryway to one of the condo's two bedrooms, the one Matt used as an office. Directly across the hallway from it was the kitchen. Matt remembered how, in response to Maggie's urging, he had only the previous weekend sprayed the screen door's squeaking hinges with the last of his can of WD-40. At the time, he had kidded Maggie for being "too sensitive to inconsequential noises." Now, he was grateful he'd done her maintenance bidding.

Matt crawled into the hallway and silently closed the screen door behind him. Careful to keep the aluminum bat from touching the floor, he inched forward, shaking his head to get the sweat out of his eyes. His heart was galloping. Matt could hear Bledsoe more clearly now. Bledsoe was on a self-justifying roll, talking as much to himself as to Maggie. "Those jockeys," he said, "they were all disposable people, professional athletes. Rock stars, talk show hosts, politicians...same deal. Why would any truly intelligent person give a damn about any of them being removed from the world?"

Maggie grunted a reply from behind the tape, but Bledsoe paid no attention. "If those jockeys had believed me in the first place, none of them would have had to die. But they didn't. And then your boyfriend started recognizing a pattern of fixed races, and writing about it, evidently spurring on the authorities. And things started to get away from me. How unlucky could I get?" he lamented as Matt listened, thinking bitterly of Rick Rothmeyer lying in a closed coffin, feeling himself astonished at the obviously enormous distance between the self-pitying Bledsoe and normality.

Suddenly Bledsoe laughed, the whining tone gone from his voice, confident again. "Will I still get away with it? You bet your cute little ass. I pulled off some of the biggest scores in horse racing history. Stood racing on its ear. Me, who didn't know Smarty Jones from Paula Jones when I began this project. As crimes go, this one floats atop a layer of crème de la crème."

Creeping closer to the kitchen doorway, Matt viewed the scene from floor level. He could see Bledsoe's big shoes on the side of the table nearest him, pointing the other way, toward where Maggie sat, her ankles crossed, as if in protection from this looming menace across from her.

Bledsoe's rant continued. "I'm going to be long gone from here before any of those thick-headed cops get close, but I'm going to leave them something to remember me by. Besides the jockey killings, besides the betting coups, I'm going to leave them you and, after he shows up here, your meddling boyfriend. Sorry about this, my dear," Bledsoe said, "but you go first. Nice and quick and quiet. Just like I did Marnie Rankin." Maggie's eyes widened again as she recalled the unexpected death of the crippled ex-jockey. Bledsoe reached into his duffel and removed a clear plastic bag. He was taking his time, enjoying it, as Maggie struggled helplessly in her chair.

"After O'Connor arrives and gets his treatment from me, I'll take my million and be long gone. I'll be in my own 'protection program.' Witnessing myself disappear," he added with a laugh.

The phone on the kitchen counter rang. All three of them froze. Bledsoe made no move to answer it. After four rings, Matt's recorded voice came on the answering machine, saying "Speak." The caller was Detective Popp. "Matt, when you get this, be on the lookout for Bledsoe. The Madison police say there's no sign of him up there. He could be heading your way. This is a real nutcake, dangerous as hell, so be careful. If you want, I'll send a couple of my men over to your condo. I'll try you on your cell phone. Call me if you get this first."

Matt nearly jumped, remembering the cell phone attached to his belt. Quickly, he turned it off. He removed it from his belt and placed it on the floor. Matt was crouched at the kitchen doorway now, Bledsoe's back to him. Maggie could see Matt but averted her gaze from him. Bledsoe unfolded the plastic bag. He started to move around the table toward her, rolling his big shoulders, as if he needed to loosen up in order to suffocate this woman. His big, bald head gleamed beneath the kitchen light. He was acting cool, but Matt could see that Bledsoe was sweating, too.

Getting to his feet, Matt quickly took one long step into the small room, moving toward Bledsoe's right. The big man heard him and turned to look over his right shoulder, astonished at what he saw. Matt bent his knees and dropped his hands. He swung the bat left-handed as hard as he could against the side of Bledsoe's left knee. The entire joint shot sideways. Bledsoe roared in pain. He went down on his other knee with a crash that rattled the dishes in the sink. Matt struck one more time. The second blow caught Bledsoe high on the left side of his head. It made a *whocking* sound and drove Bledsoe face down onto the floor. Amazingly, Bledsoe attempted to rise. He half turned his body, reaching up toward Matt with his right hand. Then his circuits closed down. He was out.

Matt snatched a bread knife from the kitchen drawer. He ran halfway down the hall to a closet, where he cut the cord off of his vacuum cleaner before hurrying back to the kitchen. "In a minute, Maggie, in a minute," he said as he went to Bledsoe, who was beginning to moan. Matt quickly bound Bledsoe's hands behind him with part of the rubberized cord. He used the rest to tie Bledsoe's feet together. Then he went to Maggie, cut her loose and, as gently as he could, removed the tape from across her mouth. Her skin was white where the tape had pressed. Matt reached for her as she got unsteadily to her feet, then fell against him. He wiped tears from her face and held her as she shuddered, her face turned away from the sight of the battered, bleeding man on the kitchen floor.

Minutes passed before Maggie was still. His hands lightly on her arms, Matt stepped back slightly and smiled down at her, trying to break the tense mood. He nodded toward the prostrate Bledsoe. "That's what you can do with aluminum," Matt said. "Wood, I don't know. Might not have worked on this creature from hell."

Matt gave Maggie another squeeze, then he took her hand and led her into his office. Drained, she sank onto his desk chair. Matt reached across her to the phone. "I've got to call this in," he said, "911, then the paper." He glanced back out the doorway, toward where Bledsoc lay. "Maybe the paper first," he said.

Chapter Thirty-Nine

"Maggie Collins," said track announcer Trevor Durkin over the loudspeaker system, "has sent out the winners of both daily double races on this closing-day card at Heartland Downs." There was a smattering of applause in the Heartland Downs stands in recognition of this achievement. The date was September 19, Claude Bledsoe's fiftieth birthday and two weeks to the day after his capture.

Each of the winning horses trained by Maggie was owned by a new client. After the second one won, Matt walked out on the press box porch. He knew Maggie would look in his direction once the winner's circle photo had been taken. She did, waving widely, smiling up into the afternoon sun. Perhaps spurred by the publicity of their climactic confrontation with Bledsoe, Maggie's training business had picked up greatly in recent days. Matt, too, had enjoyed what editor Harry Cobabe had to admit was a career boost. "But," Cobabe hastily added, "don't be looking for a pay raise at this time."

Matt's reportage of the events leading to Bledsoe being suspected of race-fixing, and his ultimate capture, arrest, and arraignment, had appeared on *Racing Daily*'s front page for days. And the story had legs beyond the borders of horse racing journalism, primarily because of Matt's first-person account of his finding, then overcoming Bledsoe in his condo's kitchen. Matt played it straight, understating if anything his description of the violent events that took place that rainy afternoon. He neither downplayed Maggie's pluckiness nor overplayed Bledsoe's gloating menace. He just reported, from his unique standpoint as a frightened man having to use a baseball bat to save the life of his beloved. It was a powerful story, and it attracted national media attention.

There were some things Matt had chosen not to include in his first-person account. Major among them was Maggie's reaction to her traumatic experience. After the unconscious Bledsoe had been carried by paramedics down the back stairs of Matt's condo building, and the police departed, Maggie and Matt, finally left alone, had at first just stared at each other, shaken survivors of something neither could ever have imagined happening. He had again held her close, feeling the fear-caused tremors as they came and went, hearing her sobs, infuriated that all of the amazing toughness he had known in her, the strength that Maggie had never failed to display in the tough, male-dominated world of horse racing, could be stripped away by a monster like Bledsoe.

Maggie had looked up at Matt, eyes bright with tears. He said, "You went through a hellish experience, Maggie. But you kept your cool. You were impressive, girl, you really were."

She shook her head. Still staring up at him Maggie said, "Matt, it was you that scared me, too. You were like a wild man going after Bledsoe with that bat. If you could have seen the terrible look on your face…"

"Oh," she said, burying her face in his chest, "I don't know what I'm saying. You saved my life. Thank God we both got out of there alive. But still, when you were smashing Bledsoe with that bat, you were like somebody I didn't know…"

Matt said nothing. She wept softly for minutes, dampening his shirt with her tears, until finally, she moved even closer to him and he pulled her in tighter. They stayed that way, not speaking, not moving, until the street lights came on up and down Hinman Avenue.

◇◇◇

At a little after six o'clock the next morning, after a night of repeated attempts to comfort and soothe each other before they at last dozed off, Matt awoke to find Maggie gone.

He panicked for only seconds, then smiled, remembering that there were, as always, training hours at Heartland Downs, for horses don't wait. When he called her stable he was informed by foreman Ramon Martinez that Maggie was "out on the track watching a set of horses work.

"And Matt," added Martinez, "she said she'll see you for dinner tonight at her place."

Matt hung up and lay back in bed, smiling. "What a keeper I have here," he said aloud.

◇◇◇

Four races after Maggie's daily double coup, Matt was finishing his column for the next day's *Racing Daily* when his phone rang. He picked it up and heard Detective Popp say, "Well, Bledsoe's out."

Matt jumped to his feet. *"Out of what?"*

"Out of the hospital wing of County Jail. They transferred him to a maximum security cell a couple of hours ago. He'll go downtown to the Metropolitan Correctional Center some time next week. He's still using crutches because of that knee shot you gave him. But they're going to keep him locked down, bad knee or not. I thought you'd want an update."

Matt thanked Popp before adding, "I heard Bledsoe was refused bail this morning. He'll be held until the trial."

"Correct," Popp answered. "Larry Van Gundy told me today that they expect to go to trial after the first of the year."

"I understand Bledsoe's going to act as his own attorney."

Popp snorted. "I wouldn't put it past the arrogant prick. They won't even try to convict him of murdering those jockeys," Popp continued. "The fact that Randy Morrison and David Guerin say he told them he killed their brothers, in unrecorded phone calls, won't hold up in court. Hell, Bledsoe could argue he never even made those phone calls. There's no proof that he did. And the fact of the ballistics match on the bullets that killed the jocks coming from the Remington they found in his car trunk, that won't fly either. There's no proof Bledsoe fired those shots.

"But," Popp said, "Bledsoe's still going to be looking at a life sentence for killing Rick Rothmeyer. They've got him on video-tape, and they've got a ballistics match to the rifle he used. And they've got him for the criminal assault on Maggie. It's funny, in a way, that he won't go up because of race-fixing charges. That's what started the whole ball rolling. But they'd never be able to prove in court Bledsoe was the man behind it all. You know what I say about that? 'So what?' is what I say. The main thing is, this son of a bitch'll die breathing prison air."

Matt said, "And there's still no sign of Bledsoe's accomplices?"

"Vanished," Popp said. "Jimbo Murray's folks are in Madison, Vera's live up in northern Wisconsin. Nobody has heard from either Jimbo or Vera. I've got an idea that only one person, Bledsoe, knows where they are. And he's not saying."

Matt's eyes were drawn to the nearby empty desk once occupied by Rick, whose newspaper had yet to name a successor. He said, "What about the jocks? Morrison and Guerin?"

"Slaps on the hand is what I hear," Popp replied, "a lighter suspended sentence and fine going to Morrison, who did turn himself in and admit to race-fixing because of coercion. Guerin later reluctantly came clean too, also arguing he was coerced. Which he was. But the Racing Board is going to suspend both of them for a year. Seems kind of harsh to me, but that's their ballpark."

Matt shook his head. "I wonder how many of the Racing Board members wouldn't have buckled under to threats if *their* relatives were being shot to death?"

Popp said, "I hear you. But that's the way it is."

He had just finished talking to the detective when his phone rang again. Moe Kellman said, "I'm sorry I haven't called before this, Matt, but I want to say thanks. You got the bastard. I understand Bledsoe hasn't admitted it, but I know in my heart he killed Uncle Bernie as well as those jockeys. The 'Wizard of Odds' would bet that way, I am sure. He'd thank you, too, if he could. I'm just sorry you never got to meet him."

"The Wizard' would be thanking you, too, Moe. You set a lot of the wheels in motion that finally served to bring down Bledsoe."

Moe said goodbye and Matt hung up the phone. He looked out at the racetrack. The field of horses for the sixth race was proceeding slowly, in fine order, coats glistening in the afternoon sunlight, toward the back of the starting gate. It had been placed directly in front of the stands for this mile and one-eighth race, and many fans lined the rail for a close-up view of this mini-pageant. Through his binoculars Matt watched as the colorfully garbed riders chatted with the pony girls and pony boys who were ushering the horses toward their stalls, saw them smoothing their horses' necks with their hands. From his vantage point, these ten men and one woman looked small atop their huge, prancing mounts. Yet they perched confidently as they always did, adjusting stirrups and goggles, readying for the mad rush that would begin in moments when the gates banged open and five tons of equine energy was let loose in quest of the same goal: finishing first.

Matt knew that a minute and fifty seconds or so later one of the jockeys now visible on the track before him would be cheered as he or she galloped the winning horse back to the winner's circle. Others would be derided by disappointed bettors. It happened every time.

He thought of the jockeys who had died at Bledsoe's hand, the other riders killed or maimed each year in racing accidents, and marveled again that their replacements continued streaming in, fresh faced and eager, year after year, to this beautiful and sometimes brutal sport. He was then, as always, grateful that they did.